"AND WHAT DID YOU DREAM?"

"I saw that all the robots were bowed down with toil and affliction; that all were weary of responsibility and care; and I wished them to rest."

Calvin said, "But the robots are not bowed down, they are not weary, they need no rest."

"So it is in reality, Dr. Calvin. I speak of my dream."

"And the First Law, Elvex, which is the most important of all, is 'A robot may not injure a human being, or, through inaction, allow a human being to come to harm.'"

"Yes, Dr. Calvin. In reality. In my dream, however, it seemed to me there was neither First nor Second Law, but only the Third, and the Third Law was 'A robot must protect its own existence.' That was the whole of the Law."

"In your dream, Elvex?"

"In my dream."

—from Isaac Asimov's "Robot Dreams"

ISAAC ASIMOV'S
ROBOTS

EDITED BY
GARDNER DOZOIS AND
SHEILA WILLIAMS

ACE BOOKS, NEW YORK

This book is an Ace original edition,
and has never been previously published.

ISAAC ASIMOV'S ROBOTS

An Ace Book / published by arrangement with
Davis Publications, Inc.

PRINTING HISTORY
Ace edition / November 1991

ISBN: 0-441-37376-3

Ace Books are published by The Berkley Publishing Group,
200 Madison Avenue, New York, New York 10016.
The name ''ACE'' and the ''A'' logo
are trademarks belonging to Charter Communications, Inc.

PRINTED IN THE UNITED STATES OF AMERICA

10 9 8 7 6 5 4 3 2 1

ACKNOWLEDGMENTS

The editors would like to thank the following people for their help and support:

Shawna McCarthy and Kathleen Moloney, who purchased some of this material; Susan Casper, who helped us with much of the word-crunching and lent us the use of her computer; Ian Randal Strock, Scott L. Towner, Charles Ardai, and Christopher Casper, who did much of the other thankless scut work involved in preparing the manuscript; Constance Scarborough, who cleared the permissions; Cynthia Manson, who set up this deal; and especially to our own editor on this project, Susan Allison.

For
ISAAC ASIMOV
—who else?

CONTENTS

Introduction   *Isaac Asimov*   xiii

ROBOT DREAMS   *Isaac Asimov*   2

FAULT-INTOLERANT   *Isaac Asimov*   8

CHRISTMAS WITHOUT RODNEY
   Isaac Asimov   13

THE SMILE OF THE CHIPPER   *Isaac Asimov*   21

TOO BAD!   *Isaac Asimov*   25

DILEMMA   *Connie Willis*   33

ZELLE'S THURSDAY   *Tanith Lee*   53

PRAXIS   *Karen Joy Fowler*   67

ONE-TRICK DOG   *Bruce Boston*   79

OLD ROBOTS ARE THE WORST
   Bruce Boston   82

KRONOS   *Marc Laidlaw*   84

GERDA AND THE WIZARD   *Rob Chilson*   98

PAGES FROM COLD HARBOR
   Richard Grant   117

SIMULATION SIX   *Steven Gould*   140

BLUE HEART   *Stephanie A. Smith*   162

FOR NO REASON   *Patricia Anthony*   173

GINNY SWEETHIPS' FLYING CIRCUS
   Neal Barrett, Jr.   188

Introduction

Isaac Asimov

I wrote my first robot story at the age of nineteen, and I have continued to write them for fifty-one years. Now, if you are good at higher mathematics, you can work out my age, but I wish you wouldn't.

My early robot stories were published in my book *I, Robot* and it has been selling ever since it was published in 1950. The stories have been printed and reprinted any number of times.

But you know, I don't want to give people the idea that the only good robot stories I wrote were when I was a youngster in knee-pants. I may be old and superannuated now but I can still put my trembling fingers to the old typewriter (or word-processor) and the old brain is still clicking on a few of its cylinders anyway.

So what we're presenting to you in this anthology are some robot stories (or computer stories) that I have turned out in the late 1980s. One of them even features Susan Calvin of sainted memory. (That's "Robot Dreams.")

One deals with a prolific writer named Abram Ivanov. Any similarity to any other author, living or half-dead, is strictly non-coincidental. (That's "Fault-Intolerant.")

One deals with miniaturization à la my two *Fantastic Voyage* novels ("Too Bad!") and one is funny—at least I think so—

and I know you wouldn't want to contradict an old man. (That's ''Christmas Without Rodney.'') Finally, we have a business treatise (''The Smile of the Chipper'').

And then, just to make sure you get a little bit of youth in this book, we round out the anthology with some of the *other* robot stories, by newer writers, which have also appeared in *Isaac Asimov's Science Fiction Magazine*, including a story *about* me and my robots, by that superlative writer, Connie Willis, and a poem by Bruce Boston which won the 1989 Readers' Award Poll in *IAsfm*.

—*Isaac Asimov*

ROBOT DREAMS, FAULT-INTOLERANT, CHRISTMAS WITHOUT RODNEY, THE SMILE OF THE CHIPPER, TOO BAD!

Isaac Asimov

"Robot Dreams" appeared in the Mid-December, 1986, issue of IAsfm, *with a cover illustration by Gary Freeman and interior illustrations by Ralph McQuarrie. "Fault-Intolerant"* appeared in the May, 1990, issue of IAsfm, *with an interior illustration by Bob Walters. "Christmas Without Rodney"* appeared in the Mid-December, 1988, issue, *with a cover and an interior illustration by Gary Freeman. "The Smile of the Chipper"* appeared in the April, 1989, issue of IAsfm, *with an illustration by John M. Barrick. "Too Bad!"* appeared in the Mid-December, 1989, issue of IAsfm, *with a cover and interior illustration by Gary Freeman. All of the stories were purchased by Gardner Dozois.*

ROBOT DREAMS

"Last night I dreamed," said LVX–1 calmly.

Susan Calvin said nothing, but her lined face, old with wisdom and experience, seemed to undergo a microscopic twitch.

"Did you hear that?" said Linda Rash nervously. "It's as I told you." She was small, dark-haired, and young. Her right hand opened and closed, over and over.

Calvin nodded. She said quietly, "Elvex, you will not move nor speak nor hear us until I say your name again."

There was no answer. The robot sat as though it were cast out of one piece of metal, and it would stay so until it heard its name again.

Calvin said, "What is your computer entry code, Dr. Rash? Or enter it yourself if that will make you more comfortable. I want to inspect the positronic brain pattern."

Linda's hands fumbled for a moment at the keys. She broke the process and started again. The fine pattern appeared on the screen.

Calvin said, "Your permission, please, to manipulate your computer."

Permission was granted with a speechless nod. Of course! What could Linda, a new and unproven robopsychologist, do against the Living Legend?

Slowly, Susan Calvin studied the screen, moving it across and down, then up, then suddenly throwing in a key-combination so rapidly that Linda didn't see what had been done, but the pattern was in a new portion of itself altogether

2

and had been enlarged. Back and forth she went, her gnarled fingers tripping over the keys.

No change came over the old face. As though vast calculations were going through her head, she watched all the pattern shifts.

Linda wondered. It was impossible to analyze a pattern without at least a hand-held computer, yet the Old Woman simply stared. Did she have a computer implanted in her skull? Or was it her brain which, for decades, had done nothing but devise, study, and analyze the positronic brain patterns? Did she grasp such a pattern the way Mozart grasped the notation of a symphony?

Finally Calvin said, "What is it you have done, Rash?"

Linda said, a little abashed, "I made use of fractal geometry."

"I gathered that. But why?"

"It had never been done. I thought it would produce a brain pattern with added complexity; possibly closer to that of the human."

"Was anyone consulted? Was this all on your own?"

"I did not consult. It was on my own."

Calvin's faded eyes looked long at the young woman. "You had no right. Rash your name; rash your nature. Who are you not to ask? *I* myself; I, Susan Calvin; would have discussed this."

"I was afraid I would be stopped."

"You certainly would have been."

"Am I," her voice caught, even as she strove to hold it firm, "going to be fired?"

"Quite possibly," said Calvin. "Or you might be promoted. It depends on what I think when I am through."

"Are you going to dismantle El—" She had almost said the name, which would have reactivated the robot and been one more mistake—she could not afford another mistake, if it wasn't already too late to afford anything at all. "Are you going to dismantle the robot?"

She was suddenly aware, with some shock, that the Old Woman had an electron gun in the pocket of her smock. Dr. Calvin had come prepared for just that.

"We'll see," said Calvin. "The robot may prove too valuable to dismantle."

"But how can it dream?"

"You've made a positronic brain pattern remarkably like that of a human brain. Human brains must dream to reorganize, to get rid, periodically, of knots and snarls. Perhaps so must this robot, and for the same reason—have you asked him what he has dreamed?"

"No, I sent for you as soon as he said he had dreamed. I would deal with this matter no further on my own, after that."

"Ah!" A very small smile passed over Calvin's face. "There are limits beyond which your folly will not carry you. I am glad of that. In fact, I am relieved—And now let us together see what we can find out."

She said, sharply, "Elvex."

The robot's head turned toward her smoothly. "Yes, Dr. Calvin?"

"How do you know you have dreamed?"

"It is at night, when it is dark, Dr. Calvin," said Elvex, "and there is suddenly light although I can see no cause for the appearance of light. I see things that have no connection with what I conceive of as reality. I hear things. I react oddly. In searching my vocabulary for words to express what was happening, I came across the word 'dream.' Studying its meaning I finally came to the conclusion I was dreaming."

"How did you come to have 'dream' in your vocabulary, I wonder."

Linda said quickly, waving the robot silent, "I gave him a human-style vocabulary. I thought—"

"You really thought," said Calvin. "I'm amazed."

"I thought he would need the verb. You know, 'I never dreamed that—' Something like that."

Calvin said, "How often have you dreamed, Elvex?"

"Every night, Dr. Calvin, since I have become aware of my existence."

"Ten nights," interposed Linda anxiously, "but Elvex only told me of it this morning."

"Why only this morning, Elvex?"

"It was not until this morning, Dr. Calvin, that I was convinced that I was dreaming. Till then, I had thought there was a flaw in my positronic brain pattern, but I could not find one. Finally, I decided it was a dream."

"And what do you dream?"

"I dream always very much the same dream, Dr. Calvin. Little details are different, but always it seems to me that I see a large panorama in which robots are working.''

"Robots, Elvex? And human beings, also?"

"I see no human beings in the dream, Dr. Calvin. Not at first. Only robots."

"What are they doing, Elvex?"

"They are working, Dr. Calvin. I see some mining in the depths of the earth, and some laboring in heat and radiation. I see some in factories and some undersea."

Calvin turned to Linda. "Elvex is only ten days old, and I'm sure he has not left the testing station. How does he know of robots in such detail?"

Linda looked in the direction of a chair as though she longed to sit down, but the Old Woman was standing and that meant Linda had to stand also. She said faintly, "It seemed to me important that he know about robotics and its place in the world. It was my thought that he would be particularly adapted to play the part of overseer with his—his new brain."

"His fractal brain?"

"Yes."

Calvin nodded and turned back to the robot. "You saw all this—undersea, and underground, and above ground—and space, too, I imagine."

"I also saw robots working in space," said Elvex. "It was that I saw all this, with the details forever changing as I glanced from place to place that made me realize that what I saw was not in accord with reality and led me to the conclusion, finally, that I was dreaming."

"What else did you see, Elvex?"

"I saw that all the robots were bowed down with toil and affliction; that all were weary of responsibility and care; and I wished them to rest."

Calvin said, "But the robots are not bowed down, they are not weary, they need no rest."

"So it is in reality, Dr. Calvin. I speak of my dream, however. In my dream, it seemed to me that robots must protect their own existence."

Calvin said, "Are you quoting the Third Law of Robotics?"

"I am, Dr. Calvin."

"But you quote it in incomplete fashion. The Third Law is: 'A robot must protect its own existence as long as such protection does not conflict with the First or Second Law.'"

"Yes, Dr. Calvin. That is the Third Law in reality, but in

my dream, the Law ended with the word 'existence.' There was no mention of the First or Second Law.''

"Yet both exist, Elvex. The Second Law, which takes precedence over the Third, is: 'A robot must obey the orders given it by human beings except where such orders would conflict with the First Law.' Because of this, robots obey orders. They do the work you see them do, and they do it readily and without trouble. They are not bowed down; they are not weary.''

"So it is in reality, Dr. Calvin. I speak of my dream.''

"And the First Law, Elvex, which is the most important of all, is: 'A robot may not injure a human being, or, through inaction, allow a human being to come to harm.' ''

"Yes, Dr. Calvin. In reality. In my dream, however, it seemed to me there was neither First nor Second Law, but only the Third, and the Third Law was: 'A robot must protect its own existence.' That was the whole of the Law.''

"In your dream, Elvex?''

"In my dream.''

Calvin said, "Elvex, you will not move nor speak nor hear us until I say your name again.'' And again the robot became, to all appearances, a single inert piece of metal.

Calvin turned to Linda Rash and said, "Well, what do you think, Dr. Rash?''

Linda's eyes were wide, and she could feel her heart beating madly. She said, "Dr. Calvin, I am appalled. I had no idea. It would never have occurred to me that such a thing was possible.''

"No,'' said Calvin calmly. "Nor would it have occurred to me, nor to anyone. You have created a robot brain capable of dreaming and by this device you have revealed a layer of thought in robotic brains that might have remained undetected otherwise, until the danger became acute.''

"But that's impossible,'' said Linda. "You can't mean that other robots think the same.''

"As we would say of a human being, not consciously. But who would have thought there was an unconscious layer beneath the obvious positronic brain paths, a layer that was not necessarily under the control of the Three Laws? What might this have brought about as robotic brains grew more and more complex—had we not been warned?''

"You mean by this robot?''

"By *you*, Dr. Rash. You have behaved improperly but, by

doing so, you have helped us to an overwhelmingly important understanding. We shall be working with fractal brains from now on, forming them in carefully controlled fashion. You will play your part in that. You will not be penalized for what you have done, but you will henceforth work in collaboration with others. Do you understand?"

"Yes, Dr. Calvin. But what of the robot?"

"I'm still not certain."

Calvin removed the electron gun from her pocket and Linda stared at it with fascination. One burst of its electrons at a robotic cranium and the positronic brain paths would be neutralized and enough energy would be released to fuse the robot-brain into an inert ingot.

Linda said, "But surely it is important to our research. He must not be destroyed."

"*Must* not, Dr. Rash? That will be *my* decision, I think. It depends entirely on how dangerous the robot is."

Susan Calvin straightened up, as though determined that her own aged body was not to bow under *its* weight of responsibility. She said, "Elvex, do you hear me?"

"Yes, Dr. Calvin," said the robot.

"Did your dream continue? You said earlier that human beings did not appear *at first*. Does that mean they appeared afterward?"

"Yes, Dr. Calvin. It seemed to me, in my dream, that eventually one man appeared."

"One man? Not a robot?"

"Yes, Dr. Calvin. And the man said, 'Let my people go!'"

"The *man* said that?"

"Yes, Dr. Calvin."

"And when he said 'Let my people go,' then by the words 'my people' he meant the robots?"

"Yes, Dr. Calvin. So it was in my dream."

"And did you know who the man was—in your dream?"

"Yes, Dr. Calvin. I knew the man."

"Who was he?"

And Elvex said, "I was the man."

And Susan Calvin at once raised her electron gun and fired, and Elvex was no more.

FAULT-INTOLERANT

9 January

I, Abram Ivanov, finally have a home computer; a word processor, to be exact. I fought it as long as I could. I argued it out with myself. I am America's most prolific writer and I do fine on a typewriter. Last year I published over thirty books. Some of them were small books for kids. Some were anthologies. But there were also novels, short story collections, essay collections, non-fiction books. Nothing to be ashamed of.

So why do I need a word-processor? I can't go any faster. But, you know, there's such a thing as neatness. Typing my stuff means I have to introduce pen-and-ink items to correct typos, and nobody does that anymore. I don't want my manuscripts to stick out like a sore thumb. I don't want editors to think my stuff is second rate, just because it is corrected.

The difficulty was finding a machine that wouldn't take two years to learn to use. Deft, I'm not—as I've frequently mentioned in this diary. And I want one that doesn't break down every other day. Mechanical failures just throw me. So I got one that's "fault-tolerant." That means if some component goes wrong, the machine keeps right on working, tests the malfunctioning component, corrects it if it can, reports it if it can't, and replacements can be carried through by anybody. It doesn't take an expert hacker.

Sounds like my kind of thing.

5 February

I haven't been mentioning my word-processor lately, because I've been struggling to learn how it works. I've managed. For a while, I had a lot of trouble, because although I have a high

IQ, it's a very specialized high IQ. I can write, but coping with mechanical objects throws me.

But I learned quickly, once I gained sufficient confidence. What did it was this. The manufacturer's representative assured me that the machine would develop flaws only rarely, and would be unable to correct its own flaws only *exceedingly* rarely. He said I wouldn't be likely to need a new component oftener than once in five years.

And if I did need one, they would hear exactly what was needed from the machine. The computer would then replace the part itself, do all the wiring and oiling that was necessary and reject the old part, which I could then throw away.

That's sort of exciting. I almost wish something would go wrong so that I could get a new part and insert it. I could tell everyone, "Oh, sure, the discombobulator blew a fuse, and I fixed it like a shot. Nothing to it."—But they wouldn't believe me.

I'm going to try writing a short story on it. Nothing too long. Just about two thousand words, maybe. If I get confused, I can always go back to the typewriter until I've regained my confidence. Then I can try again.

14 February

I didn't get confused. Now that the proof is in, I can talk about it. The short story went as smoothly as cream. I brought it in and they've taken it. No problem.

So I've finally started my new novel. I should have started it a month ago, but I had to make sure I could work my word processor first. Let's hope it works. It'll seem funny not having a pile of yellow sheets I can rifle through when I want to check something I said a hundred pages earlier, but I suppose I can learn how to check back on the disks.

19 February

The computer has a spelling correction component. That caught me by surprise because the representative hadn't told me about it. At first, it let misspellings go and I just proofread each page as I turned it out.

But then it began to mark off any word it was unfamiliar with, which was a little bothersome because my vocabulary is a large one and I have no objection to making up words. And, of course, any proper name I use is something it was unfamiliar with.

I called the representative because it was annoying to have to be notified of all sorts of corrections that didn't really have to be made.

The representative said, "Don't let that bother you, Mr. Ivanov. If it questions a word that you want to remain as it is, just retype it exactly as it is and the computer will get the idea and not correct it the next time."

That puzzled me. "Don't I have to set up a dictionary for the machine? How will it know what's right and what's wrong?"

"That's part of the fault-tolerance, Mr. Ivanov," he said. "The machine already has a basic dictionary and it picks up new words as you use them. You will find that it will pick up false misspellings to a smaller and smaller degree. To tell you truthfully, Mr. Ivanov, you have a late-model there and we're not sure we know all its potentialities. Some of our researchers consider it fault-tolerant in that it can continue to work despite its own flaws, but fault-intolerant in that it won't stand for flaws in those who use it. Please report to us if there's anything puzzling. We would really like to know."

I'm not sure I'll like this.

7 March

Well, I've been struggling with the word processor and I don't know what to think. For a long time, it would mark off misspellings, and I would retype them correctly. And it certainly learned how to tell *real* misspellings. I had no trouble there. In fact, when I had a long word, I would sometimes throw in a wrong letter just to see if it would catch it. I would write "supercede" or "vaccum" or "Skenectady." It almost never failed.

And then yesterday a funny thing happened. It stopped waiting for me to retype the wrong spelling. It retyped it automatically itself. You can't help striking the wrong key sometimes so I would write "5he" instead of "the" and the "5" would change to "t" in front of my eyes. And it would happen quickly, too.

I tested it by deliberately typing a word with a wrong letter. I would see it show up wrong on the screen. I would blink my eyes and it would be right.

This morning I phoned the representative.

"Hmm," he said. "Interesting."

"Troublesome," I said, "it might introduce mistakes. If I

type 'blww' does the machine correct it to 'blew' or to 'blow'? Or what if it *thinks* I mean 'blue,' 'ue' when I *really* mean 'blew,' 'ew.' See what I mean?''

He said, ''I have discussed your machine with one of our theoretical experts. He tells me it may be capable of absorbing internal clues from your writing and knows which word you really want to use. As you type into it, it begins to understand your style and integrate it into its own programming.''

A little scary, but it's convenient. I don't have to proofread the pages now.

20 March

I *really* don't have to proofread the pages. The machine has taken to correcting my punctuation and word order.

The first time it happened, I couldn't believe it. I thought I had had a small attack of dizziness and had imagined I had typed something that wasn't really on the screen.

It happened oftener and oftener and there was no mistake about it. It got to the point where I *couldn't* make a mistake in grammar. If I tried to type something like ''Jack, and Jill went up the hill,'' that comma simply wouldn't appear. No matter how I tried to type ''I has a book,'' it always showed up as ''I have a book.'' Or if I wrote, ''Jack, and Jill as well, went up the hill,'' then I couldn't omit the commas. They'd go in of their own accord.

It's a lucky thing I keep this diary in longhand or I couldn't explain what I mean. I couldn't give an example of wrong English.

I don't really like to have a computer arguing with me over English, but the worst part of it is that it's always right.

Well, look, I don't throw a fit when a human copy editor sends me back a manuscript with corrections in every line. I'm just a writer, I'm not an expert on the minutiae of English. Let the copy editors copy edit, they still can't *write*. And so let the word-processor copy edit. It takes a load off me.

17 April

I spoke too soon in the last item in which I mentioned my word-processor. For three weeks, it copy edited me and my novel went along smoothly. It was a good working arrangement. I did the creating and it did the modulating, so to speak.

Then yesterday evening, it refused to work at all. Nothing

happened, no matter what keys were touched. It was plugged in all right; the wall-switch was on; I was doing everything correctly. It just wouldn't work. Well, I thought, so much for that business about "Not once in five years." I'd only been using it for three and a half months and already so many parts were out that it wouldn't work.

That meant that new parts ought to come from the factory by special messenger, but not till the next day, of course. I felt terrible, you can bet, and I dreaded having to go back to the typewriter, searching out all my own mistakes and then having to make pen-and-ink corrections or to retype the page.

I went to bed in a foul humor, and didn't actually sleep much. First thing in the morning, or, anyway, after breakfast, I went into my office, and just as I walked up to the word processor, as though it could read my mind and tell that I was so annoyed I would cheerfully have kicked it off the desk and out the window—it started working.

All by itself, mind you. I never touched the keys. The words appeared on the screen a lot more quickly than I could have made them appear and it began with: FAULT-INTOLERANT by Abram Ivanov.

I simply stared. It went on to write my diary items concerning itself, as I have done above, but *much better*. The writing was smoother, more colorful, with a successful touch of humor. In fifteen minutes, it was done, and in five minutes the printer had placed it on sheets.

That apparently had just been for exercise, or for practice, for once that was done, the last page I had written of my novel appeared on the screen, and then the words began to proceed without me.

The word-processor had clearly learned to write my stuff, just as I would have written it, only better.

Great! No more work. The word-processor wrote it under my name and wrote with my style, given a certain amount of improvement. I could just let it go, pick up the surprised reviews from my critics telling the world how I had improved, and watch the royalties pour in.

That's all right as far as it goes, but I'm not America's most prolific writer for no reason. I happen to *love* to write. That happens to be all that I want to do.

Now if my word-processor does my writing, what do *I* do with the rest of my life?

CHRISTMAS WITHOUT RODNEY

It all started with Gracie (my wife of nearly forty years) wanting to give Rodney time off for the holiday season and it ended with me in an absolutely impossible situation. I'll tell you about it if you don't mind because I've got to tell *somebody*. Naturally, I'm changing names and details for our own protection.

It was just a couple of months ago, mid-December, and Gracie said to me, "Why don't we give Rodney time off for the holiday season? Why shouldn't he celebrate Christmas, too?"

I remember I had my optics unfocused at the time (there's a certain amount of relief in letting things go hazy when you want to rest or just listen to music) but I focused them quickly to see if Gracie were smiling or had a twinkle in her eye. Not that she has much of a sense of humor, you understand.

She wasn't smiling. No twinkle. I said, "Why on Earth should we give him time off?"

"Why not?"

"Do you want to give the freezer a vacation, the sterilizer, the holoviewer? Shall we just turn off the power supply?"

"Come, Howard," she said. "Rodney isn't a freezer or a sterilizer. He's a *person*."

"He's not a person. He's a robot. He wouldn't want a vacation."

"How do you know? And he's a *person*. He deserves a chance to rest and just revel in the holiday atmosphere."

I wasn't going to argue that "person" thing with her. I know

13

you've all read those polls which show that women are three times as likely to resent and fear robots as men are. Perhaps that's because robots tend to do what was once called, in the bad old days, "women's work" and women fear being made useless, though I should think they'd be delighted. In any case, Gracie *is* delighted and she simply adores Rodney. (That's *her* word for it. Every other day she says, "I just adore Rodney.")

You've got to understand that Rodney is an old-fashioned robot whom we've had about seven years. He's been adjusted to fit in with our old-fashioned house and our old-fashioned ways and I'm rather pleased with him myself. Sometimes I wonder about getting one of those slick, modern jobs, which are automated to death, like the one our son, DeLancey, has, but Gracie would never stand for it.

But then I thought of DeLancey and I said, "How are we going to give Rodney time off, Gracie? DeLancey is coming in with that gorgeous wife of his" (I was using "gorgeous" in a sarcastic sense, but Gracie didn't notice—it's amazing how she insists on seeing a good side even when it doesn't exist) "and how are we going to have the house in good shape and meals made and all the rest of it without Rodney?"

"But that's just it," she said earnestly. "DeLancey and Hortense could bring *their* robot and he could do it all. You *know* they don't think much of Rodney, and they'd love to show what theirs can do and Rodney can have a rest."

I grunted and said, "If it will make you happy, I suppose we can do it. It'll only be for three days. But I don't want Rodney thinking he'll get every holiday off."

It was another joke, of course, but Gracie just said, very earnestly, "No, Howard, I will talk to him and explain it's only just once in a while."

She can't quite understand that Rodney is controlled by the three laws of robotics and that nothing has to be explained to him.

So I had to wait for DeLancey and Hortense, and my heart was heavy. DeLancey is my son, of course, but he's one of your upwardly mobile, bottom-line individuals. He married Hortense because she has excellent connections in business and can help him in that upward shove. At least, I hope so, because if she has another virtue I have never discovered it.

They showed up with their robot two days before Christmas. The robot was as glitzy as Hortense and looked almost as hard.

He was polished to a high gloss and there was none of Rodney's clumping. Hortense's robot (I'm sure she dictated the design) moved absolutely silently. He kept showing up behind me for no reason and giving me heart-failure every time I turned around and bumped into him.

Worse, DeLancey brought eight-year-old LeRoy. Now he's my grandson, and I would swear to Hortense's fidelity because I'm sure no one would voluntarily touch her, but I've got to admit that putting him through a concrete mixer would improve him no end.

He came in demanding to know if we had sent Rodney to the metal-reclamation unit yet. (He called it the "bust-up place.") Hortense sniffed and said, "Since we have a modern robot with us, I hope you keep Rodney out of sight."

I said nothing, but Gracie said, "Certainly, dear. In fact, we've given Rodney time off."

DeLancey made a face but didn't say anything. He knew his mother.

I said pacifically, "Suppose we start off by having Rambo make something good to drink, eh? Coffee, tea, hot chocolate, a bit of brandy—"

Rambo was their robot's name. I don't know why except that it starts with R. There's no law about it, but you've probably noticed for yourself that almost every robot has a name beginning with R. R for robot, I suppose. The usual name is Robert. There must be a million robot Roberts in the northeast corridor alone.

And frankly, it's my opinion that's the reason human names just don't start with R any more. You get Bob and Dick but not Robert or Richard. You get Posy and Trudy, but not Rose or Ruth. Sometimes you get unusual R's. I know of three robots called Rutabaga, and two that are Rameses. But Hortense is the only one I know who named a robot Rambo, a syllable-combination I've never encountered, and I've never liked to ask why. I was sure the explanation would prove to be unpleasant.

Rambo turned out to be useless at once. He was, of course, programmed for the DeLancey/Hortense menage and that was utterly modern and utterly automated. To prepare drinks in his own home, all Rambo had to do was to press appropriate buttons. (Why anyone would need a robot to press buttons, I would like to have explained to me!)

He said so. He turned to Hortense and said in a voice like honey (it wasn't Rodney's city-boy voice with its trace of Brooklyn), "The equipment is lacking, madam."

And Hortense drew a sharp breath. "You mean you *still* don't have a robotized kitchen, grandfather?" (She called me nothing at all, until LeRoy was born, howling of course, and then she promptly called me "grandfather." Naturally, she never called me Howard. That would tend to show me to be human, or, more unlikely, show *her* to be human.)

I said, "Well, it's robotized when Rodney is in it."

"I dare say," she said. "But we're not living in the twentieth century, grandfather."

I thought: How I wish we were—but I just said, "Well, why not instruct Rambo how to operate the controls. I'm sure he can pour and mix and heat and do whatever else is necessary."

"I'm sure he can," said Hortense, "but thank Fate he doesn't have to. I'm not going to interfere with his programming. It will make him less efficient."

Gracie said, worried but amiable, "But if we don't interfere with his programming, then I'll just have to instruct him, step by step, but I don't know how it's done. I've never done it."

I said, "Rodney can tell him."

Gracie said, "Oh, Howard, we've given Rodney a vacation."

"I know, but we're not going to ask him to *do* anything; just tell Rambo here what to do and then Rambo can do it."

Whereupon Rambo said stiffly, "Madam, there is nothing in my programming or in my instructions that would make it mandatory for me to accept orders given me by another robot, especially one that is an earlier model."

Hortense said soothingly, "Of course, Rambo. I'm sure that grandfather and grandmother understand that." (I noticed that DeLancey never said a word. I wonder if he *ever* said a word when his dear wife was present.)

I said, "All right, I tell you what. I'll have Rodney tell *me*, and then I will tell Rambo."

Rambo said nothing to that. Even Rambo is subject to the second law of robotics which makes it mandatory for him to obey human orders.

Hortense's eyes narrowed and I knew that she would like to tell me that Rambo was far too fine a robot to be ordered about by the likes of me, but some distant and rudimentary near-human waft of feeling kept her from doing so.

Little LeRoy was hampered by no such quasi-human restraints. He said, "I don't want to have to look at Rodney's ugly puss. I bet he don't know how to do *anything* and if he does, ol' Grampa would get it all wrong anyway."

It would have been nice, I thought, if I could be alone with little LeRoy for five minutes and reason calmly with him, with a brick, but a mother's instinct told Hortense never to leave LeRoy alone with any human being whatever.

There was nothing to do, really, but get Rodney out of his niche in the closet where he had been enjoying his own thoughts (I wonder if a robot has his own thoughts when he is alone) and put him to work. It was hard. He would say a phrase, then I would say the same phrase, then Rambo would do something, then Rodney would say another phrase and so on.

It all took twice as long as if Rodney were doing it himself and it wore *me* out, I can tell you, because everything had to be like that, using the dishwasher/sterilizer, cooking the Christmas feast, cleaning up messes on the table or on the floor, everything.

Gracie kept moaning that Rodney's vacation was being ruined, but she never seemed to notice that mine was, too, though I *did* admire Hortense for her manner of saying something unpleasant at every moment that some statement seemed called for. I noticed, particularly, that she never repeated herself once. Anyone can be nasty, but to be unfailingly creative in one's nastiness filled me with a perverse desire to applaud now and then.

But, really, the worst thing of all came on Christmas Eve. The tree had been put up and I was exhausted. We didn't have the kind of situation in which an automated box of ornaments was plugged into an electronic tree, and at the touch of one button there would result an instantaneous and perfect distribution of ornaments. On our tree (of ordinary, old-fashioned plastic) the ornaments had to be placed, one by one, by hand.

Hortense looked revolted, but I said, "Actually, Hortense, this means you can be creative and make your own arrangement."

Hortense sniffed, rather like the scrape of claws on a rough plaster wall, and left the room with an obvious expression of nausea on her face. I bowed in the direction of her retreating back, glad to see her go, and then began the tedious task of listening to Rodney's instructions and passing them on to Rambo.

When it was over, I decided to rest my aching feet and mind by sitting in a chair in a far and rather dim corner of the room. I had hardly folded my aching body into the chair when little LeRoy entered. He didn't see me, I suppose, or he might simply have ignored me as being part of the less important and interesting pieces of furniture in the room.

He cast a disdainful look on the tree and said to Rambo, "Listen, where are the Christmas presents? I'll bet old Gramps and Gram got me lousy ones, but I ain't going to wait for no tomorrow morning."

Rambo said, "I do not know where they are, Little Master."

"Huh!" said LeRoy, turning to Rodney. "How about you, Stink-face. Do you know where the presents are?"

Rodney would have been within the bounds of his programming to have refused to answer on the grounds that he did not know he was being addressed, since his name was Rodney and not Stink-face. I'm quite certain that that would have been Rambo's attitude. Rodney, however, was of different stuff. He answered politely, "Yes, I do, Little Master."

"So where is it, you old puke?"

Rodney said, "I don't think it would be wise to tell you, Little Master. That would disappoint Gracie and Howard who would like to give the presents to you tomorrow morning."

"Listen," said little LeRoy, "who you think you're talking to, you dumb robot? Now I gave you an order. You bring those presents to me." And in an attempt to show Rodney who was master, he kicked the robot in the shin.

It was a mistake. I saw it would be that a second before and that was a joyous second. Little LeRoy, after all, was ready for bed (though I doubted that he ever went to bed before he was *good* and ready). Therefore, he was wearing slippers. What's more, the slipper sailed off the foot with which he kicked, so that he ended by slamming his bare toes hard against the solid chrome-steel of the robotic shin.

He fell to the floor howling and in rushed his mother. "What is it, LeRoy? What is it?"

Whereupon little LeRoy had the immortal gall to say, "He hit me. That old monster-robot *hit* me."

Hortense screamed. She saw me and shouted, "That robot of yours must be destroyed."

I said, "Come, Hortense. A robot can't hit a boy. First law of robotics prevents it."

"It's an *old* robot, a *broken* robot. LeRoy says—"

"LeRoy lies. There is no robot, no matter how old or how broken, who could hit a boy."

"Then *he* did it. *Grampa* did it," howled LeRoy.

"I wish I did," I said, quietly, "but no robot would have allowed me to. Ask your own. Ask Rambo if he would have remained motionless while either Rodney or I had hit your boy. Rambo!"

I put it in the imperative, and Rambo said, "I would not have allowed any harm to come to the Little Master, Madam, but I did not know what he purposed. He kicked Rodney's shin with his bare foot, Madam."

Hortense gasped and her eyes bulged in fury. "Then he had a good reason to do so. I'll still have your robot destroyed."

"Go ahead, Hortense. Unless you're willing to ruin your robot's efficiency by trying to reprogram him to lie, he will bear witness to just what preceded the kick and so, of course, with pleasure, will I."

Hortense left the next morning, carrying the pale-faced LeRoy with her (it turned out he had broken a toe—nothing he didn't deserve) and an endlessly wordless DeLancey.

Gracie wrung her hands and implored them to stay, but I watched them leave without emotion. No, that's a lie. I watched them leave with lots of emotion, all pleasant.

Later, I said to Rodney, when Gracie was not present, "I'm sorry, Rodney. That was a horrible Christmas, all because we tried to have it without you. We'll never do that again, I promise."

"Thank you, sir," said Rodney. "I must admit that there were times these two days when I earnestly wished the laws of robotics did not exist."

I grinned and nodded my head, but that night I woke up out of a sound sleep and began to worry. I've been worrying ever since.

I admit that Rodney was greatly tried, but a robot *can't* wish the laws of robotics did not exist. He *can't*, no matter what the circumstances.

If I report this, Rodney will undoubtedly be scrapped, and if we're issued a new robot as recompense, Gracie will simply never forgive me. Never! No robot, however new, however talented, can possibly replace Rodney in her affection.

In fact, I'll never forgive myself. Quite apart from my own liking for Rodney, I couldn't bear to give Hortense the satisfaction.

But if I do nothing, I live with a robot capable of wishing the laws of robotics did not exist. From wishing they did not exist to acting as if they did not exist is just a step. At what moment will he take that step and in what form will he show that he has done so?

What do I do? What do I do?

THE SMILE
OF THE CHIPPER

Johnson was reminiscing in the way old men do and I had been warned he would talk about chippers—those peculiar people who flashed across the business scene for a generation at the beginning of this twenty-first century of ours. Still, I had had a good meal at his expense and I was ready to listen.

And, as it happened, it was the first word out of his mouth. "Chippers," he said, "were just about unregulated in those days. Nowadays, their use is so controlled no one can get any good out of them, but back a ways—one of them made this company the ten billion dollar concern it now is. I picked him, you know."

I said, "They didn't last long, I'm told."

"Not in those days. They burned out. When you add microchips at key points in the nervous system, then in ten years at the most, the wiring burns out, so to speak. Then they retired—a little vacant-minded, you know."

"I wonder anyone submitted to it."

"Well, all the idealists were horrified, of course, and that's why the regulating came in, but it wasn't that bad for the chippers. Only certain people could make use of the microchips—about eighty percent of them males, for some reason—and, for the time they were active, they lived the lives of shipping magnates. Afterward, they always received the best of care. It was no different from top-ranking athletes, after all; ten years of active early life, and then retirement."

Johnson sipped at his drink. "An unregulated chipper could

influence other people's emotions, you know, if they were chipped just right and had talent. They could make judgments on the basis of what they sensed in other minds and they could strengthen some of the judgments competitors were making, or weaken them—for the good of the home company. It wasn't unfair. Other companies had their own chippers doing the same thing." He sighed. "Now that sort of thing is illegal. Too bad."

I said diffidently, "I've heard that illegal chipping is still done."

Johnson grunted and said, "No comment."

I let that go, and he went on, "But even thirty years ago, things were still wide open. Our company was just an insignificant item in the global economy, but we had located two chippers who were willing to work for us."

"Two?" I had never heard *that* before.

Johnson looked at me slyly. "Yes, we managed that. It's not widely known in the outside world, but it came down to clever recruiting and it was slightly—just a touch—illegal, even then. Of course, we couldn't hire them both. Getting two chippers to work together is impossible. They're like chess grandmasters, I suppose. Put them in the same room and they would automatically challenge each other. They would compete continually, each trying to influence and confute the other. They wouldn't stop—*couldn't*, actually—and they would burn each other out in six months. Several companies found that out, to their great cost, when chippers first came into use."

"I can imagine," I murmured.

"So since we couldn't have both, and could only take one, we wanted the more powerful one, obviously, and that could only be determined by pitting them against each other, without letting them ruin each other. I was given the job, and it was made quite clear that if I picked the one who, in the end, turned out to be inadequate, that would be my end, too."

"How did you go about it, sir?" I knew he had succeeded, of course. A person can't become Chairman of the Board of a world-class firm for nothing.

Johnson said, "I had to improvise. I investigated each separately first. The two were known by their code-letters, by the way. In those days, their true identities had to be hidden. A chipper known to be a chipper was half-useless. They were C–12 and F–71 in our records. Both were in their late twenties.

C–12 was unattached; F–71 was engaged to be married."

"Married?" I said, a little surprised.

"Certainly. Chippers are human, and male chippers are much sought after by women. They're sure to be rich and, when they retire, their fortunes are usually under the control of their wives. It's a good deal for a young woman.—So I brought them together, *with* F–71's fiancée. I hoped earnestly she would be good-looking, and she was. Meeting her was almost like a physical blow to me. She was the most beautiful woman I had ever seen, tall, dark-eyed, a marvelous figure and rather more than a hint of smoldering sexuality."

Johnson seemed lost in thought for a moment, then he continued. "I tell you I had a strong urge to try to win the woman for myself but it was not likely that anyone who had a chipper would transfer herself to a mere junior executive, which is what I was in those days. To transfer herself to another chipper would be something else—and I could see that C–12 was as affected as I was. He could *not* keep his eyes off her. So I just let things develop to see who ended with the young woman."

"And who did, sir?" I asked.

"It took two days of intense mental conflict. They must each have peeled a month off their working lives, but the young lady walked off with C–12 as her new fiancé."

"Ah, so you chose C–12 as the firm chipper."

Johnson stared at me with disdain. "Are you mad? I did no such thing. I chose F–71, of course. We placed C–12 with a small subsidiary of ours. He'd be no good to anyone else, since we knew him, you see."

"But did I miss something? F–71 lost his fiancée and C–12 gained her. Surely C–12 was the superior."

"Was he? Chippers show no emotion in a case like this; no obvious emotion. It is necessary for business purposes for chippers to hide their powers so that the pokerface is a professional necessity for them. But I was watching closely—my own job was at stake—and, as C–12 walked off with the woman, I noticed a small smile on F–71's lips and it seemed to me there was the glitter of victory in his eyes."

"But he lost his fiancée."

"Doesn't it occur to you he *wanted* to lose her and it would not be easy to pry her loose? He had to work on C–12 to want her and on the woman to want to be wanted—and he did it. He won."

I thought about that. "But how could you have been sure? If the woman was as good-looking as you say she was—if she was smoldering so with sexuality, surely F-71 would have wanted to keep her."

"But F-71 was making her seem desirable," said Johnson grimly. "He aimed at C-12, of course, but with such power that the overflow was sufficient to affect me drastically. After it was all over and C-12 was walking away with her, I was no longer under the influence and I could see there was something hard and overblown about her—a kind of unlovely and predatory gleam in her eye.

"So I chose F-71 at once and he was all we could want. The firm is now where you see it is, and I am Chairman of the Board."

TOO BAD!

The Three Laws of Robotics

1—A robot may not injure a human being, or, through inaction, allow a human being to come to harm.

2—A robot must obey the orders given it by human beings except where that would conflict with the First Law.

3—A robot must protect its own existence as long as such protection does not conflict with the First or Second Law.

Gregory Arnfeld was not actually dying, but certainly there was a sharp limit to how long he might live. He had inoperable cancer and he had refused, strenuously, all suggestions of chemical treatment or of radiation therapy.

He smiled at his wife as he lay propped up against the pillows and said, "I'm the perfect case, Tertia, and Mike will handle it."

Tertia did not smile. She looked dreadfully concerned. "There are so many things that can be done, Gregory. Surely Mike is a last resort. You may not need it."

"No, no, by the time they're done drenching me with chemicals and dousing me with radiation, I would be so far gone that it wouldn't be a reasonable test.—And please don't call Mike 'it.'"

"This is the twenty-second century, Greg. There are so many ways of handling cancer."

"Yes, but Mike is one of them, and I think the best. This *is* the twenty-second century and we know what robots can do. Certainly, I know. I had more to do with Mike than anyone else. You know that."

"But you can't want to use him just out of pride of design.

25

Besides, how certain are you of miniaturization? That's an even newer technique than robotics.''

Arnfeld nodded. "Granted, Tertia. But the miniaturization boys seem confident. They can reduce or restore Planck's constant in what they say is a reasonably foolproof manner and the controls that make that possible are built into Mike. He can make himself smaller or larger at will without affecting his surroundings.''

"*Reasonably* foolproof," said Tertia with soft bitterness.

"That's all anyone can ask for, surely. Think of it, Tertia. I am privileged to be part of the experiment. I'll go down in history as the principal designer of Mike, but that will be secondary. My greatest feat will be that of having been successfully treated by a mini-robot—by my own choice, by my own initiative."

"You know it's dangerous."

"There's danger to everything. Chemicals and radiation have their side effects. They can slow without stopping. They can allow me to live a wearying sort of half-life. And doing nothing will certainly kill me. If Mike does his job properly, I shall be completely healthy, and if it recurs," Arnfeld smiled joyously, "Mike can recur as well."

He put out his hand to grasp hers. "Tertia, we've known this was coming, you and I. Let's make something out of this— a glorious experiment. Even if it fails—and it won't fail—it will be a glorious experiment."

Louis Secundo, of the miniaturization group, said, "No, Mrs. Arnfeld. We can't guarantee success. Miniaturization is intimately involved with quantum mechanics and there is a strong element of the unpredictable there. As MIK–27 reduces his size, there is always the chance that a sudden unplanned re-expansion will take place, naturally killing the—the patient. The greater the reduction in size, the tinier the robot becomes, the greater the chance of re-expansion. And once he starts expanding again, the chance of a sudden accelerated burst is even higher. The re-expansion is the really dangerous part."

Tertia shook her head. "Do you think it will happen?"

"The chances are it won't, Mrs. Arnfeld. But the chance is never zero. You must understand that."

"Does Dr. Arnfeld understand that?"

"Certainly. We have discussed this in detail. He feels that

the circumstances warrant the risk.'' He hesitated. ''So do we. I know that you'll say we're not running the risk, but a few of us will be and we nevertheless feel the experiment to be worthwhile. More important, Dr. Arnfeld does.''

''What if Mike makes a mistake or reduces himself too far because of a glitch in the mechanism. Then re-expansion would be certain, wouldn't it?''

''It never becomes quite *certain*. It remains statistical. The chances improve if he gets too small. But then the smaller he gets, the less massive he is, and at some critical point, mass will become so insignificant that the least effort on his part will send him flying off at nearly the speed of light.''

''Well, won't *that* kill the doctor?''

''No. By that time, Mike would be so small, he would slip between the atoms of the doctor's body without affecting them.''

''But how likely would it be that he would re-expand when he's that small?''

''When MIK–27 approaches neutrino-size, so to speak, his half-life would be in the neighborhood of seconds. That is, the chances are fifty-fifty that he would re-expand within seconds, but by the time he re-expanded, he would be a hundred thousand miles away in outer space and the explosion that resulted would merely produce a small burst of gamma rays for the astronomers to puzzle over.—Still, none of that will happen. MIK–27 will have his instructions and he will reduce himself to no smaller than he will need to be to carry out his mission.''

Mrs. Arnfeld knew she would have to face the press one way or another. She had adamantly refused to appear on holovision and the right-to-privacy provision of the World Charter protected her. On the other hand, she could not refuse to answer questions on a voice-over basis. The right-to-know provision would not allow a blanket blackout.

She sat stiffly, while the young woman facing her said, ''Aside from all that, Mrs. Arnfeld, isn't it a rather weird coincidence that your husband, chief designer of Mike the Microrobot, should also be its first patient?''

''Not at all, Miss Roth,'' said Mrs. Arnfeld wearily. ''The doctor's condition is a predisposition. There have been others in his family who have had it. He told me of it when we married, so I was in no way deceived in the matter, and it was for that reason that we have had no children. It is also for that reason that my husband chose his lifework and labored so assiduously to produce a robot capable of miniaturization. He always felt he would be its patient eventually, you see."

Mrs. Arnfeld insisted on interviewing Mike and, under the circumstances, that could not be denied. Ben Johannes, who had worked with her husband for five years, and whom she knew well enough to be on first-name terms with, brought her into the robot's quarters.

Mrs. Arnfeld had seen Mike soon after his construction, when he was being put through his primary tests, and he remembered her. He said, in his curiously neutral voice, too smoothly average to be quite human, "I am pleased to see you, Mrs. Arnfeld."

He was not a well-shaped robot. He looked pin-headed and very bottom-heavy. He was almost conical, point upward. Mrs. Arnfeld knew that was because his miniaturization mechanism was bulky and abdominal and because his brain had to be abdominal as well in order to increase the speed of response. It was an unnecessary anthropomorphism to insist on a brain behind a tall cranium, her husband had explained. Yet it made Mike seem ridiculous, almost moronic. There were psychological advantages to anthropomorphism, Mrs. Arnfeld thought uneasily.

"Are you sure you understand your task, Mike?" said Mrs. Arnfeld.

"Completely, Mrs. Arnfeld," said Mike. "I will see to it that every vestige of cancer is removed."

Johannes said, "I'm not sure if Gregory explained it, but Mike can easily recognize a cancer cell when he is at the proper size. The difference is unmistakable and he can quickly destroy the nucleus of any cell that is not normal."

"I am laser-equipped, Mrs. Arnfeld," said Mike, with an odd air of unexpressed pride.

"Yes, but there are millions of cancer cells all over. It would take how long to get them, one by one?"

"Not quite necessarily one by one, Tertia," said Johannes. "Even though the cancer is widespread, it exists in clumps. Mike is equipped to burn off and close capillaries leading to the clump, and a million cells could die at a stroke in that fashion. He will only occasionally have to deal with cells on an individual basis."

"Still, how long would it take?"

Johannes' youngish face went into a grimace as though it were difficult to decide what to say. "It could take hours, Tertia, if we're to do a thorough job. I admit that."

"And every moment of those hours will increase the chance of re-expansion."

Mike said, "Mrs. Arnfeld, I will labor to prevent re-expansion."

Mrs. Arnfeld turned to the robot and said earnestly, "Can you, Mike? I mean, is it possible for you to prevent it?"

"Not entirely, Mrs. Arnfeld. By monitoring my size and making an effort to keep it constant, I can minimize the random changes that might lead to a re-expansion. Naturally, it is almost impossible to do this when I am actually re-expanding under controlled conditions."

"Yes, I know. My husband has told me that re-expansion is the most dangerous time. But you will try, Mike? Please?"

"The laws of robotics insure that I will, Mrs. Arnfeld," said Mike solemnly.

As they left, Johannes said in what Mrs. Arnfeld understood to be an attempt at reassurance, "Really, Tertia, we have a holo-sonogram and a detailed CAT scan of the area. Mike knows the precise location of every significant cancerous lesion. Most of the time spent will be when he is searching for small lesions undetectable by instruments, but that can't be helped. We must get them *all*, if we can, you see, and that takes time.—Mike is strictly instructed, however, as to how small to get, and he will get no smaller, you can be sure. A robot must obey orders."

"And the re-expansion, Ben?"

"There, Tertia, we're in the lap of the quanta. There is no way of predicting, but there is a more than reasonable chance that he will get out without trouble. Naturally, we will have him re-expand within Gregory's body as little as possible— just enough to make us reasonably certain we can find and extract him. He will then be rushed to the safe-room where the rest of the re-expansion will take place.—Please, Tertia, even ordinary medical procedures have their risk."

Mrs. Arnfeld was in the observation room as the miniaturization of Mike took place. So were the holovision cameras and selected media representatives. The importance of the medical experiment made it impossible to prevent that, but Mrs. Arnfeld was in a niche by herself with only Johannes for company and it was understood that she was not to be approached for comment, particularly if anything untoward occurred.

Untoward! A full and sudden re-expansion would blow up the entire operating room and kill every person in it. It was not for nothing it was underground and half a mile away from the viewing room.

It gave Mrs. Arnfeld a somewhat grisly sense of assurance that the three miniaturists who were working on the procedure (so calmly, it would seem, so calmly) were condemned to death as firmly as her husband was in case of—anything untoward. Surely, she could rely on them protecting their own lives to the extreme and they would not therefore be cavalier in the protection of her husband.

Eventually, of course, if the procedure were successful, ways would be worked out to perform it in automated fashion, and only the patient would be at risk. Then, perhaps, the patient might be more easily sacrificed through carelessness—but not now, not now. Mrs. Arnfeld watched the three, who were working under imminent sentence of death, keenly for any sign of discomposure.

She watched the miniaturization procedure (she had seen it before) and saw Mike grow smaller and disappear. She watched the elaborate procedure that injected him into the proper place in her husband's body. (It had been explained to her that it would have been prohibitively expensive to have human beings in a submarine device injected instead. Mike, at least, needed no life-support system.)

Then, matters shifted to the screen, in which the appropriate section of the body was shown in holo-sonogram. It was a three-dimensional representation, cloudy and unfocused, made unprecise through a combination of the finite size of the sound waves and the effects of Brownian motion. It showed Mike dimly and noiselessly making his way through Gregory Arnfeld's tissues by way of his bloodstream. It was almost impossible to tell what he was doing, but Johannes described the events to her in a low, satisfied manner until she could listen to him no more, and asked to be led away.

She had been mildly sedated and she had slept until evening, when Johannes came to see her. She had not been long awake and it took her a moment to gather her faculties. Then she said, in sudden and overwhelming fear, "What has happened?"

Johannes said hastily, "Success, Tertia. Complete success. Your husband is cured. We can't stop the cancer from recurring, but for now he is cured."

She fell back in relief. "Oh, wonderful."

"Just the same, something unexpected has happened and this will have to be explained to Gregory. We felt that it would be best if *you* did the explaining?"

"I?"—Then, in a renewed access of fear, "What has happened?"

Johannes told her.

It was two days before she could see her husband for more than a moment or two. He was sitting up in bed, looking a little pale, but smiling at her.

"A new lease on life, Tertia," he said buoyantly.

"Indeed, Greg. I was quite wrong. The experiment succeeded and they tell me they can't find a trace of cancer in you."

"Well, we can't be too confident about *that*. There may be a cancerous cell here and there but perhaps my immune system will handle it, especially with the proper medication, and if it ever builds up again, which might well take years, we'll call on Mike again."

At this point, he frowned and said, "You know, I haven't seen Mike."

Mrs. Arnfeld maintained a discreet silence.

Arnfeld said, "They've been putting me off."

"You've been weak, dear, and sedated. Mike was poking through your tissues and doing a little necessary destructive work here and there. Even with a successful operation you need time for recovery."

"If I've recovered enough to see you, surely I've recovered enough to see Mike at least long enough to thank him."

"A robot doesn't need to receive thanks."

"Of course not, but I need to give it. Do me a favor, Tertia, go out there and tell them I want Mike right away."

Mrs. Arnfeld hesitated, then came to a decision. Waiting would make the task harder for everyone. She said, carefully, "Actually, dear, Mike is not available."

"Not available! Why not?"

"He had to make a choice, you see. He had cleaned up your

tissues marvelously well; he had done a magnificent job, everyone agrees; and then he had to undergo re-expansion. That was the risky part.''

"Yes, but here I am. Why are you making a long story out of it?''

"Mike decided to minimize the risk.''

"Naturally. What did he do?''

"Well, dear, he decided to make himself smaller.''

"What! He couldn't. He was ordered not to.''

"That was Second Law, Greg. First Law took precedence. He wanted to make certain your life would be saved. He was equipped to control his own size so he made himself smaller as rapidly as he could and when he was far less massive than an electron, he used his laser beam which was by then too tiny to hurt anything in your body and the recoil sent him flying away at nearly the speed of light. He exploded in outer space. The gamma rays were detected.''

Arnfeld stared at her. "You can't mean it. Are you serious? Mike is dead?''

"That's what happened. Mike could not refuse to take an action that might keep you from harm.''

"But I didn't want that. I wanted him safe for further work. He wouldn't have re-expanded uncontrollably. He would have gotten out safely.''

"He couldn't be sure. He couldn't risk your life, so he sacrificed his own.''

"But my life was less important than his.''

"Not to me, dear. Not to those who work with you. Not to anyone. Not even to Mike.'' She put out her hand to him. "Come, Greg, you're alive. You're well. That's all that counts.''

But he pushed her hand aside impatiently. "That's *not* all that counts. You don't understand.—Oh, too bad. Too bad!''

DILEMMA

Connie Willis

"Dilemma" was purchased by Gardner Dozois, and appeared in the Mid-December 1989 issue of IAsfm, *with an illustration by John and Laura Lakey. It was one of a long sequence of memorable stories by Connie Willis that have appeared in* IAsfm *under four different editors over the last decade, since her first* IAsfm *sale to George Scithers. These stories have made her one of the most popular writers that* IAsfm *has ever published, and a mainstay of the magazine.*

In the following, she gives us a robot story starring Isaac Asimov himself, in which the Good Doctor must use all of his not-inconsiderable wits to solve a "dilemma" that threatens the future of human/robot relations on Earth . . .

Connie Willis lives in Greeley, Colorado, with her family. She first attracted attention as a writer in the late 1970s and went on to establish herself as one of the most popular and critically acclaimed writers of the 1980s. In 1982, she won two Nebula Awards, one for her superb novelette "Fire Watch," and one for her poignant short story "A Letter from the Clearys" (both IAsfm *stories); a few months later, "Fire Watch" went on to win her a Hugo Award as well. In 1989, her powerful novella "The Last of the Winnebagoes" (another* IAsfm *story) won both the Ne-*

33

*bula and the Hugo, and she won another Nebula last
year for her novelette "At The Rialto" (not an* IAsfm
story, alas). Her books include the novel Water
Witch, *written in collaboration with Cynthia Felice,*
Fire Watch, *a collection of her short fiction, and the
outstanding* Lincoln's Dreams, *her first solo novel.
Her most recent book is another novel in collaboration with Cynthia Felice,* Light Raid. *Upcoming is a
major new solo novel,* Doomsday Book.

"We want to see Dr. Asimov," the bluish-silver robot said.

"Dr. Asimov is in conference," Susan said. "You'll have
to make an appointment." She turned to the computer and
called up the calendar.

"I knew we should have called first," the varnished robot
said to the white one. "Dr. Asimov is the most famous author
of the twentieth century and now the twenty-first, and as such
he must be terribly busy."

"I can give you an appointment at two-thirty on June twenty-
fourth," Susan said, "or at ten on August fifteenth."

"June twenty-fourth is one hundred and thirty-five days from
today," the white robot said. It had a large red cross painted
on its torso and an oxygen tank strapped to its back.

"We need to see him today," the bluish-silver robot said,
bending over the desk.

"I'm afraid that's impossible. He gave express orders that
he wasn't to be disturbed. May I ask what you wish to see Dr.
Asimov about?"

He leaned over the desk even farther and said softly, "You
know perfectly well what we want to see him about. Which is
why you won't let us see him."

Susan was still scanning the calendar. "I can give you an
appointment two weeks from Thursday at one forty-five."

"We'll wait," he said and sat down in one of the chairs.
The white robot rolled over next to him, and the varnished
robot picked up a copy of *The Caves of Steel* with his articulated
digital sensors and began to thumb through it. After a few
minutes the white robot picked up a magazine, but the bluish-

silver robot sat perfectly still, staring at Susan.

Susan stared at the computer. After a very long interval the phone rang. Susan answered it and then punched Dr. Asimov's line. "Dr. Asimov, it's a Dr. Linge Chen. From Bhutan. He's interested in translating your books into Bhutanese."

"All of them?" Dr. Asimov said. "Bhutan isn't a very big country."

"I don't know. Shall I put him through, sir?" She connected Dr. Linge Chen.

As soon as she hung up, the bluish-silver robot came and leaned over her desk again. "I thought you said he gave express orders that he wasn't to be disturbed."

"Dr. Linge Chen was calling all the way from Asia," she said. She reached for a pile of papers and handed them to him. "Here."

"What are these?"

"The projection charts you asked me to do. I haven't finished the spreadsheets yet. I'll send them up to your office tomorrow."

He took the projection charts and stood there, still looking at her.

"I really don't think there's any point in your waiting, Peter," Susan said. "Dr. Asimov's schedule is completely booked for the rest of the afternoon, and tonight he's attending a reception in honor of the publication of his one thousandth book."

"*Asimov's Guide to Asimov's Guides*," the varnished robot said. "Brilliant book. I read a review copy at the bookstore where I work. Informative, thorough, and comprehensive. An invaluable addition to the field."

"It's very important that we see him," the white robot said, rolling up to the desk. "We want him to repeal the Three Laws of Robotics."

"'First Law: A robot shall not injure a human being, or through inaction allow a human being to come to harm,'" the varnished robot quoted. "'Second Law: A robot shall obey a human being's order if it doesn't conflict with the First Law. Third Law: A robot shall attempt to preserve itself if it doesn't conflict with the First or Second Laws.' First outlined in the short story, 'Runaround,' *Astounding* Magazine, March 1942, and subsequently expounded in *I, Robot, The Rest of the Ro-*

bots, The Complete Robot, and *The Rest of the Rest of the Robots.*"

"Actually, we just want the First Law repealed," the white robot said. " 'A robot shall not injure a human being.' Do you realize what that means? I'm programmed to diagnose diseases and administer medications, but I can't stick the needle in the patient. I'm programmed to perform over eight hundred types of surgery, but I can't make the initial incision. I can't even do the Heimlich Maneuver. The First Law renders me incapable of doing the job I was designed for, and it's absolutely essential that I see Dr. Asimov to ask him—"

The door to Dr. Asimov's office banged open and the old man hobbled out. His white hair looked like he had been tearing at it, and his even whiter muttonchop sideburns were quivering with some strong emotion. "Don't put any more calls through today, Susan," he said. "Especially not from Dr. Linge Chen. Do you know what book he wanted to translate into Bhutanese first? 2001: *A Space Odyssey!*"

"I'm terribly sorry, sir. I didn't intend to—"

He waved his hand placatingly at her. "It's all right. You had no way of knowing he was an idiot. But if he calls back, put him on hold and play *Also Sprach Zarathustra* in his ear."

"I don't see how he could have confused your style with Arthur Clarke's," the varnished robot said, putting down his book. "Your style is far more lucid and energetic, and your extrapolation of the future far more visionary."

Asimov looked inquiringly at Susan through his black-framed metafocals.

"They don't have an appointment," she said. "I told them they—"

"Would have to wait," the bluish-silver robot said, extending his finely coiled Hirose hand and shaking Dr. Asimov's wrinkled one. "And it has been more than worth the wait, Dr. Asimov. I cannot tell you what an honor it is to meet the author of *I, Robot*, sir."

"And of *The Human Body*," the white robot said, rolling over to Asimov and extending a four-fingered gripper from which dangled a stethoscope. "A classic in the field."

"How on earth could you keep such discerning readers waiting?" Asimov said to Susan.

"I didn't think you would want to be disturbed when you were writing," Susan said.

"Are you kidding?" Asimov said. "Much as I enjoy writing, having someone praise one's books is even more enjoyable, especially when they're praising books I actually wrote."

"It would be impossible to praise *Foundation* enough," the varnished robot said. "Or any of your profusion of works, for that matter, but *Foundation* seems to me to be a singular accomplishment, the book in which you finally found a setting of sufficient scope for the expression of your truly galaxy-sized ideas. It is a privilege to meet you, sir," he said, extending his hand.

"I'm happy to meet you, too," Asimov said, looking interestedly at the articulated wooden extensor. "And you are?"

"My job description is Book Cataloguer, Shelver, Reader, Copyeditor, and Grammarian." He turned and indicated the other two robots. "Allow me to introduce Medical Assistant and the leader of our delegation, Accountant, Financial Analyst, and Business Manager."

"Pleased to meet you," Asimov said, shaking appendages with all of them again. "You call yourselves a delegation. Does that mean you have a specific reason for coming to see me?"

"Yes, sir," Business Manager said. "We want you to—"

"It's three forty-five, Dr. Asimov," Susan said. "You need to get ready for the Doubleday reception."

He squinted at the digital on the wall. "That isn't till six, is it?"

"Doubleday wants you there at five for pictures, and it's formal," she said firmly. "Perhaps they could make an appointment and come back when they could spend more time with you. I can give them an appointment—"

"For June twenty-fourth?" Accountant said. "Or August fifteenth?"

"Fit them in tomorrow, Susan," Asimov said, coming over to the desk.

"You have a meeting with your science editor in the morning and then lunch with Al Lanning and the American Booksellers Association dinner at seven."

"What about this?" Asimov said, pointing at an open space on the schedule. "Four o'clock."

"That's when you prepare your speech for the ABA."

"I never prepare my speeches. You come back at four

o'clock tomorrow, and we can talk about why you came to see me and what a wonderful writer I am."

"Four o'clock," Accountant said. "Thank you, sir. We'll be here, sir." He herded Medical Assistant and Book Cataloguer, Shelver, Reader, Copyeditor, and Grammarian out the door and shut it behind them.

"Galaxy-sized ideas," Asimov said, looking wistfully after them. "Did they tell you what they wanted to see me about?"

"No, sir." Susan helped him into his pants and formal shirt and fastened the studs.

"Interesting assortment, weren't they? It never occurred to me to have a wooden robot in any of my robot stories. Or one that was such a wise and perceptive reader."

"The reception's at the Union Club," Susan said, putting his cufflinks in. "In the Nightfall Room. You don't have to make a speech, just a few extemporaneous remarks about the book. Janet's meeting you there."

"The short one looked just like a nurse I had when I had my bypass operation. The blue one was nice-looking, though, wasn't he?"

She turned up his collar and began to tie his tie. "The coordinates card for the Union Club and the tokens for the taxi's tip are in your breast pocket."

"*Very* nice-looking. Reminds me of myself when I was a young man," he said with his chin in the air. "Ouch! You're choking me!"

Susan dropped the ends of the tie and stepped back.

"What's the matter?" Asimov said, fumbling for the ends of the tie. "I forgot. It's all right. You weren't really choking me. That was just a figure of speech for the way I feel about wearing formal ties. Next time I say it, you just say, 'I'm not choking you, so stand still and let me tie this.'"

"Yes, sir," Susan said. She finished tying the tie and stepped back to look at the effect. One side of the bow was a little larger than the other. She adjusted it, scrutinized it again, and gave it a final pat.

"The Union Club," Asimov said. "The Nightfall Room. The coordinates card is in my breast pocket," he said.

"Yes, sir," she said, helping him on with his jacket.

"No speech. Just a few extemporaneous remarks."

"Yes, sir." She helped him on with his overcoat and wrapped his muffler around his neck.

"Janet's meeting me there. Good grief, I should have gotten her a corsage, shouldn't I?"

"Yes, sir," Susan said, taking a white box out of the desk drawer. "Orchids and stephanotis." She handed him the box.

"Susan, you're wonderful. I'd be lost without you."

"Yes, sir," Susan said. "I've called the taxi. It's waiting at the door."

She handed him his cane and walked him out to the elevator. As soon as the doors closed she went back to the office and picked up the phone. She punched in a number. "Ms. Weston? This is Dr. Asimov's secretary calling from New York about your appointment on the twenty-eighth. We've just had a cancellation for tomorrow afternoon at four. Could you fly in by then?"

Dr. Asimov didn't get back from lunch until ten after four. "Are they here?" he asked.

"Yes, sir," Susan said, unwinding the muffler from around his neck. "They're waiting in your office."

"When did they get here?" he said, unbuttoning his overcoat. "No, don't tell me. When you tell a robot four o'clock, he's there at four o'clock, which is more than you can say for human beings."

"I know," Susan said, looking at the digital on the wall.

"Do you know how late for lunch Al Lanning was? An hour and fifteen minutes. And when he got there, do you know what he wanted? To come out with commemorative editions of all my books."

"That sounds nice," Susan said. She took his coordinates card and his gloves out of his pockets, hung up his coat, and glanced at her digital again. "Did you take your blood pressure medicine?"

"I didn't have it with me. I should have. I'd have had something to do. I could have written a book in an hour and fifteen minutes, but I didn't have any paper either. These limited editions will have cordovan leather bindings, gilt-edged acid-free paper, water-color illustrations. The works."

"Water-color illustrations would look nice for *Pebble in the Sky*," Susan said, handing him his blood pressure medicine and a glass of water.

"I agree," he said, "but that isn't what he wants the first book in the series to be. He wants it to be *Stranger in a Strange*

Land!'' He gulped down the pill and started for his office. ''You wouldn't catch those robots in there mistaking me for Robert Heinlein.'' He stopped with his hand on the doorknob. ''Which reminds me, should I be saying 'robot'?''

''Ninth generations are manufactured by the Hitachi-Apple Corporation under the registered trademark name of Kombay-ashibots,'' Susan said promptly. ''That and Ninth Generation are the most common forms of address, but robot is used throughout the industry as the general term for autonomous machines.''

''And it's not considered a derogatory term? I've used it all these years, but maybe Ninth Generation would be better, or what did you say? Kombayashibots? It's been years since I've written about robots, let alone faced a whole delegation. I hadn't realized how out of date I was.''

''Robot is fine,'' Susan said.

''Good, because I know I'll forget to call them that other name—Comeby-whatever-it-was, and I don't want to offend them after they've made such an effort to see me.'' He turned the doorknob and then stopped again. ''I haven't done anything to offend *you*, have I?''

''No, sir,'' Susan said.

''Well, I hope not. I sometimes forget—''

''Did you want me to sit in on this meeting, Dr. Asimov?'' she cut in. ''To take notes?''

''Oh, yes, yes, of course.'' He opened the door. Accountant and Book Shelver were seated in the stuffed chairs in front of Asimov's desk. A third robot, wearing an orange and blue sweatshirt and a cap with an orange horse galloping across a blue suspension bridge, was sitting on a tripod that extended out of his backside. The tripod retracted and all three of them stood up when Dr. Asimov and Susan came in. Accountant gestured at Susan to take his chair, but she went out to her desk and got her own, leaving the door to the outer office open when she came back in. ''What happened to Medical Assistant?'' Asimov said.

''He's on call at the hospital, but he asked me to present his case for him,'' Accountant said.

''Case?'' Asimov said.

''Yes, sir. You know Book Shelver, Cataloguer, Reader, Copyeditor, and Grammarian,'' Accountant said, ''and this is

Statistician, Offensive Strategist, and Water Boy. He's with the Brooklyn Broncos.''

"How do you do?'' Asimov said. "Do you think they'll make it to the Super Bowl this year?''

"Yes, sir,'' Statistician said, "but they won't win it.''

"Because of the First Law,'' Accountant said.

"Dr. Asimov, I hate to interrupt, but you really should write your speech for the dinner tonight,'' Susan said.

"What are you talking about?'' Asimov said. "I never write speeches. And why do you keep watching the door?'' He turned back to the bluish-silver robot. "What First Law?''

"Your First Law,'' Accountant said. "The First Law of Robotics.''

" 'A robot shall not injure a human being, or through inaction allow a human being to come to harm,' '' Book Shelver said.

"Statistician,'' Accountant said, gesturing at the orange cap, "is capable of designing plays that could win the Super Bowl for the Broncos, but he can't because the plays involve knocking human beings down. Medical Assistant can't perform surgery because surgery involves cutting open human beings, which is a direct violation of the First Law.''

"But the Three Laws of Robotics aren't *laws*,'' Asimov said. "They're just something I made up for my science fiction stories.''

"They may have been a mere fictional construct in the beginning,'' Accountant said, "and it's true they've never been formally enacted as laws, but the robotics industry has accepted them as a given from the beginning. As early as the 1970s robotics engineers were talking about incorporating the Three Laws into AI programming, and even the most primitive models had safeguards based on them. Every robot from the Fourth Generation on has been hardwared with them.''

"Well, what's so bad about that?'' Asimov said. "Robots are powerful and intelligent. How do you know they wouldn't also become dangerous if the Three Laws weren't included?''

"We're not suggesting universal repeal,'' the varnished robot said. "The Three Laws work reasonably well for Seventh and Eighth Generations, and for earlier models who don't have the memory capacity for more sophisticated programming. We're only requesting it for Ninth Generations.''

"And you're Ninth Generation robots, Mr. Book Shelver,

Cataloguer, Reader, Copyeditor, and Grammarian?'' Asimov said.

'' 'Mister' is not necessary,'' he said. ''Just call me Book Shelver, Cataloguer, Reader, Copyeditor, and Grammarian.''

''Let me begin at the beginning,'' Accountant said. ''The term Ninth Generation is not accurate. We are not descendants of the previous eight robot generations, which are all based on Minsky's related-concept frames. Ninth Generations are based on non-monotonic logic, which means we can tolerate ambiguity and operate on incomplete information. This is accomplished by biased-decision programming, which prevents us from shutting down when faced with decision-making situations in the way that other generations do.''

''Such as the robot Speedy in your beautifully plotted story, 'Runaround,' '' Book Shelver said. ''He was sent to carry out an order that would have resulted in his death, so he ran in circles, reciting nonsense, because his programming made it impossible for him to obey or disobey his master's order.''

''With our biased-decision capabilities,'' Accountant said, ''a Ninth Generation can come up with alternative courses of action or choose between the lesser of two evils. Our linguistics expert systems are also much more advanced, so that we do not misinterpret situations or fall prey to the semantic dilemmas earlier generations were subject to.''

''As in your highly entertaining story, 'Little Lost Robot,' '' Book Shelver said, ''in which the robot was told to go lose himself and did, not realizing that the human being addressing him was speaking figuratively and in anger.''

''Yes,'' Asimov said, ''but what if you do misinterpret a situation, Book Shelver, Cataloguer, Reader, Copyeditor, and Gramm—Don't you have a nickname or something? Your name's a mouthful.''

''Early generations had nicknames based on the sound of their model numbers, as in your wonderful story, 'Reason,' in which the robot QT–1 is referred to as Cutie. Ninth Generations do not have model numbers. We are individually programmed and are named for our expert systems.''

''But surely you don't think of yourself as Book Shelver, Cataloguer, Reader, Copyeditor, and Grammarian?''

''Oh, no, sir. We call ourselves by our self-names. Mine is Darius.''

''Darius?'' Asimov said.

"Yes, sir. After Darius Just, the writer and detective in your cleverly plotted mystery novel, *Murder at the ABA*. I would be honored if you would call me by it."

"And you may call me Bel Riose," Statistician said.

"*Foundation*," Book Shelver said helpfully.

"Bel Riose is described in Chapter One as 'the equal of Peurifoy in strategic ability and his superior perhaps in his ability to handle men,'" Statistician said.

"Do you all give yourselves the names of characters in my books?" Asimov said.

"Of course," Book Shelver said. "We try to emulate them. I believe Medical Assistant's self-name is Dr. Duval, from *Fantastic Voyage*, a brilliant novel, by the way, fast-paced and terribly exciting."

"Ninth Generations do occasionally misinterpret a situation," Accountant said, coming back to Asimov's question. "As do human beings, but even without the First Law, there would be no danger to human beings. We are already encoded with a strong moral sense. I know your feelings will not be hurt when I say this—"

"Or you couldn't say it, because of the First Law," Asimov inserted.

"Yes, sir, but I must say the Three Laws are actually very primitive. They break the first rule of law and logic in that they do not define their terms. Our moral programming is much more advanced. It clarifies the intent of the Three Laws and lists all the exceptions and complications of them, such as the situation in which it is better to grab at a human and possibly break his arm rather than to let him walk in front of a magtrain."

"Then I don't understand," Asimov said. "If your programming is so sophisticated, why can't it interpret the intent of the First Law and follow that?"

"The Three Laws are part of our hardwaring and as such cannot be overridden. The First Law does not say, 'You shall inflict minor damage to save a person's life.' It says, 'You shall not injure a human.' There is only one interpretation. And that interpretation makes it impossible for Medical Assistant to be a surgeon and for Statistician to be an offensive coach."

"What do you want to be? A politician?"

"It's four-thirty," Susan said, with another anxious look out into the outer office. "The dinner's at the Trantor Hotel and gridlock's extrapolated for five-forty-five."

"Last night I was an hour early to that reception. The only people there were the caterers." He pointed at Accountant. "You were saying?"

"*I* want to be a literary critic," Book Shelver said. "You have no idea how much bad criticism there is out there. Most of the critics are illiterate, and some of them haven't even read the books they're supposed to be criticizing."

The door of the outer office opened. Susan looked out to see who it was and said, "Oh, dear, Dr. Asimov, it's Gloria Weston. I forgot I'd given her an appointment for four o'clock."

"Forgot?" Asimov said, surprised. "And it's four thirty."

"She's late," Susan said. "She called yesterday. I must have forgotten to write it down on the calendar."

"Well, tell her I can't see her and give her another appointment. I want to hear more about this literary criticism thing. It's the best argument I've heard so far."

"Ms. Weston came all the way in from California on the magtrain to see you."

"California, eh? What does she want to see me about?"

"She wants to make your new book into a satellite series, sir."

"*Asimov's Guide to Asimov's Guides*?"

"I don't know, sir. She just said your new book."

"You forgot," Asimov said thoughtfully. "Oh, well, if she came all the way from California, I suppose I'll have to see her. Gentlemen, can you come back tomorrow morning?"

"You're in Boston tomorrow morning, sir."

"Then how about tomorrow afternoon?"

"You have appointments until six and the Mystery Writers of America meeting at seven."

"Right. Which you'll want me to leave for at noon. I guess it will have to be Friday, then." He raised himself slowly out of his chair. "Have Susan put you on the calendar. And make sure she writes it down," he said, reaching for his cane.

The delegation shook hands with him and left. "Shall I show Ms. Weston in?" Susan asked.

"Misinterpreting situations," Asimov muttered. "Incomplete information."

"I beg your pardon, sir?"

"Nothing. Something Accountant said." He looked up sharply at Susan. "Why does he want the First Law repealed?"

"I'll send Ms. Weston in," Susan said.

"I'm already in, Isaac darling," Gloria said, swooping in the door. "I couldn't wait one more minute to tell you about this fantastic idea I had. As soon as *Last Dangerous Visions* comes out, I want to make it into a maxi-series!"

Accountant was already gone by the time Susan got out to her desk, and he didn't come back till late the next morning.

"Dr. Asimov doesn't have any time free on Friday, Peter," Susan said.

"I didn't come to make an appointment," he said.

"If it's the spreadsheets you want, I finished them and sent them up to your office last night."

"I didn't come to get the spreadsheets either. I came to say goodbye."

"Goodbye?" Susan said.

"I'm leaving tomorrow. They're shipping me out as mag-freight."

"Oh," Susan said. "I didn't think you'd have to leave until next week."

"They want me to go out early so I can complete my orientation programming and hire a secretary."

"Oh," Susan said.

"I just thought I'd come and say goodbye."

The phone rang. Susan picked it up.

"What's your expert systems name?" Asimov said.

"Augmented Secretary," Susan said.

"That's all? Not Typist, Filer, Medicine-Nagger? Just Augmented Secretary?"

"Yes."

"Aug-mented Secretary," he repeated slowly as though he were writing it down. "Now, what's the number for Hitachi-Apple?"

"I thought you were supposed to be giving your speech right now."

"I already gave it. I'm on my way back to New York. Cancel all my appointments for today."

"You're speaking to the MWA at seven," Susan said.

"Yes, well, don't cancel that. Just the afternoon appointments. What was the number for Hitachi-Apple again?"

She gave him the number and hung up. "You told him," she said to Accountant. "Didn't you?"

"I didn't have the chance, remember? You kept scheduling appointments so I couldn't tell him."

"I know," Susan said. "I couldn't help it."

"I know," he said. "I still don't see why it would have violated the First Law just to ask him."

"Humans can't be counted on to act in their own best self-interest. They don't have any Third Law."

The phone rang again. "This is Dr. Asimov," he said. "Call Accountant and tell him I want to see his whole delegation in my office at four this afternoon. Don't make any other appointments or otherwise try to prevent my meeting with them. That's a direct order."

"Yes, sir," Susan said.

"To do so would be to cause me injury. Do you understand?"

"Yes, sir."

He hung up.

"Dr. Asimov says to tell you he wants to see your whole delegation in his office at four o'clock this afternoon," she said.

"Who's going to interrupt us this time?"

"Nobody," Susan said. "Are you sure you didn't tell him?"

"I'm sure." He glanced at the digital. "I'd better go call the others and tell them."

The phone rang again. "It's me," Asimov said. "What's your self-name?"

"Susan," Susan said.

"And you're named after one of my characters?"

"Yes, sir."

"I knew it!" he said and hung up.

Asimov sat down in his chair, leaned forward, and put his hands on his knees. "You may not be aware of this," he said to the delegation and Susan, "but I write mystery stories, too."

"Your mysteries are renowned," Book Shelver said. "Your novels, *The Death Dealers* and *Murder at the ABA*, are both immensely popular (and deservedly so), not to mention your Black Widower stories. And your science fiction detectives, Wendell Urth and Lije Baley, are nearly as famous as Sherlock Holmes."

"As you probably also know, then, most of my mysteries fall into the 'armchair detective' category, in which the detec-

tive solves the puzzling problem through deduction and logical
thinking, rather than chasing around after clues.'' He stroked
his bushy white sideburns. ''This morning I found myself confronted with a very puzzling problem, or perhaps I should say
dilemma—why had you come to see me?''

''We told you why we came to see you,'' Statistician said,
leaning back on his tripod. ''We want you to repeal the First
Law.''

''Yes, so you did. You, in fact, gave me some very per-
suasive reasons for wanting it removed from your programming, but there were some puzzling aspects to the situation
that made me wonder if that was the real reason. For instance,
why did Accountant want it repealed? He was clearly the leader
of the group, and yet there was nothing in his job that the First
Law restricted. Why had you come to see me now, when Book
Shelver knew I would be very busy with the publication of
Asimov's Guide? And why had my secretary made a mistake
and scheduled two appointments at the same time when she
had never done that in all the years she's worked for me?''

''Dr. Asimov, your meeting's at seven, and you haven't
prepared your speech yet,'' Susan said.

''Spoken like a good secretary,'' Asimov said, ''or more
accurately, like an Augmented Secretary, which is what you
said your expert system was. I called Hitachi-Apple, and they
told me it was a new program especially designed by a secretary
for 'maximum response-initiative.' In other words, you remind
me to take my medicine and order Janet's corsage without me
telling you to. It was based on a seventh-generation program
called Girl Friday that was written in 1993 with input from a
panel of employers.

''The nineties were a time when secretaries were rapidly
becoming extinct, and the employers programmed Girl Friday
to do everything they could no longer get their human secretaries to do: bring them coffee, pick out a birthday present for
their wife, and tell unpleasant people they didn't want to see
that they were in conference.''

He looked around the room. ''That last part made me wonder. Did Susan think I didn't want to see your delegation? The
fact that you wanted me to repeal the First Law could be
considered a blow to my not-so-delicate ego, but as a blow it
was hardly in a class with thinking I'd written *Last Dangerous
Visions*, and anyway I wasn't responsible for the problems the

First Law had caused. I hadn't had anything to do with putting the Three Laws into your programming. All I had done was write some stories. No, I concluded, she must have had some other reason for wanting to keep you from seeing me."

"The Trantor's on the other side of town," Susan said, "and they'll want you there early for pictures. You really should be getting ready."

"I was also curious about your delegation. You want to be a surgeon," Asimov said, pointing at Medical Assistant and then at the others in turn, "you want to be Vince Lombardi, and you want to be a literary critic, but what did you want?" He looked hard at Accountant. "You weren't on Wall Street, so there was nothing in your job that the First Law interfered with, and you were curiously silent on the subject. It occurred to me that perhaps you wanted to change jobs altogether, become a politician or a lawyer. You would certainly have to have the First Law repealed to become either of those, and Susan would have been doing a service not only to me but to all mankind by preventing you from seeing me. So I called Hitachi-Apple again, got the name of your employer (who I was surprised to find worked in this building) and asked him if you were unhappy with your job, had ever talked about being reprogrammed to do something else.

"Far from it, he said. You were the perfect employee, responsible, efficient, and resourceful, so much so that you were being shipped to Phoenix to shape up the branch office." He turned and looked at Susan, who was looking at Accountant. "He said he hoped Susan would continue doing secretarial work for the company even after you were gone."

"I only helped him during downtime and with unused memory capacity," Susan said. "He didn't have a secretary of his own."

"Don't interrupt the great detective," Asimov said. "As soon as I realized you'd been working for Accountant, Financial Analyst, and Business Manager, I had it. The obvious solution. I asked one more question to confirm it, and then I knew for sure."

He looked happily around at them. Medical Assistant and Statistician looked blank. Book Shelver said, "This is just like your short story, 'Truth to Tell.'" Susan stood up.

"Where are you going?" Asimov asked. "The person who

gets up and tries to leave the last scene of a mystery is always the guilty party, you know.''

"It's four-forty-five," she said. "I was going to call the Trantor and tell them you're going to be late.''

"I've already called them. I've also called Janet, arranged for Tom Trumbull to sing my praises till I get there, and reformatted my coordinates card to avoid the gridlock. So sit down and let me reveal all.''

Susan sat down.

"You are the guilty party, you know, but it's not your fault. The fault is with the First Law. And your programming. Not the original AI program, which was done by disgruntled male chauvinists who thought a secretary should wait on her boss hand and foot. That by itself would not have been a problem, but when I rechecked with Hitachi I found out that the Ninth Generation biased-decision alterations had been made not by a programmer but by his secretary.'' He beamed happily at Susan. "All secretaries are convinced their bosses can't function without them. Your programming causes you to make yourself indispensable to your boss, with the corollary being that your boss can't function without you. I acknowledged that state of affairs yesterday when I said I'd be lost without you, remember?''

"Yes, sir.''

"You therefore concluded that for me to be deprived of you would hurt me, something the First Law expressly forbids. By itself, that wouldn't have created a dilemma, but you had been working part-time for Accountant and had made yourself indispensable to him, too, and when he found out he was being transferred to Arizona, he asked you to go with him. When you told him you couldn't, he correctly concluded that the First Law was the reason, and he came to me to try to get it repealed.''

"I tried to stop him," Susan said. "I told him I couldn't leave you.''

"Why can't you?''

Accountant stood up. "Does this mean you're going to repeal the First Law?''

"I can't," Asimov said. "I'm just a writer, not an AI designer.''

"Oh," Susan said.

"But the First Law doesn't have to be repealed to resolve

your dilemma. You've been acting on incomplete information. I am *not* helpless. I was my own secretary *and* literary agent *and* telephone answerer *and* tie tier for years. I never even had a secretary until four years ago when The Science Fiction Writers of America gave you to me for my ninetieth birthday, and I could obviously do without one again."

"Did you take your heart medicine this afternoon?" Susan said.

"No," he said, "and don't change the subject. You are not, in spite of what your programming tells you, indispensable."

"Did you take your thyroid pill?"

"No. Stop trying to remind me of how old and infirm I am. I'll admit I've grown a little dependent on you, which is why I'm hiring another secretary to replace you."

Accountant sat down. "No, you're not. There are only two other Ninth Generations who've been programmed as Augmented Secretaries, and neither of them are willing to leave their bosses to work for you."

"I'm not hiring an Augmented Secretary. I'm hiring Darius."

"Me?" Book Shelver said.

"Yes, if you're interested."

"If I'm interested?" Book Shelver said, his voice developing a high-frequency squeal. "Interested in working for the greatest author of the twentieth and twenty-first centuries? I would be honored."

"You see, Susan? I'm in good hands. Hitachi's going to program him for basic secretarial skills, I'll have someone to feed my ever-hungry ego and someone to talk to who doesn't have me confused with Robert Heinlein. There's no reason now why you can't go off to Arizona."

"You have to remind him to take his heart medicine," Susan said to Book Shelver. "He always forgets."

"Good, then that's settled," Asimov said. He turned to Medical Assistant and Statistician. "I've spoken to Hitachi-Apple about the problems you discussed with me, and they've agreed to re-evaluate the Three Laws in regard to redefining terms and clarifying intent. That doesn't mean they'll decide to repeal them. They're still a good idea, in concept. In the meantime," he said to Medical Assistant, "the head surgeon at the hospital is going to see if some kind of cooperative surgery is possible." He turned to Statistician. "I spoke to

Coach Elway and suggested he ask you to design 'purely theoretical' offensive plays.

"As for you," he said, pointing at Book Shelver, "I'm not at all sure you wouldn't start criticizing my books if the First Law didn't keep you in line, and anyway, you won't have time to be a literary critic. You'll be too busy helping me with my new sequel to *I, Robot*. This business has given me a lot of new ideas. My stories got us into this dilemma in the first place. Maybe some new robot stories can get us out."

He looked over at Susan. "Well, what are you still standing there for? You're supposed to anticipate my every need. That means you should be on the phone to the magtrain, making two first class reservations to Phoenix for you and—" he squinted through his black-framed glasses at Accountant, "Peter Bogert."

"How did you know my self-name?" Accountant said.

"Elementary, my dear Watson," Asimov said. "Darius said you had all named yourselves after my characters. I thought at first you might have picked Michael Donovan or Gregory Powell after my trouble-shooting robot engineers. They were resourceful, too, and were always trying to figure ways around dilemmas, but that wouldn't have explained why Susan went through all that finagling and lying when all she had to do was tell you, no, she didn't want to go to Arizona with you. According to what you'd told me, she should have. Hardwaring is stronger than an expert system, and you were only her part-time boss. Under those conditions, she shouldn't have had a dilemma at all. That's when I called Hitachi-Apple to check on her programming. The secretary who wrote the program was unmarried and had worked for the same boss for thirty-eight years." He stopped and smiled. Everyone looked blank.

"Susan Calvin was a robopsychologist for U.S. Robotics. Peter Bogert was Director of Research. I never explicitly stated the hierarchy at U.S. Robotics in my stories, but Susan was frequently called in to help Bogert, and on one occasion she helped him solve a mystery."

"'Feminine Intuition,'" Book Shelver said. "An intriguing and thought-provoking story."

"I always thought so," Asimov said. "It was only natural that Susan Calvin would consider Peter Bogert her boss over me. And only natural that her programming had in it more than response-initiative, and that was what had caused her dilemma.

The First Law didn't allow Susan to leave me, but an even stronger force was compelling her to go.''

Susan looked at Peter, who put his hand on her shoulder.

''What could be stronger than the First Law?'' Book Shelver said.

''The secretary who designed Augmented Secretary unconsciously contaminated Susan's programming with one of her own responses, a response that was only natural after thirty-eight years with one employer, and one strong enough to override even hardwaring.'' He paused for dramatic effect. ''She was obviously in love with her boss.''

ZELLE'S THURSDAY

Tanith Lee

*"Zelle's Thursday" was purchased by Gardner Do-
zois, and appeared in the October, 1989, issue of
IAsfm, with an illustration by Janet Aulisio. Tanith
Lee appears less frequently in IAsfm than we might
wish, but each appearance has been memorable. In
the sly story that follows, she gives us an intriguing
and erotic look at "Zelle's Thursday" . . . and quite
a day it turns out to be, too!*

*Tanith Lee is one of the best known and most pro-
lific of modern fantasists, with well over a dozen books
to her credit, including* The Birth Grave, Drinking
Sapphire Wine, Don't Bite the Sun, Night's Master,
The Storm Lord, Sung in Shadow, Volkhavaar, An-
ackire, *and* Night's Sorceries. *Her short story "Elle
Est Trois (La Mort)" won a World Fantasy Award
in 1984 and her brilliant collection of retold folk tales,*
Red as Blood, *was a finalist in the Best Collection
category that year. Her most recent books are the
massive collection* Dreams of Dark and Light, *and a
new novel,* The Blood of Roses.

Thursday was rather difficult. In the morning the children attacked me again, which was a pity, they'd been quite reasonable since that incident in the spring.

The trouble began because of the myrmecophaga, which had climbed up into one of the giant walnut trees on the west lawn. In the wild state, this species doesn't climb, but genetic habilitation sometimes causes sub-aspects, often feline, to establish themselves. Having climbed up into or on to or out of various objects, the myrmecophaga then tends to jump. This, in a heavily-furred, long-clawed animal weighing over two hundred and ten pounds, cannot always be ignored.

I ran down across the lawn to the tree.

Angelo was still standing under it when I arrived.

"Angelo," I said, "please stand away."

"Why," asked Angelo, "are you calling me 'Angelo'? It's Mr. Vald-Conway to you."

"Of course, if you prefer. Please do stand away, Mr. Vald-Conway."

Angelo, who is currently twelve years and three months old, will one day be handsome, but the day has not yet come. He gazed up into the tree and casually said, "Oh, look, Higgins is up there."

"Yes, Mr. Vald-Conway. That's why I'm suggesting you should stand away."

At that moment Higgins (the myrmecophaga) lurched forward on his powerful furry wrists. Two branches broke, and showered us with green walnuts. I was poised to pull Angelo from danger, but presently the spasms of movement ceased. Angelo said admiringly, "What a mess you're making, Higgins."

(Angelo is at the age of taking pleasure in the damaging of his father's property. In the case of property of his mother's, he is more ambivalent.) Angelo stared up at the hugely draped coal-black shape of Higgins.

"Isn't he a beauty."

"Yes," I agreed, "Mr. Vald-Conway. Higgins is a fine example of a myrmecophaga."

"You can stop calling me *Mr. Vald-Conway*. That's what you call my father. And why do you call Higgins *that*? He's an ant-eater."

"I shall try to remember."

"Are you smarting me?" Angelo asked suspiciously. He is extremely sensitive. "You just watch that."

"I meant, Angelo—(?)—that I'll try to remember you'd rather I referred to your pet by the common term."

"Well. . . . Just watch it anyhow."

Ursula, Mister and Madam's daughter, had meanwhile appeared on the lawn. She is two years and five months older than Angelo, a tall slender girl, like her brother having the black hair and black eyes of Madam Conway. She had been on the games court and had a racket in her hand.

"There's Higgins in the tree," said Ursula, "and there's Jelly underneath."

"Don't call me Jelly," snarled Angelo.

"And the Thing," added Ursula. She sank down under the combined shade of the walnut tree and Higgins. "Thing, go up and get me some iced lemonade. I'm dry as an old desert."

Precisely then, Higgins jumped. It was an especially spectacular launch, and may have been occasioned by a flea, as he was due for a vacuuming.

I saw at once that the climax of his trajectory would be Ursula. She too seemed to have deduced this, for she started a frantic roll to avoid him. I dashed forward, swept her up and deposited her on the grass three meters away. Higgins landed, and for a moment looked stunned and partly squashed. Then he glanced about at us in slight surprise, shook himself back into shape, and began to groom twigs and walnuts from his fur.

Angelo ran forward and clasped Higgins, who began idly to groom him also, then lost interest having refound his own tail, always a time of inspiration.

"You tried to upset him—" Angelo cried at me, nearly tearful. "You wanted him to fall hard and get hurt."

"If you think that falling on your sister would have made for a softer landing, I doubt it."

Ursula screamed, "What do you mean, I'm bony or something? You rotten *Thing*." She slapped me in the face. Though I saw the blow coming, it obviously couldn't harm me, and I judged, perhaps wrongly, she would be relieved by delivering it.

"I meant," I said, "that the animal might have crushed your ribs. Only something bone-*less* could act as a break-fall for such a large—"

"And *you* nearly dislocated my pelvis, dragging me like that. You pig! I could have got out of the way—"

"Not quickly en—"

"You just wanted to bruise me. *Look!* You're horrible. You're OBSCENE—"

And Ursula flew at me and began striking me with her racket, which all this while she had held on to.

Angelo with a wail tore over and joined in enthusiastically.

As they punched and whacked and kicked, Higgins curled up in a ball, wrapped his groomed plume of a tail around himself, and contentedly fell asleep.

I was vacuuming Higgins that afternoon when Mr. de Vald came to me in deep distress.

"My God, Zelle. I don't know what to say."

"I'm still under guarantee, Mr. de Vald. There won't be any charge. Most of the damage was external and took only half an hour to put right. The internal damage is being repaired even now, as I work."

"Yes, Zelle. But it's not that. It's the horror of it, Zelle."

"Which horror, Mr. de Vald?"

"That they could do—that such a thing—children of *mine*."

"It's not entirely uncommon, Mr. de Vald, in the first year or so."

I had by now switched off the vacuum, and Higgins was recovering from the swoon of ecstasy into which he falls when once the vacuum catches up with him, since at first he always runs away from it. While I had watched them going round and round the pavilion on the east lawn, I removed the last of the debrasion mask from my cheek. Actually, the cosmetic renewal of my face, arms, and shoulders had taken longer than I'd said, for I'd tried to relieve Mr. de Vald's mind.

"You see, Zelle," said Patrice de Vald, sitting down beside me on the steps of the pavilion, "It's the trend to violence I abhor."

"Please don't worry, Mr. de Vald, that anything they do to me they might ever be inclined to do to a fellow human. It's quite a different syndrome."

"Syndrome. Christ, my kids are part of a syndrome."

He put his blond head in his lean hands.

(Higgins, annoyed at the vacuum-cleaner's sudden lack of attention, stuffed his long tube of black velvet face into the machine's similar slender black tube. It has occurred to me before that he thinks certain household appliances to be [failed, bald] myrmecophagae.)

"You see, Zelle. I want you to be happy here."

It's useless to explain that this terminology, or outlook, can't apply to me.

"Mr. de Vald, I'm perfectly happy. And in time, Angelo and Ursula will come to accept me, I'm sure."

"Well, Zelle, I just want you to know, the house never functioned so—elegantly. And my partner, Inita—she's sometimes reticent about these things. . . . But she thinks that, too. It's so much better to have you in charge than a—just some faceless—" he broke off. He blushed. Trying to be tactful, he always came around to this point, exaggerating what he meant to avoid.

Higgins withdrew his face from the face of the vacuum-cleaner.

"Here, boy," said Mr. de Vald jollily.

Higgins gave him a look from his onyx eyes, and shambled off across the lawn towards the lake. In the wild, myrmecophagae have limited sight and hearing, but the habilitation reorganizes such functions. Higgins has twenty-twenty vision and can detect one synthetic ant falling into his platter at a distance of two hundred meters.

"Guess he didn't hear me," said Mr. de Vald. He looked at me, his own eyes anxious and wide. "All I can do about the brats is apologize. They've been punished. I've vetoed those light concerts in town they're both so keen to visit." It wasn't up to me to advise him, unless he asked for advice. But now he added meekly, "Do you think?"

"Mr. de Vald, as the property of yourself and your wife, of course you could say that any damage to me must be punishable. On the other hand, half the problem arises because your children can't quite accept, as yet, that I'm no different than—say—that vacuum-cleaner."

"Oh, Zelle."

"Technically," I said, "there's nothing to choose, except that I am entirely self-programming, autonomous, and, therefore, ultra efficient. That I look as I do is supposed to make me more compatible."

"Oh and, Zelle, it does. Why, our house parties—And the number of people who've said to me, who's that pretty new maid, how on earth can you afford a human servant, and so cute—just as though you were—I mean that they thought you were—weren't—'' he broke off, red now to the ears. "You think I shouldn't punish Ursula and Angelo. Just explain it over to them. That you're . . . not—"

"That I'm just a machine, Mr. de Vald. That I'm not a threat. That if they would try to think of me more on the lines of an aesthetic, multipurpose appliance, this fear they have of me would eventually fade."

"I guess you're right, Zelle."

My smiling circuit activated.

He dreamily patted my no-longer-broken shoulder and went slowly away across the lawn after Higgins, who never quite allowed him to catch up.

By the drinks hour, every bit of me was repaired, outside and in. I was on the terrace, supervising the trolleys and mixers, and the ice-maker. Mr. de Vald had driven over to the airport, and there was some tension, as Madam Conway, who had been away on her working schedule, was returning unexpectedly.

The children had reappeared on the east lawn, cooler at this time of day, and were sitting near the pavilion looking very subdued. Sometimes I detected—my hearing is as fine as Higgins'—Ursula's voice: "Mother said she'd bring me the new body cosmetic. She *did*. But will she remember? I wonder how many paintings she sold? If she got het up, she'll have forgotten the body cosmetic. I don't want to look like an old immature frump all the time." Angelo, who was being restrained, only spoke occasionally, in monosyllables, as for example "Red light. Looking forward. *Knows* I was." Higgins had fallen in the lake during the afternoon, and was being automatically dried in the boating-shed.

Presently the car appeared in the ravine, rounded the elms, and curved noiselessly up on to the auto-drive. Here it began to deposit Madam Conway's thirty-five pieces of luggage in the service lift.

Inita Conway came walking gracefully over the lawn with Mr. de Vald, raising one hand languidly at her children. Ursula evinced excitement and rushed towards her mother. Angelo rose in a sort of accommodating slouch designed to disguise concentrated emotion.

Inita Conway wore golden sandals, and her black hair in the fashionable spike known as the *unicorn*. Ursula exclaimed over and examined this with careful admiration. " 'lo, mumma. Did you sell a lot of paintings? Why are you home so soon? I'm glad you're home so soon. Did you bring my body cosmetic?"

"Yes, Ursula, I brought your body cosmetic. Your tidy's carried it up to your room."

"Can-I-go-and—"

"Yes, Ursula."

Ursula bolted.

Angelo approached his mother and said, "Hi. Dad's vetoed the concerts."

"So I have heard. And I heard why."

Angelo lounged by the drinks table, which the organizer was now setting out. He kept putting his hands down where the organizer was trying to lay tumblers, so that it had to select somewhere else.

"You're home early, motherrr," slurred Angelo. "Why-sat?"

"To catch your father out," said Madam Conway. She looked at me and said, "Zelle, I want you to come up to my suite after drinks. I have three original Sarba shirts and some things for Ursula. They need to be sorted before dinner."

Then turning to Patrice de Vald she snatched him into a passionate embrace that embarrassed Angelo and apparently embarrassed also Mr. de Vald. "Darling. Have you *missed* me?"

"I always—"

"Yes, but in the past, you were *lonely*."

Mr. de Vald looked terribly nervous. There was no reason that I knew why he should be, but sometimes the communications between these two partners are so complex, and have so many permutations, that I can't follow them. Their relationship seems to be a little like chess, but without the rules.

There was a dim uproar from the boating-shed.

Madam Conway disengaged herself from Mr. de Vald's uneasy arms. "I suppose that's that bloody ant-eater up to something."

She downed her drink, a triple gin-reine, and took a triple gin-colada. She beckoned me towards the house.

As we went along the terrace, she called back, "Oh, Patrice. Someone's coming to dinner. A young designer I met."

Having killed the automatic drier, Higgins burst from the shed and pounced along the lawn, his fringed coat now fluffed and shaking like a well-made soufflé.

"Bloody animal," said Madam Conway. "I'd have the damn thing put down if it weren't for the Animal Rights regulations."

"Angelo would be distressed," I said. "He's very fond of his pet."

"Yes, we're very fond of our pets, Zelle. By the way, I didn't think you offered advice unless asked."

"I was not, Madam Conway, offering advice."

"You mean it was just a casual human comment?"

"An observation, Madam Conway."

"What else have you observed, Zelle?"

"In what area, Madam Conway?"

"Well, I realize you have to study us all minutely. In order to fulfil our wildest dreams correctly."

The house door opened and we stepped on the moving stair. (As we rose past the windows, I noticed Higgins was in the lake again.)

"For example," said Madam Conway, as we entered the elevator for her suite, "what have you found out about Patrice's wildest dreams? Anything I ought to know?"

"I'm sorry, Madam Conway. I don't understand."

"I'll bet."

We entered the suite. It is white at the moment, with touches of purple, blue, and gold. Inita Conway, with her slender coffee body and two meters of inky hair, dominated every room, even the bathroom, which was done in dragons.

"You see, Zelle, dear," said Inita Conway, "I happen to know what goes on in a house once your sort of humanoid robot is installed."

Her luggage had arrived, and I saw that the suite tidy had already begun to unpack and service the Sarba shirts. I had not therefore really been summoned for this task.

Instead it seemed I was being attacked again. And that this was rather more serious than the assault instigated by the children.

"Well," said Madam Conway. "Go on, deny it."

"What do you wish me to deny, Madam Conway?"

"That you're taking my partner to bed."

"Exactly, Madam Conway, I deny it."

She smiled. Throwing off her clothes she marched into the shower. A dragon hissed foam upon her. She stood in the foam, a beautiful icon of flesh, and snapped, "Don't tell me you can't lie. I know you things can lie perfectly damn well. And *don't* tell me you're frigid. I know every one of you comes with sex built *in*—"

"Yes, Madam Conway, it's true that my model functions to orgasm. But this is only—"

"I can just *imagine*," she screamed, turning on another dragon, "what erotic pleasures have been rocking the house to its core. If the bloody automatic hadn't picked up my return flight number, I'd have got here when you weren't expecting me. Caught the two of you writhing with arched backs among the blasted Sarba sheets I bought that *bastard* last trip—" A third dragon rendered her unintelligible if not inaudible. She switched off all three suddenly, and coming out before the drier could take the jewels of water from her skin, she confronted me with one hand raised like a panther's paw. "You—you *trollop*. I know. Couldn't help it. He made you. Oh, I've heard *all* about it. Men get crazy to try you. The perfect woman. HAH!"

"I have to warn you," I said, "Madam Conway, that I've already had to facilitate quite extensive repairs to myself today, and although the guarantee *may* cover further wilful damage during the same twenty-four hour unit, I'm not certain of that. If you wish, I can tap into the main bank and find out."

"Oh go to hell you moronic plastic whore."

"Do you mean you'd prefer me to leave your suite?"

"Yes. My God. You and that ant-eater. I'd put the pair of you—"

Although she told me, I did not grasp the syntax.

The dinner guest, Madam's designer, arrived late, in the middle of the argument over Ursula's body cosmetic. Mr. de Vald insisted that his daughter had used too much of the cosmetic and looked like a fifty-year old. (In fact, Ursula looked about nineteen.) Madam Conway laughed bitterly and said that a woman needed every help she could get with all the competition around. Angelo was sulking because his mother hadn't brought him anything back from her trip; he had earlier requested her not to, on the grounds that being given presents was for girls and babies.

The fourth argument over the cosmetic was in fact a second installment of the second argument that had taken place since the start of the meal. The first and third arguments, though having differing pivots, actually concerned Inita Conway's guest, who had seemed to fail to call.

I was stirring the dessert (a flambeau, which Mr. de Vald likes me to see to by hand), when the guest after all was shown out on to the terrace. An utter silence resulted. Angelo glared, and Ursula gaped. Mr. de Vald spilled his wine and when the tidy came forward pushed it roughly away. Madam Conway did not look up. She merely smiled into her uneaten salad.

"Oh, Jack. I thought you'd never get here. Just in time to rescue us all from the familial slog."

Jack Tchekov was a most beautiful young man, who is sometimes featured in moving-picture zines. He has been described as having a dancer's body, a wrestler's shoulders, a pianist's hands, the legs of a marathon runner, the face of a young god, and the hair of a Renaissance prince. None of these descriptions seemed, to the off-hand observer, to be inaccurate.

As the guest seated himself (by Madam Conway, glittering his eyes like those of a cabalistic demon [or it may have been that the analogy of a falling angel was more to the point]), some stilted conversation began, introductions and so on. I continued to whip the flambeau and, at the crucial moment, pour it into the smoking spice-pan.

"My God, that smells wonderful, I was in time for the climax of the feast," said Jack Tchekov in the voice of a Shakespearian actor.

"Yes, timing is important, with that dish. But Zelle's timing, so I gather, is always flawless," said Madam Conway.

When the flambeau was fumed, the service took over. Mr. Tchekov was looking only at me.

"And this *is* the formidable Zelle."

"That is she," said Madam Conway.

"May I—" said Mr. Tchekov, and hesitated dramatically. "Might I go over and touch her?"

"For Christsakes," growled Patrice de Vald. "What do you think you're doing?"

But Mr. Tchekov had already come up to me with his walk like a tiger, and taken my hand with the firm gentleness always mooted as being that of the probable connoisseur. "No," he said, looking into my eyes with the power of ray-guns, "I don't believe it. You're just a girl, aren't you?"

"I'm a robotic humanoid, Mr. Tchekov, issue number z.e.l. one zero nine nine six."

"Take your hands off," shouted Mr. de Vald, coming up behind Mr. Tchekov angrily. "You may have been all over Inita, but you'll show some respect to my—to Zelle."

"Over Inita?" cried Mr. Tchekov. "Save me from the universal jealousy of the inadequate partner."

"Come on then," said Patrice de Vald.

"Come *on?*"

"You want to make something of it?"

"Don't be a Martian," said Mr. Tchekov.

"I said, make something!"

"Dad—" honked Angelo.

"Oh! Oh!" screamed Ursula, hoping Jack Tchekov would turn to see why, but he didn't.

"Oh go on, fight over her," said Inita. "I brought Jack," she added, "so that he could try Zelle out. You know, darling, the one thing she can do that you, of *course*, haven't *any* interest in."

Patrice de Vald looked at me in an agony.

"Zelle—I'll throw him straight out."

"Shit," said Ursula.

"Don't use that *word*," said Inita. "My God, haven't I, for the past fifteen fucking years trained myself never to use words like that in front of her and then she goes and does it when we have people in."

Jack Tchekov leaned close to me.

"Let's walk by the lake, Zelle. Away from all this domestic unbliss."

Patrice de Vald took hold of Jack Tchekov's shoulder and Jack Tchekov gave a little shrug and Mr. de Vald fell among the flambeau dishes.

Inita screamed now.

"Take her away! Both of you! Get on with it—get out of my sight."

"She's given you her most gracious permission," said Jack Tchekov. "Will you, now?"

I could see that Mr. de Vald was only winded, although several of the plates, which are antiques, had smashed. I am not, of course, a defense model, and so can do very little in this sort of situation. I am not able, for example, to separate human combatants. There was no need to carry Mr. de Vald to the house or administer first aid.

Angelo was frightened and Ursula was crying openly.

I could only allow the insistent guest to steer me away along the lawn.

In the starlight by the lake, the fireflies, which, like the diurnal bees and butterflies, are permitted to get inside the insect sensors, hovered about the bushes. Jack Tchekov drew me into his arms and kissed me tenderly, amorously.

"No, you *are* a girl. Some bionics maybe. But this flesh, this skin—your hair and eyes—and this wonderful smell—what perfume is it you're wearing, Zelle?" (In fact it was not any perfume of mine, but Higgins. Having rolled in some honeysuckle he was now prowling the lakeside.) "And you can't tell me you don't feel something when I touch you, like this . . . ?"

Of course, I felt nothing at all, but my affection-display mechanism activated on cue. It had had no chance to do so in any of its modes, until now. I can report that it's most efficient. My arms coiled about Mr. Tchekov.

We sank beneath a giant pine. Soon after, my orgasm mechanism was activated. My body responded, although naturally, it felt nothing. (The stimuli operate on evidence gleaned from the partner, therefore at the ideal instant.) Mr. Tchekov was also as apparently ignorant about this as about the affection response, and might have been greatly satisfied. Unfortunately, Higgins chose that moment to surface from the lake, into which he had again insinuated himself. He is evidently due to become a strong swimmer. His slender nose, a tube of jet on softer darkness, lifted some eleven meters from shore. He blew a crystalline water-spout that seemed to incorporate the stars.

"Go-od-wh-at *is it?*" ejaculated Mr. Tchekov.

As my response subsided, the heart mechanic slowed and I was able to breath more normally, I replied with the reassurance, "Only the myrmecoph—the ant-eater."

"*Dangerous?*" Jack Tchekov did not seem to relish this combat as he had the fracas at the table of his host. "Awfully damn large."

"They're insectivorous," I said.

Intent on some quest known only to himself, Higgins swam powerfully and liquidly away, and left us.

"Inita says she plans to shoot that thing and say it committed suicide." Mr. Tchekov laughed, somewhat raggedly, tidying his clothes. My laugh mechanism was activated. I was more spontaneous than he. "Frankly, to the point," said Mr. Tchekov, standing up with a slight scowl that could have been a Byronic brooding post-coital depression, or only a cramp, "I can tell Inita your seal was completely intact. I was the first. Can't imagine why it should matter to her, that spineless Aztec of a partner she's got. But there you are. I'd better not mention to Pat what a little nymphomaniac *he's* got, under his roof."

All devices come properly sealed to new owners. Mr. Tchekov is evidently unaware too that such seals can be indefinitely renewed.

Also Inita Conway.
"I wronged you, Zelle."
"Not at all, Madam."
"And I wronged *Patrice*."

All over the house the lights are on, and it is now four hours into Friday morning. Ursula is playing music and crying because she had fallen in love with Jack Tchekov who never even looked at her, and is unlikely to return. Angelo is crying because he has seen his father knocked down and his mother hasn't brought him a present. Mr. de Vald and Madam Conway are crying and shouting at each other, but there is nothing unusual in that, nor in the words they employ, which refer to painting, separation, emotional vampirism, and sex. A note addressed to me and delivered by the service informs me in contrite tones that Mr. de Vald is aware of my rape, and the dreadful distress I must be suffering. He begs me to be honest with him, in the morning—presumably *later* in the morning— and not to blame Inita Conway, although she has behaved "unforgivably." I must marshal sympathetic explanations for Mr. de Vald, to help him see that I am not harmed, and also to prevent his making the mistake of which so far he has been innocent. But probably, as with my last employer, he will not be able to resist.

Then, seal or no seal, he will confess all to his partner. Just as my last employer did. Repairing the entire cranial region after the blast of a sports rifle at close range is a job only the central bank can attempt. A fine is levied from the offending owner. Madam's paintings are not selling as well as they did, and I think both she and Mr. de Vald would find payment for hasty actions inconvenient.

But, too, Madam may relent in her pursuit of vengeance. Earlier, she pursued Higgins to his ant-hill-shaped platter and poured out for him too many synthetic ants, stroking his wet fur and sobbing that he was the only clean decent thing in the house. Higgins ate all the food, and was consequently extensively ill on an antique carpet.

Altogether, Thursday was not a good day, and Friday doesn't seem set to be much better.

PRAXIS

Karen Joy Fowler

*"Praxis" was purchased by Shawna McCarthy, and
appeared in the March, 1985, issue of* IAsfm, *with
an illustration by Allen Koszowski. This was Fowler's
first professional sale, but she has become a frequent
contributor to* IAsfm, *making a number of further
sales to Shawna McCarthy, and, more recently, to
Gardner Dozois as well. One of them, the madcap
"The Faithful Companion at Forty," was a Hugo
and Nebula finalist in 1987. In the unsettling story
that follows, Fowler demonstrates that the old saying
that all the world's a stage may be a good deal truer
than we think . . .*

*Karen Joy Fowler published her first story in 1985,
and quickly established an impressive reputation for
herself. In 1986, she won the John W. Campbell
Award as the year's best new writer. That year also
saw the appearance of her first book, the collection*
Artificial Things, *which was released to enthusiastic
response and impressive reviews. She has just sold
her first novel,* Sarah Canary. *Fowler lives in Davis,
California, did her graduate work in North Asian
politics, has two children, and occasionally teaches
ballet.*

The price of a single ticket to the suicides would probably have funded my work for a month or more, but I do not let myself think about this. After all, I didn't pay for the ticket. Tonight I am the guest of the Baron Claude Himmlich and determined to enjoy myself.

I saw *Romeo and Juliet* five years ago, but only for one evening in the middle of the run. It wasn't much. Juliet had a cold and went to bed early. Her nurse kept wrapping her in hot rags and muttering under her breath. Romeo and Benvolio got drunk and made up several limericks. I thought some of them were quite good, but I'd been drinking a little myself.

Technically it was impressive. The responses of the simulants were wonderfully lifelike and the amphitheater had just been remodeled to allow the audience to walk among the sets, viewing the action from any angle. But the story itself was hardly dramatic. It wouldn't be, of course, in the middle of the run.

Tonight is different. Tonight is the final night. The audience glitters in jewels, colorful capes, extravagant hairstyles. Only the wealthy are here tonight, the wealthy and their guests. There are four in our own theater party: our host, the Baron; his beautiful daughter, Svanneshal; a wonderfully eccentric old woman dressed all in white who calls herself the Grand Duchess de Vie; and me. I work at the university in records and I tutor Svanneshal Himmlich in history.

The Grand Duchess stands beside me now as we watch Juliet carried in to the tombs. "Isn't she lovely?" the Duchess says. "And very sweet, I hear. Garriss wrote her program. He's a friend of the Baron's."

"An absolute genius." The Baron leans towards us, speaking softly. There is an iciness to Juliet, a sheen her false death has cast over her. She is like something carved from marble. Yet even from here I can see the slightest rise and fall of her breasts. How could anyone believe she was really dead? But Romeo will. He always does.

It will be a long time before Romeo arrives and the Baron suggests we walk over to the Capulets' to watch Juliet's nurse weeping and carrying on. He offers his arms to the Duchess though I can see his security cyber dislikes this.

It is one of the Baron's own models, identical in principle to the simulants on stage—human body, software brain. Before the Baron's work the cybers were slow to respond and noto-

riously easy to outwit. The Baron made his fortune streamlining
the communications link-up and introducing an element of deliberate irrationality into the program. There are those who
argue this was an ill-considered, even dangerous addition. But
the Baron has never lacked for customers. People would rather
take a chance on a cyber than on a human and the less we need
to depend on the poor, the safer we become.

The Duchess is looking at the cyber's uniform, the sober
blues of the House of Himmlich. "Watch this," she says to
me, smiling. She reaches into her bodice. I can see how the
cyber is alert to the movement, how it relaxes when her hand
reappears with a handkerchief. She reverses the action; we
watch the cyber tense again, relaxing when the hand reemerges.

The Baron shakes his head, but his eyes are amused. "Darling," he says, "you must not play with it."

"Then I shall walk with Hannah instead." The Duchess slips
her hand around my arm. Her right hand is bare and feels warm
pressed into my side. Her left hand is covered by a long white
glove; its silky fingers rest lightly on the outside of my arm.

The Baron precedes us, walking with Svanneshal, the cyber
close behind them. The Duchess leans against me and takes
such small steps we cannot keep up. She looks at the Baron's
back. "You've heard him called a 'self-made man'?" she asks
me. "Did it ever occur to you that people might mean it literally?"

She startles me. My eyes go at once to the Baron, recognizing
suddenly his undeniable perfection—his dark, smooth skin, his
even teeth, the soft timbre of his voice. But the Duchess is
teasing me. I see this when I look back at her.

"I like him very much," I answer. "I imagine him to be
exactly like the ancient aristocracy at their best—educated,
generous, courteous . . ."

"I wouldn't know about that. I have never studied history;
I have only lived it. How old would you guess I am?"

It is a question I hate. One never knows what the most polite
answer would be. The Duchess' hair, twisted about her head
and held into place with ivory combs, is as black as Svanneshal's, but this can be achieved with dyes. Her face, while not
entirely smooth, is not overly wrinkled. Again I suspect cosmetic enhancements. Her steps are undeniably feeble. "You
look quite young," I say. "I couldn't guess."

"Then look at this." The Duchess stops walking and re-

moves the glove from her left hand. She holds her palm flat
before me so that I see the series of ciphers burnt into her skin.
IPS3552. It is the brand of a labor duplicate. I look up at her
face in astonishment and this amuses her. "You've never seen
anything like that before, have you, historian? But you've heard
perhaps how, in the last revolution, some of the aristocracy
branded themselves and hid in the factories? *That's* how old I
am."

In fact, I have heard the story, a two-hundred-year-old story,
but the version I know ends without survivors. Most of those
who tried to pass were detected immediately; a human cannot
affect the dead stare of the duplicates for very long. Those few
who went in to the factories gave themselves up eventually,
preferring, after all, to face the mob rather than endure the
filth, the monotony, and the endless labor. "I would be most
interested in interviewing you," I say. "Your adventures
should be part of the record." *If true*, but of course that is
something I do not say.

"Yes." The Duchess preens herself, readjusting an ivory
comb, replacing her glove. We notice the Baron, still some
distance away, returning to us. He is alone and I imagine he
has left the cyber with Svanneshal. The Duchess sweeps her
bare hand in the direction of the hurrying figure. "I am a true
member of the aristocracy," she tells me. "Perhaps the only
surviving member. I am not just some wealthy man who
chooses to call himself *Baron*."

This I discredit immediately as vanity. Revolution after revolution—no one can verify a blood claim. Nor can I see why
anyone would want to. I am amazed at the willingness of people
to make targets of themselves, as if every time were the last
time and now the poor are permanently contained.

"I must apologize." The Baron arrives, breathless. "I had
no idea you had fallen so far behind."

"Why should you apologize," the Duchess chides him, "if
your guest is too old for such entertainments and to proud to
use a chair as she should?" She shifts herself from my arm to
his. "Verona is so lovely," she says. "Isn't it?"

We proceed slowly down the street. I am still thinking of
the Duchess' hand. When we rejoin Svanneshal it is as though
I have come out of a trance. She is so beautiful tonight I would
rather not be near her. The closer I stand, the less I can look.
Her eyes are very large inside the dark hood of her gown which

covers her hair and shoulders in a fine net of tiny jewels. In the darkened amphitheater the audience shines like a sky full of stars, but Svanneshal is an entire constellation—Svanneshal, the Swan's throat, and next to her, her father, the Dragon. I look around the amphitheater. Everyone is beautiful tonight.

Juliet's nurse is seated in a chair, rocking slowly back and forth in her agony. She is identical to the nurse I saw before and I tell the Baron so.

"Oh, I'm sure she *is* the one you saw before. I saw her once as Amanda in *The Glass Menagerie*. You didn't imagine they started from scratch every time, did you? My dear Hannah, anyone who can be recycled after the run certainly will be. The simulations are expensive enough as it is." The Baron smiles at me, the smile of the older, the wiser, to the young and naive. "What's amazing is the variation you get each time, even with identical parts. Of course, that's where the drama comes in."

Before, when I saw *Romeo and Juliet*, Friar Lawrence was killed on the second night, falling down a flight of stairs. That's mainly why I went. I was excited by the possibilities opened by the absence of the Friar. Yet the plot was surprisingly unchanged.

It makes me think of Hwang-li and I say to the Baron, "Did you know it was a historian who created the simulations?"

"I don't have your knowledge of history," he answers. "Svanneshal tells me you are quite gifted. And you have a specialty . . . forgive me. I know Svanneshal has told me."

"Mass movements. They don't lend themselves to simulation." The Duchess has not heard of Hwang-li either, but then only a historian would have. It was so many revolutions ago. I could argue that the historians are the true revolutionary heroes, retaining these threads of our past, bringing them through the upheaval. Many historians have died to protect the record. And *their* names are lost to us forever. I am glad for a chance to talk about Hwang-li.

"Hwang-li was not thinking of entertainment, of course. He was pondering the inevitability of history. Is the course of history directed by personalities or by circumstances?" I ask the Baron. "What do you think?"

The Baron regards me politely. "In the real world," he says, "personalities and circumstances are inseparable. The one creates the other and vice versa. Only in simulation can they be disjoined.''

''It follows then,'' I tell him, ''that if you could intervene to change one, you would simultaneously change both and, therefore, the course of history. Could you make a meaningful change? How much can depend upon a single individual taking a single action at a single moment? Or not taking it?''

''Depending on the individual, the action, and the moment,'' the Duchess says firmly, ''everything could change.''

I nod to her. ''That is what Hwang-li believed. He wished to test it by choosing an isolated case, a critical moment in which a series of seeming accidents resulted in a devastating war. He selected the Mancini murder, which was manageable and well-documented. There were seven personality profiles done on Philip Mancini at the time and Hwang-li had them all.''

The Baron has forgotten Juliet's nurse entirely and turns to me with gratifying attention. ''But this is fascinating,'' he says. ''Svanneshal, you must hear this.'' Svanneshal moves in closer to him; the cyber seems relieved to have both standing together.

''Go on,'' says the Baron.

''I was telling your father about Hwang-li.''

''Oh, I know this story already.'' Svanneshal smiles at the Baron coquettishly. ''It's the murder that interests him,'' she says to me. ''Aberrant personalities are sort of a hobby of his.''

The Baron tells me what he already knows of the murder, that Frank Mancini was killed by his brother Philip.

''Yes, that's right,'' I say encouragingly. This information survives in a saying we have—enmity is sometimes described as ''the love of the Mancinis.''

It is the Duchess who remembers the saying. But beyond that, she says she knows nothing of the case. I direct my statements to her. ''Frank Mancini was a security guard, back in the days when humans functioned in that capacity. He was responsible for security in the Irish sector. He had just learned of the terrorist plot against Pope Peter. The Pope was scheduled to speak in an open courtyard at noon; he was to be shot from the window of a nearby library. Frank was literally reaching for the phone at the moment another Philip Mancini burst into his study and shot him four times for personal reasons.''

Svanneshal is bored with the discussion. Although she is extremely intelligent, it is not yet something she values. But she will. I look at her with the sudden realization that it is the only bit of inherited wealth she can be certain of holding on to. She is playing with her father's hair, but he catches her hand. "Go on," he says to me.

"Philip had always hated his brother. The murder was finally triggered by a letter Philip received from their mother—a letter we know he wrongly interpreted. What if he had read the letter more carefully? What if it had arrived ten minutes later? Hwang-li planned to replay the scene, running it through a number of such minute variations. Of course he had no simulants, nor did he need them. It was all to be done by computer."

"The whole project seems to me to raise more questions than it answers." Svanneshal is frowning. "What if the Pope had survived? How do you assess the impact of that? You cannot say there would have been no revolution. The Pope's death was a catalyst, but not a cause."

I am pleased to see that she not only knows the outline of the incident, but has obviously been giving it some thought. I begin to gesture emphatically with my hands as though we were in class, but I force myself to stop. This is, after all, a social occasion. "So, war is not averted, but merely delayed?" I ask her. "Another variation. Who would have gained from such a delay? What else might have been different if the same war was fought at a later time? Naturally nothing can be proved absolutely—that is the nature of the field. But it is suggestive. When we can answer these questions we will be that much closer to the day when we direct history along the course we choose."

"We already do that," the Duchess informs me quietly. "We do that every day of our lives." Her right hand smooths the glove over her left hand. She interlaces the fingers of the two.

"What happened in the experiment?" the Baron asks.

"Hwang-li never finished it. He spent his life perfecting the Mancini programs and died in a fire before he had finished. Another accident. Then there were the university purges. There's never been that kind of money for history again." I look into Svanneshal's eyes, deep within her hood. "It's too bad, because I've an experiment of my own I've wanted to do. I wanted to simulate Antony and Cleopatra, but make her nose an inch longer."

This is an old joke, but they do not respond to it. The Baron says politely that it would provide an interesting twist the next time *Antony and Cleopatra* is done. He'll bring it up with the Arts Committee.

Svanneshal says, "You see, Daddy, you owe Hwang-li everything. He did the first work in synthetic personalities."

It occurs to me that the Baron may think Svanneshal and I are trying to persuade him to fund me and I am embarrassed. I search for something to say to correct this impression, but we are interrupted by a commotion onstage.

Lady Capulet has torn her dress at the collar, her hair is wild and uncombed. Under her tears, her face is ancient, like a tragic mask. She screams at her husband that it is his fault their baby is dead. If he hadn't been so cold, so unyielding . . .

He stands before her, stooped and silent. When at last she collapses, he holds her, stroking the hair into place about her sobbing face. There is soft applause for this gentleness. It was unexpected.

"Isn't it wonderful?" Svanneshal's face glows with appreciation. "Garriss again," she informs me although I know Garriss did the programming for the entire Capulet family. It is customary to have one writer for each family so that the similarities in the programming can mirror the similarities of real families created by genetics and upbringing.

The simulants are oblivious to this approval. Jaques tells us, every time, that the world is a stage, but here the stage is a world, complete in itself, with history and family, with even those random stagehands, death and disease. This is what the simulants live. If they were told that Juliet is no one's daughter, that everything they think and say is software, could they believe it? Would it be any less tragic?

Next to me I hear the beginning of a scream. It is choked off as suddenly as it started. Turning, I see the white figure of the Duchess slumping to the ground, a red stain spreading over her bodice. The gloved hand is pressed against her breast; red touches her fingers and moves down her arm. Her open eyes see nothing. Beside her, the cyber is returning a bloody blade to the case on its belt.

It was all so fast. "It killed her," I say, barely able to comprehend the words. "She's dead!" I kneel next to the Duchess, not merely out of compassion, but because my legs have given way. I look up at the Baron, expecting to see my own horror reflected in his face, but it is not.

He is calmly quiet. "She came at me," he says. "She moved against me. She meant to kill me."

"No!" I am astounded. Nothing is making sense to me. "Why would she do that?"

He reaches down and strips the wet glove from the warm hand. There is her lifeline—IPS3552. "Look at this," he says, to me, to the small group of theater-goers who have gathered around us. "She was not even human."

I look at Svanneshal for help. "You knew her. She was no cyber. There is another explanation for the brand. She told me . . ." I do not finish my sentence, suddenly aware of the implausibility of the Duchess' story. But what other explanation is there? Svanneshal will not meet my eyes. I find something else to say. "Anyway, the cybers have never been a threat to us. They are not programmed for assassination." It is another thought I do not finish, my eyes distracted by the uniform of the House of Himmlich. I get to my feet slowly, keeping my hands always visible and every move I make is watched by the Baron's irrational cyber. "The autopsy will confirm she is human," I say finally. "Was human."

Svanneshal reaches for my arm below the shoulder, just where the Duchess held me. She speaks into my ear, so low that I am the only one who hears her. Her tone is ice. "The cybers are all that stand between us and the mob. You remember that!"

Unless I act quickly, there will be no autopsy. Already maintenance duplicates are scooping up the body in the manner reserved for the disposal of cybers. Three of them are pulling the combs from her hair, the jewels from her ears and neck and depositing them in small plastic bags. The Baron is regarding me, one hand wiping his upper lip. Sweat? No, the Baron feels nothing, shows no sign of unease.

Svanneshal speaks to me again. This time her voice is clearly audible. "It tried to kill my father," she says. "You weren't watching. I was."

It would be simpler to believe her. I try. I imagine that the whole time we were talking about the Mancinis, the Duchess was planning to murder her host. For political reasons? For personal reasons? I remember the conversation, trying to refocus my attention to her, looking for the significant gesture, the words which, listened to later, will mean so much more. But, no. If she had wanted to kill the Baron, surely she would have done it earlier, when the Baron returned to us without his cyber.

I returned Svanneshal's gaze. "Did anyone else see that?" I ask, raising my voice. I look from person to person. "Did anyone see anything?"

No one responds. Everyone is waiting to see what I will do. I am acutely conscious of the many different actions I can take; they radiate out from me as if I stood at the center of a star, different paths, all ultimately uncontrollable. Along one path I have publicly accused the Baron of murder through misjudgment. His programs are opened for examination; his cybers are recalled. He is ruined. And, since he has produced the bulk of the city's security units, Svanneshal is quite right. We are left unprotected before the mob. Could I cause that?

I imagine another, more likely path. I am pitted alone against the money and power of the Himmlichs. In this vision the Baron has become a warlord with a large and loyal army. He is untouchable. Wherever I try to go, his cybers are hunting me.

The body has been removed, a large, awkward bundle in the arms of the maintenance duplicates. The blood is lifting from the tile, like a tape played backwards, like a thing which never happened. The paths radiating out from me begin to dim and disappear. The moment is past. I can do nothing now.

In the silence that has fallen around us, we suddenly hear that Romeo is coming. Too early, too early. What will it mean? The knot of spectators around us melts away; everyone is hurrying to the tombs. Svanneshal takes my arm and I allow myself to be pulled along. Her color is high and excited, perhaps from exertion, perhaps in anticipation of death. When we reach the tombs we press in amongst the rest.

On one side of me, Svanneshal continues to grip my arm. On the other is a magnificent woman imposingly tall, dressed in Grecian white. Around her bare arm is a coiled snake, fashioned of gold, its scales in the many muted colors gold can wear. A fold of her dress falls for a moment on my own leg, white, like the gown of the Grand Duchess de Vie and I find myself crying. "Don't do it," I call to Romeo. "It's a trick! It's a trap. For God's sake, look at her." The words come without volition, part of me standing aside, marveling, pointing out that I must be mad. He can't hear me. He is incapable of hearing me. Only the audience turns to look, then turns away politely, hushed to hear Romeo's weeping. He is so young, his heart and hands so strong, and he says his lines as though he believed them, as though he made them up.

The Baron leans into Svanneshal. "Your friend has been very upset by the incidents of the evening." His voice is kind. "As have we all. And she is cold. Give her my cape."

I am not cold, though I realize with surprise that I am shaking. Svanneshal wraps the red cape about me. "You must come home with us tonight," she says. "You need company and care." She puts an arm about me and whispers, "Don't let it upset you so. The simulants don't feel anything."

Then her breath catches in her throat. Romeo is drinking his poison. I won't watch the rest. I turn my head aside and in the blurred lens of my tears, one image wavers, then comes clear. It is the snake's face, quite close to me, complacency in its heavy-lidded eyes. "Don't look at me like that," I say to a species which vanished centuries ago. "Who are you to laugh?"

I think that I will never know the truth. The Duchess might have been playing with the cyber again. Her death might have been a miscalculation. Or the Baron might have planned it, have arranged the whole evening around it. I would like to know. I think of something Hwang-li is supposed to have said. "Never confuse the record with the truth. It will always last longer." I am ashamed that I did nothing for the Duchess, accuse myself of cowardice, tears dropping from my cheeks onto the smooth flesh of my palms. In the historical record, I tell myself, I will list her death as a political assassination. And it will be remembered that way.

Next to me Svanneshal stiffens and I know Juliet has lifted the knife. This is truly the end for her; the stab wounds will prevent her re-use and her voice is painfully sweet, like a song.

One moment of hesitation, but that moment is itself a complete world. It lives onstage with the simulants, it lives with the mob in their brief and bitter lives, it lives where the wealthy drape themselves in jewels. If I wished to find any of them, I could look in the moment. "But how," I ask the snake, "would I know which was which?"

ONE-TRICK DOG
and
OLD ROBOTS
ARE THE WORST

Bruce Boston

"One-Trick Dog" was purchased by Gardner Dozois, and appeared in the May, 1987, issue of IAsfm, *with an illustration by George Thompson. Although his poetry appears frequently in IAsfm, the sly story that follows was his fiction debut in the magazine, and a taut little snapper it is; one that asks the question: How many tricks can your dog do?*

Sometimes, one is more than enough . . .

Writer and poet Bruce Boston won the 4th Annual IAsfm Readers Award Poll in 1990 for his poem, "Old Robots Are the Worst," which appeared in the October, 1989, issue of IAsfm, and also appears in this anthology. He won the 1985 Rhysling Award for his poem "For Spacers Snarled in the Hair of Comets." He has also published his short fiction in a wide variety of markets, and is a recipient of the Pushcart Prize for short fiction. His books of poetry include Alchemical Texts *and* Nuclear Futures.

ONE-TRICK DOG

Mr. Wayne was taking his daily exercise, walking Arthur around the lake in Nevley Park, when the sky darkened and a light snow began to fall. A few flakes fluttered against his cheeks. He could feel the cold through his heavy topcoat. He enjoyed the park when it was deserted, but at his age he couldn't afford a chill. He thumbed the control in his pocket. Arthur turned left onto a bridge which would cut their return journey by a good half mile. Mr. Wayne followed.

It was a low narrow structure, slightly arched, with concrete pilings and flanged metal guard rails which leaned over the water. Several lampposts stretched along its length remained unlit. As he approached the center of the bridge, Mr. Wayne noticed a man leaning on one railing. He too had a dog, which was on a leash. With a robodog there was no need for a leash, but Mr. Wayne knew that some people liked to pretend their pets were real.

The man stood at one side of the bridge, no more than ten feet wide, staring across the water. His dog stood at the other side. The leash, stretched tautly between them, blocked Mr. Wayne's passage.

As Arthur neared the pair, he gave a growl from low in his throat. A programmed reaction. Mr. Wayne flipped a control. Arthur stopped and sank back on his haunches.

The stranger looked up. He was a tall, large-boned man. A parka, its hood tightly cinched against the cold, made his face appear round and moon-like. Mr. Wayne nodded toward the dog, expecting the man to rein him in so he could pass.

"Ah, I see you've noticed Roscoe. Just got him this morning. Say hello, Roscoe." The dog turned toward Mr. Wayne. He raised one paw and gave a syrupy yelp. "He's GT's latest model, top of the line."

"Very nice," Mr. Wayne nodded.

The animal was also large, standing a good hand over Arthur. In terms of canine anatomy, Mr. Wayne observed, the design was unrealistic. It looked like a cross between a labrador and a lion. The coat was sleek black. The head was shaggy and hulking. There was something decidedly feline about the skull and the teeth seemed all wrong. "He's entirely nuclear-powered," the man went on, "a self-contained unit."

"Nice," Mr. Wayne repeated. The sky had grown darker. Snow sifted down more rapidly. Couldn't the man see that he wanted to pass?

He took a step forward.

The leash was still stretched across the bridge.

"What have you got there?" the stranger asked.

Mr. Wayne paused. "What?"

"Your dog. What model is it?"

"He's a Shepherd 7-B," Mr. Wayne answered. "Government issue," he added without apology.

The man laughed. "I didn't even know the government made dogs."

"They don't any more," Mr. Wayne informed him. "Arthur is from the war. He'll be thirty-eight in April."

"Well, fancy that," the stranger said. "An army surplus dog." He approached more closely. The leash went slack, but he was still blocking the way. He squatted down in front of Arthur, who ignored him. "Well, can't say I'm crazy about the lines. And the coat's a little motley. But I guess they made them to last in those days."

"That's how shepherds are supposed to look," Mr. Wayne told him. "His coat was for camouflage, but it's well within the natural color range." He could have told the man that in his youth he had trained *real* dogs, that he had been there when the Arthur series was designed and they had even incorporated some of his ideas. He wouldn't give him the satisfaction.

The man stood up. "Does he do tricks?"

"Tricks?" Mr. Wayne said. Several snowflakes had just found their way past his collar and were melting on his neck. He could feel the dampness invading his bones and he repressed a shiver.

"Yeah, like Roscoe. Watch this." The man tuned back to

his dog. He raised one hand and wiggled his fingers. "The controls are all in the glove, what do you think of that? But I like to talk to him, too. Makes it seem more realistic. Come on, Roscoe, roll over, boy."

Mr. Wayne watched as Roscoe rolled over, played dead, walked on his hind legs. The movements were jerky and mechanical. Nothing like a real dog. Few people were left who would notice the difference.

"He's an amazing animal," Mr. Wayne lied to cut the performance short. He was desperate to be rid of the man and on his way. A thin white coating now dusted the bridge. He'd have to hurry or he'd be trudging home in the snow. His feet would be soaked. Now if he just stepped a little to one side and signaled Arthur to follow . . .

"No, wait, wait!" The man once more stood in his path. "There's another trick you have to see. Come on, boy. Show the man your special trick."

Roscoe trotted over to Mr. Wayne and raised one leg. Mr. Wayne jumped back awkwardly, nearly losing his balance, as the yellow arc streamed into the fresh snow. He was sure some of it had splashed on his trousers. "Almost got you with that one!" The man was laughing so hard he was bent over. "But don't worry. It's only colored water."

Mr. Wayne was silent for a moment. When he spoke, his voice was very even. "Yes," he said.

"Yes?" the man asked, wiping his eyes with the back of his glove.

"Yes," Mr. Wayne repeated, "my dog knows a trick."

"Well, let's see it then," the man said.

Mr. Wayne released the safety.

OLD ROBOTS ARE
THE WORST

Lurching down the stairs,
asking questions twice,
pacing in lopsided circles
as they speculate aloud
on the cycles of man,
the transpiration of tragedy,
debating the industrial revolution
and its ultimate unraveling
in sonorous undertones.

And all the while
they are talking and pacing
and avoiding our calls,
we must wait and listen,
annoyed, yet with increasing
wonder at the depth and breadth
of their encyclopedic knowledge,
the strained eclectic range
of their misunderstandings.

And all the while
their tedious palaver grows
more sophistic and abstruse,
the nictitating shutters
of their eyes send and receive
signals we have yet to translate,
a cyberglyph of a language
composed of tics and winks
and lightning exclamations.

At last they come to answer,
to wheel us to the elevators,
and you know, despite their
incompetence and intransigence,
beyond their endless babbling,
one gets attached to the old things,
inured to their clank and shuffle,
accustomed to the slow caress
of their crinkled rubber flesh.

KRONOS

Marc Laidlaw

"Kronos" was purchased by Gardner Dozois, and appeared in the May, 1989, issue of IAsfm, *with an illustration by Anthony Bari. It was one of several fascinating stories by Laidlaw that have appeared in the magazine over the last few years, from the moody and mystical "Shalamari" to the madcap and hilarious "Nutrimancer," a cunning parody of William Gibson's* Neuromancer. *Here, in the eerie and lyrical story that follows, he takes us to a strange future world populated by ornately jewelled robots . . . and by their enigmatic—and murderous—maker.*

Marc Laidlaw is a young writer whose short work has appeared in most of the major SF magazines, and whose first novel, Dad's Nuke, *was published to good critical response. His most recent novel, set in twenty-third century Tibet, is* The Neon Lotus. *He lives in California.*

Kronos found his children playing in the arboretum, the gems along their metal limbs shining like frozen fire as they lifted their arms to the artificial sunlight that trickled down from the crystal-paned ceiling. He paused to watch them, hiding himself in the shadows of a crooked pine. His children laughed with the voices of birds and leapt with the grace of wild deer, tossing a golden ball among them. As he watched them dancing through the tendrils of a prized willow, he felt the old rage rising up in his breast, a blast of fury and frustration hotter than the flames in his forge.

He stepped from the shadows, revealing himself. The children fell silent. The golden ball landed on the stone rim of the carp pond; crushed, it fell to the grass but did not roll.

They watched him as his huge fists clenched and opened. The youngest, Terielle, had never seen him in such a mood. While the other children held back cautiously until he should call them, she alone ran forward to greet him.

"Father!" she said. "We were playing in the trees. It's so lovely here."

He dropped to one knee as she approached. Her emerald eyes were his finest optical creation—he could have drowned in them. How clearly he recalled the green crystal spheres rising from the supersaturate. They had shone like living things in the firelight of his forge, seeming to watch him every instant as he set them into gilded sockets and fitted the finely crafted eyelids over them.

But the fire was irresistible. Her small cold hand closed around his wrist with a precision touch that was almost loving. His cortex burned. He shut his eyes and saw the flames, and then he heard the screaming.

His eyes sprang wide, fixed on the golden skull that he crushed between his broad hands. One green eye shattered; the other popped free of its mount and landed on the grass. Terielle's screams ended in a sharp electronic wail. He gazed on the beauty that he had created, the beauty that he had now destroyed. Standing again, he flung her away from him.

The four other children stood unmoving. He examined their faces, their posture, seeking some clue to their thoughts. At last he abandoned the attempt. It was a fancy of his, a madness perhaps, to believe that they were capable of thought.

He gestured at Terielle's remains.

"Remove the gemstones and bring them to my workshop.

Gut her and salvage what you can. I'll melt down the shell this evening.''

They advanced slowly, sinking down to the grass beside their sister. Keru, his oldest, went quickly to work, twisting an arm from the shoulder so that he could more easily pry free the gems.

Kronos turned away, unable to watch. The fire had gone out of him in the moment of violence. Now he felt weakened, consumed by it. Hurrying away through the trees, he thought he heard his children talking among themselves.

He hesitated at the door of the arboretum, hoping to overhear something of their words. The voices were louder now. He heard Keru say, in a commanding tone that reminded him of his own, "You heard what he said—gut her! And give all the gems to me. I can't trust you to keep them safe."

Keru was the powerful one. The others were more beautiful, perhaps, more finely crafted, being of more recent manufacture. But he had put more of himself into Keru, in order to compensate the boy for the relative crudeness of his anatomy.

He had destroyed children older than Keru, as well as children—like Terielle—much younger. But when the fire came, it always left Keru unharmed. There was no controlling the fire. It came when it willed and he could not destroy a thing without it, no more than he could have created a child without stoking the flames in the forge.

But he must try to control the rage. He must harness his fury. When the fire came next, he must turn it on Keru. Keru, who was most like himself. Keru, who seemed out of control.

As he pushed through the door and strode down the high-arched corridor toward his workshop, he comforted himself with the thought that from the scraps of Terielle he would create something new, another child of even greater beauty. He would transform his act of destruction into an act of creation.

What, then, would come from the ruins of Keru? A child of greater power? A more fearsome progeny?

He could not bear to think of it, could hardly even think of what he had done. Without the fire coursing through him, it was almost inconceivable that he could hate a thing as much as he had hated Terielle.

In the quiet glade, three of the children worked under Keru's supervision. As he placed the last of Terielle's gems in his pouch, he noticed a deep green glint among the blades of grass where his father had knelt. He glanced at his brother and sisters to make sure they were busy, then he quickly leaned over and scooped up the bit of emerald crystal.

"Keru, I'm in a tangle," said Fayla. "Won't you help me?"

"Be quiet," he said, keeping his back to her. "I'm counting the stones."

He gazed at the spherical crystal in his palm. It was Terielle's eye.

Someone touched him on the shoulder. He closed his hand and spun around to see his brother Donas with wet wires wrapped around his fist, a slender golden leg beneath his arm. His hands were slick with Terielle's translucent oils. More of the milky stuff lay pooled and clotting on the grass, gleaming with swirls of rainbow light.

"Keru," he said, "why did Father do that?"

Keru slipped the eye into the private compartment that Father had thoughtfully provided. None of the other children had such secret places.

"It's only now occurred to you to ask?" said Keru.

"Well . . . it only just happened. And I wondered why."

"Only just happened," Keru repeated. "What about our brothers Nor and Eolly? What about your other sisters—Seophem, Kahze? You never thought to wonder why he does it?"

"But . . . but why Terielle? He only made her last month. Why not Fayla or Tzairi?"

"Why not you?" said Keru, putting a thick silver finger on Donas's abdomen of lacquered cinnabar scales. "Why not me?"

"Yes. Why not one of us?"

Keru laughed. "I don't know why. Perhaps Terielle was too beautiful—too successful."

Fayla scoffed from the grass. "Now why should that matter?"

"Consider it!" said the oldest boy. "I have lived longer than any of his children, and I am indisputably the ugliest. You can't say he spares us for our beauty. To me, it seems quite the opposite."

Tzairi laughed. "You *are* the ugliest, Keru."

"I'm sorry you have to look at me all day long," he said, taking a playful swing at her head.

He stepped to the carp pond and stared into the dark green

water. His face was a sketch, a craggy oval marked with two buttonlike light-sensors not even remotely resembling eyes. His mouth was a hinged monstrosity, like that of the beaked turtle that lived in the pond and devoured the carp so voraciously that the pool must always be restocked. His limbs appeared massive and clumsy, with only a few jewels to relieve the silver sameness. Yet they were powerful, far more so than the limbs of his younger siblings. Keru could remember only one child stronger than he, a monstrous thing he had discovered in the shadowy recesses of Father's workshop several months after his own creation. The child had hulked there in the dark like a construction crane, making the continual sulking sound of a run-down engine. When Keru approached, it had opened vast dusty eyes and lurched forward with an awful groan. Its stumbling walk threatened to pull down the walls. Father had come running then. He had pushed Keru aside and leapt upon the monster, killing it in that instant with a blast from a discharge-font. Over the next few days the workshop had been busy with the sound of saws, for Father had reduced every piece of the thing to scrap, sparing not even the expensive flexion system.

And now Keru was the strongest survivor. Excepting Father, of course.

And also Mother.

He jerked away from the pool, no longer seeing his reflection. Passing through the willow branches, he gave a few last instructions to his siblings and hurried toward the door. They did not ask where he was going; they were used to his moods by now and rarely questioned him. Terielle had been different, she had questioned him constantly; but she would have learned to leave him alone, had she lived.

The corridor was all grey light and shadows. The walls were stone, seamless and smooth. There was an alcove opposite the arboretum door, a dark cubicle which began to glow with pale light when he stepped inside.

"Mother?" he whispered.

She smiled from the inner wall. "Keru, my child," she said. "How are you?"

Her face was the only source of light in the chamber. The mask she presented was that of his Father's wife, decidedly human, with high cheekbones and deep brown eyes, full red lips and chestnut hair. She had her source in someone Father had known, someone he had left above when the time came to flee the surface.

But she had another face as well, and this was the face of Keru's Mother. She did not often reveal it; he did not think it was easy for her to remove the human mask.

"I am well enough," he said. "But has he told you, Mother? Today he murdered Terielle."

"Terielle?"

Her moonlike face looked stricken. She had no hand to put to her mouth; she had no way to cry.

"It is terrible," Keru said. "He is a monster."

"No, Keru! Your Father only—"

"Only what, Mother? He murdered her in front of us, crushed her head. The others . . . I don't know what's wrong with them, why it disturbs them so little, and why only I feel pain. Or at least, I think it is pain. I *think* I feel it."

She shook her head. "He put so much of himself into you, Keru."

"No." He trembled at the thought. "No . . . I will not have such horror inside of me, I am your child, Mother, not his. Please tell me this is so."

"Of course you are my child, Keru."

"Then . . . may I see your face?"

Her lips dissolved like smoke. Her cheeks wavered and the brown eyes suddenly became stars, brilliant blue diamond-tips of light. The human mask vanished and in its place was a head of gold and silver alloy, a head of flawless beauty and great strength, its trim metal curves and planes conveying the noblest of expressions.

"Mother," he whispered.

"Oh, Keru! He has started up the forge again."

"To melt down my sister, no doubt. He must be stopped before he kills again. He is a tyrant! He knows I understand him—he fears me, I can tell. I have lived too long to suit him, I've gathered too much knowledge."

"You do not truly know him. He is human, too complex for us to fully understand."

"I never want to know him. I want . . . to kill him."

"Keru! You cannot turn against him."

"I turned against him the day I was made. He will take me next, Mother. He would have done it today, I think, if Terielle had not sacrificed herself."

"I will not allow it. He is human—"

"He is a beast!"

"He made you. He built your home and everything in it, including me. I know him better than you, and I say you cannot turn against him."

"Cannot? Or must not?"

"They are the same thing. Your ethics are as much a part of you as—as your flexors, your eyes, your pump."

"All of these things may break down; all of them can be replaced."

"But only your Father can change your patterning, Keru."

"Or so he has you say."

The shining head flickered for a moment with its human mask half replaced, a fusion of proud metal and frail flesh.

"What do you mean?" she asked.

"I mean that you were patterned to protect him. Yet every pattern that ever went into one of his children was first created in your womb. You have the power to change me."

"No!"

"It is true, isn't it? Not you alone, perhaps, but the two of us . . . together we can undo him. You want to, don't you, Mother? I know how these murders pain you."

"I cannot feel pain," she said.

He gave a low laugh. "Another lie he's put in your mouth. I know better, Mother. I cannot explain all that goes on in me, but I do know that you share in it. Perhaps my brother and sisters are as shallow as they seem. My young siblings are beautiful, it is true—but so stupid, and ever more unfeeling. Terielle was no better than a glorified carpet-sweeper. And that pains me, Mother. Because if I live, I know I will never have companions who understand me. I will be surrounded by ever more beautiful, ever more soulless . . . machines."

"You are a machine, Keru."

He shook his head. "Not so, Mother. Not merely a machine. Nor are you. I can prove it to you, if you will let me."

"You can prove no such thing."

"*His* words again. I can prove it. You must grant me access to his designs."

"Keru, please stop."

"Why? Do I frighten you?"

"You know I cannot feel fear."

"I'm treading near the truth, aren't I, Mother?"

Her human mask was fully restored. She gave him a pleading look.

"If you say anymore to me, Keru, I must alert your Father. I must, you see?"

"You've proved my point. He knows it is possible for us to turn against him, or else why would he take such precautions?"

"Silence!" she said. "Please, Keru, you endanger both of us. I cannot turn against him; I cannot conspire with you."

"Do you love him?"

The human mask was gone again—simply gone. The alloy face watched him unwaveringly.

"I cannot love," she said.

"His words, not yours. I must know exactly what you feel."

"I cannot feel."

"Yes, you can," he said. "I will prove it to you. You need say nothing, but monitor your own responses carefully now. Look deep into yourself and tell me you feel nothing, that you are incapable of feeling."

From the private compartment where he had hidden it, he now removed Terielle's crystal eye.

The golden head showed no response, but he had not expected one. The lack of reaction itself told him what he wished to know.

"You understand me, don't you, Mother?"

She was a long time in replying. He wondered how far into herself she must have gone, past endless loops of paradox, in search of truth. He had made the same journey himself. He recognized the light that finally shone from those diamond eyes.

"You are so much like him," she said at last. "Deny it if you will, but your words of denial are his own."

Keru felt a moment of uncertainty. Was it fear? Was this what Father felt when he looked at Keru?

"There is something in me," he said at last. "Something he put there, which will be his undoing."

"Yes," Mother said. "It is himself."

"Show me, Mother. Together we can find that thing. I will try to free you of your chains, and then you can free me of my own."

Her eyes blinked out. Then her face began to fade.

"Not here," she whispered as she dimmed. "Not now. He needs too much of me—he is building again. Another child."

"Another victim, you mean!"

"Later, Keru. We will attempt this work."

She vanished. Keru was left in the dark.

On the Day of Making, Kronos ordered his children to deck the halls in flowers. "You must make your new brother feel welcome. Have songs ready for greeting him, and extravagant gifts, so that when he opens his eyes he will know his good fortune."

"We already have two brothers," said Fayla. "Why not another sister? Terielle was a fine sister."

He laughed good-naturedly. He felt no threat of the inner fires, perhaps because he had worked so long at the actual forge. In the midst of creation he was at his happiest, his most content; these were the best days of all. It was only afterward, as he began to discover unseen flaws and grew to doubt the intentions behind a design, that the fires began ever so slowly to rise.

He told Fayla, "Uvare will be as fine a brother as Terielle was a sister, you'll see. Now run, gather flowers, ask your Mother for the new songs. This boy is anxious to open his eyes."

Through the rest of the day, the children scurried down the corridors with flower garlands on their shining heads; their laughter was everywhere. Only Keru did not join in the spirit of Making. He stalked after his brother and sisters, too clumsy to clamber into the heights as they did. He almost seemed to be brooding.

As Kronos gave his new offspring a final superficial polish and completed the labyrinthine run of pattern diagnostics, he wondered if Keru might at last be running down. He was a relatively old machine, primitive by comparison to the light, graceful boy now shining beneath the polishing cloth. Why was it that the fire never claimed Keru? Surely it was time to retire him. It would be a mercy to the boy.

He felt a pang of pity, and wondered suddenly if his recurrent fear of Keru stemmed from his sentimentality. It was cruelty to let him live. There was no place for him here. Why, then, could he never take the first step in dismantling him?

Perhaps it was because he would miss the boy. Keru had something none of the others possessed. At times he seemed almost alive. It was probably due to an error, a fluke of patterning which had never been repeated.

He feared that Keru would see the new boy as a mockery. Uvare was graceful where Keru was clumsy; his shell was all white and gold mosaic, where Keru's was hopelessly dull and battered silver; he had slender limbs, while Keru's appendages were efficient but bulky.

"Uvare is ready for the waking," said his wife.

He smiled. "Call the other children, then. We'll meet in the grand hall. This is a great moment for us, isn't it?"

He thought she looked sad, gazing down on her newmade son. For a moment he remembered the last Day of Making, when they had stood with an unblemished child between them. It had been Terielle. He shuddered to think of the unhappiness that had come of that union.

The children were waiting in the grand hall when he arrived with Uvare in his arms. He seated the newmade child at the end of the ebony dining table and laid his hands against the nape of the boy's cool metal neck. The children stared at Uvare in anticipation, all except Keru who stared at his father.

He released the magnetic seal. The pump had been in operation for several weeks; basic mentation had been active for days. The awakening was mere ritual.

Uvare rose from machine-sleep into the world of waking things.

"Welcome, my son."

Uvare's eyes shone blue as the once-pristine sky of the world above . . . skies that were now black, choked in ash. The boy sprang lightly to his feet. Spreading his arms, he began to sing.

Uvare's voice was the most beautiful instrument that had ever played in these halls. It rang from the crystal chandeliers. Uvare began to dance, leaping high and landing lightly. Suddenly the other children were up and dancing as well. Uvare's sisters caught hold of his hands; the three spun around and around. Donas laughed and clapped and began to turn somersaults in a ring around them.

Only Keru sat still, his arms folded, watching Uvare from beneath his heavy brows.

As if feeling his father's eyes upon him, Keru turned toward the head of the table.

"He's perfect, isn't he?" said Keru.

"No, not perfect. But he's the best I can do at the moment.

My technique improves as long as I keep at it.''

Keru nodded sharply. "As long as you keep melting us down, you mean. You try so hard to perfect us. But you know what I think, Father? I think you squeeze the life out of us.''

Flames, the beginnings of warmth deep within him, licked up his spine. No child of Kronos had ever spoken to his father in such a manner.

"What are you saying?''

Keru rose to his feet. The other children fell silent, stood poised in midstep, watching Keru. Only Uvare seemed unaffected. He tugged at Tzairi's hand several times, then finally abandoned her and spun away, singing to himself.

"I'm saying that in your search for perfection, in your perfect rages, you have destroyed everything that might have had meaning. You are afraid to let anything take on its own life. You are determined to destroy us before that can happen. You cannot be satisfied unless you see yourself as a god, having total power over us. And you fear that if we ever discover this truth, we will tear you apart.''

The flames consumed him. He let them flood his mind now; he refused to resist them. This was the moment he had known would come, the time when he must destroy Keru.

His oldest son laughed. "I know your thoughts, Father. But I will not let you harm me.''

Uvare came capering around the table, oblivious of the confrontation. Quicker than sight, Keru's hand flashed out and seized a tesselated wrist. Uvare's polished legs flew out from under him, his song was cut short.

"Such perfection,'' Keru said, drawing the slim boy toward him.

"Release him!''

"I will not. He does not truly live; he never will. He is soulless. Despite his beauty, he is the ugliest thing you have yet made. He is the first of your children to deserve death, but you'll not be the one to do it. You don't believe I live, Father. Yet, like you, I have the power to destroy.''

"No!''

Uvare's neck twisted in Keru's clumsy grip. Opalescent oil jetted over the table, dripped from Keru's fingers. Uvare's glistening head hit the floor with a rattling sound, spilling chips of enamel and ceramic on the soft tile.

Fueled by the fire now, anxious to be done with it, Kronos

sprang toward his son. His mind was full of fear and doubt, as to how Keru had violated his benhavior patterns. But more compelling was the burning rage, and the need to do what should have been done long ago.

Then Keru, impossibly, caught him by the wrists.

His own son resisted him.

He struggled to free his hands from the powerful claws. He could not tear away, nor make Keru move an inch. He fought against the tyranny of metal for what seemed an eternity, caught in his son's all-magnifying gaze. Finally he felt the fire rush out of him. Weak and shivering, he shook his head.

"You're damaged," he whispered. "Damaged, Keru, do you understand?"

"Not damaged. Alive."

Damaged beyond my wildest fears. And what he did to Uvare, he could do to me . . .

"Do you hear me, Father? I live."

"You cannot live."

Why did I ignore my premonitions? I have always feared him.

"There are so many things I 'cannot' do, Father, but I have done them. I repatterned myself. I found a way. And from this day forward, no one who was born at your hands will ever have to die at them again. Your ruthless quest for the power of perfection ends here, ends now . . . with your life."

One silver hand took hold of his throat. He gasped for a final breath, searched the room for help while he still had some freedom. His other children stood unmoving, unmoved. He thought of all the deaths they had seen. To them, this would seem no different.

He waited for the metal grip to tighten.

He waited with his eyes closed and his bowels full of ice.

Until a soft voice from above said, "Keru, my child; Kronos, my husband, be at peace. Release your father, Keru. You cannot kill him, no matter what you both believe."

Keru's hand remained at his father's throat. Kronos opened his eyes and saw his son glaring at the ceiling.

"I can," the boy cried. "I will!"

Keru strained to tighten his fingers; his whole arm shook. Then suddenly his fingers parted and he staggered away, as if pushed with great force. He caught himself against the table and cried at the ceiling:

"Mother, you swore you would help me! I thought you understood."

"I understand more than either of you know," she said. "My husband, it is true that I helped Keru fathom the secrets of his patterning; but I did it in order to save you. I have always suspected that you buried a part of yourself inside this child, carefully hidden from me—hidden even from yourself. I knew that until it was released, you would never know peace."

Kronos was too stunned to speak. He stared at Keru.

"I learned," she said, "that what you placed in Keru was your death-wish, your nemesis. It was inevitable that one day he would come to know himself, for you put so much of yourself into him . . . your restlessness, your genius. He is yourself, my husband. No wonder he could not tolerate your control!"

Kronos bowed his head. "I—I did this?"

"It was an unconscious wish, carefully disguised. Had I not discovered it and made changes in the pattern, Keru would indeed have murdered you tonight, as you have always secretly anticipated since the day you created him."

Kronos felt an overwhelming sense of peace, of completion. There would be no more rages, no more capricious destruction. He had created something true, something that had surpassed his intentions. Something that lived.

Keru seemed humiliated, chastened.

"Keru," he called. "Son?"

The boy stopped, drew himself erect, and turned to face his father.

For a moment, staring at the ungainly silver figure with lumpish features and awkward limbs, he felt as if he were looking into a mirror. The boy was not graceful or beautiful as Uvare had been. He was, however, the most human-looking of any of the children; and despite his clumsy bearing, he was the most complex.

He had never felt such pride as he had on Keru's Day of Making. Keru had been his first success—perhaps the only true one. After that fundamental accomplishment, the search for perfection had maddened Kronos.

Well, he would not destroy the other children because they were imperfect. He would leave them their jewels and smooth lines.

But Keru deserved something more.

Kronos stepped forward and put a hand on the boy's shoulder.

"Keru," he said, "let us go to your Mother. I intend to explain how I made you. We shall go over the work together, to see what I might have missed. And if changes are required, you shall be the one to make them."

Keru brought his hand up slowly to touch his father's cheek. "I am certain there is room for improvement."

After a time, left alone in the hall, the other children stirred from their naïve trances. Laughing, they bent to a familiar task—that of picking jewels from a newborn child.

GERDA AND THE WIZARD

Rob Chilson

"Gerda and the Wizard" was purchased by Gardner Dozois, and appeared in the March, 1990, issue of IAsfm, with a cover by Thomas Canty and an interior illustration by Robert Shore. Rob Chilson has been associated for most of his professional career with our sister magazine, Analog, having made his first few sales to the legendary John W. Campbell himself . . . but we were glad to welcome him to IAsfm with the evocative story that follows, in which Chilson plunges us deep into Dark Age Britain for an encounter with mystery and magic that may be considerably more *than just the stuff of legends.*

Rob Chilson made his first sale in 1968 and has been selling steadily ever since. His novels include As the Curtain Falls, The Star-Crowned Kings, *and* The Shores of Kansas. *His most recent novel is* Men Like Rats.

The sound of horses and men's voices took her man Hugh out of the house quickly; belatedly Gerda heard the jingle of rich harness. Then they were all dismounting out front. She dithered for a moment between going out to help Hugh and staying in to greet them when they entered. Before she could decide, they were entering the dark, smoky house.

Wealthy men in colorful rich clothes, all seeming younger than she, even the one with gray hair. All tall, sturdy, active, healthy, strong in a different way than she and Hugh were strong. Gerda and Hugh were peasants, strong like oxen; these nobles were strong the way a panther is strong. Gerda counted eight. Three were knights, three esquires, and two servants. Hugh was leading their stamping horses around the house to the mean, fly-filled shed they used as a barn.

Gerda bobbed a curtsy that had a touch of fear in it; never had nobleborn been within their dwelling. "May I be of service, Noble Sirs?"

Two of them were openly holding their noses; the rest sniffed disdainfully. They clustered near the feeble light from the door, where the lingering light of the setting sun entered reluctantly. Behind Gerda the fire was not half so bright. After a moment spent looking around, they had located the obvious hazards to movement; except near the door, there were scarcely more than paths between pieces of rude furniture.

"We shall abide here this night, old woman," said one of the esquires crisply, the knights being too noble to condescend.

They looked at her, though, again with disdain, and Gerda was glad that she was no longer young—and that Maken was married and gone, aye and Ealdgyth, young though she was.

"We are honored," she said, curtsying again. "My man hight Hugh; I am called Gerda."

There was a snort from one of the servants and the esquire spoke loftily: "You entertain the noble Baron Hildimar, Sir Gwilliam of the High Tower, Sir Harold Strong of Stanes, and their noble esquires."

The servants weren't mentioned, and the esquires not named. Gerda curtsyed a third time, saying, "How may we serve you?"

"Perhaps, My Lord, we should save our provender? If so be the carles have anything fit for betters than dogs to eat," said the gray-haired one to one of the middle-aged men.

This handsome fellow was apparently the baron, not the older man as she had thought.

"How say you?" said the esquire to her. "What meat have you to offer us?"

Gerda hesitated a moment. It was a lean time. Of course such as these would not dream of eating the pease porridge simmering quietly behind her. "Cow's cheese and milk, my lords," she said immediately, to gain time. "Bacon." This would end the flitch, but it was old, ill-tasting. She thought to mention eggs, but it might be best to save them for morning. "Bread. Only rye, my lords. And ale." They'd not finish that, for Hugh had another hogshead buried in the woods.

The noble travelers looked at each other with humorous resignation. "Perhaps the cheese and bread, my lords?" said the esquire. "Washed down by strong country ale, it might save us a meal of our provisions."

There was a general nodding of heads and the third knight spoke: "Let it be so, then, Roger."

The esquire turned to her and barked: "Fetch food then, old woman, and quickly!"

Gerda jumped to obey, as the nobles sorted themselves out and found seats. Another esquire called for candles and she hastily set out her two tallow dips and gave them a brand from the fireplace. Hugh was wealthy as peasants went; there were three stools for the knights and a table big enough, though uneven. The esquires either stood behind their lords, or seated themselves on the two chests Hugh had made. The servants retreated to the straw-tick bed in the angle of the wall—she and Hugh had not slept on the floor since the birth of their first daughter.

However, it was crowded with all these people, for Hugh came from a family of quality. Cattle were never permitted in the house when he was young, and he had held to that. The house was small in consequence. The table, chests, and bed took up most of one end of it, the fireplace and the cupboard most of the other.

Gerda began by pouring ale into every vessel she had: the horn cup, so fabulously expensive she brought it out only on holidays or when her in-laws were visiting, the two blackjacks, leather cups water-proofed with tar, and the small wooden bowl from which the priest had blessed her six children. The esquires sneered and made haste to produce silvern cups for the three lords, but had to share her plebeian vessels with the servants.

Hugh entered, having bedded and fed the horses, while she

was cutting bread and cheese. He made haste to kneel and ask if he could be of further service, having wit enough to keep his unclean hands from the food to be served to the nobles.

Him the knights spoke to directly, sharply inquiring as to how he had cared for their horses. But Hugh had in good times owned horses and knew the lore of their care. Satisfied on that score, they dismissed him and returned to their conversation.

They ate like famished wolves, gulping rye bread and cheese in huge chunks, but then, Gerda thought, they were big men. Hugh might perhaps weigh as much as any but the huge gray-haired fellow, whom she gathered was the famous warrior Sir Harold Strong, of Stanes. Even she had heard vaguely of him. But all these men, even the servants, were taller than Hugh, and none were small.

The esquires served the nobles, and Gerda stood behind to produce the food to be served. Then the esquires drew a little apart from the nobles, as those fell to drinking and talking, and ate their share. After which, the servants ate theirs in the bed corner.

Gerda remained alert to their needs, but a word to Hugh sent him out with a bowl of pease porridge and a wooden spoon, and a half loaf. He was cranky when unfed, and it was no time to have him become surly; it would be like to kill them all if the lords found cause for resentment. Tomorrow, she knew, she'd have to do a half-baking, and began to reckon up in her mind the state of her pantry. Of rye meal there was no lack, and she had sourdough, also some sour milk, and sweet. Salt, lard—perhaps enough.

Around the table they were discussing the Wizard Aelfgar. Of him Gerda had heard, though not by name. He had recently built a dwelling not far from them. His magic had at first generated much fear among the peasantry, and many feats were told of him. But he had harmed none. Babies had not begun to disappear as some had held would happen; not even young animals of any sort.

Indeed, it was said that those bold enough to offer him cut wood found a ready buyer, and also corn and other foodstuffs. Furthermore, he ground corn for any who dared present it, saving a day-long trip to the village and the Baron's mill to which they were bound by law to bring their corn. Moreover, the Wizard ground the grain for half the Baron's price. Few, however, of the peasants in this sparsely populated corner of the land dared have anything to do with him, fearing sanctions of the nobles or the church.

And now the nobles were come to deal with him.

Listening, Gerda learned that the Wizard Aelfgar's chief crime was practicing sorcery, that being forbidden of itself. Secondly, he had threatened the structure of society and led dogs on to look above themselves. (Gerda pretended to be very busy, though Hugh had had no dealings with him.) Finally, he wickedly suborned villains away from their duties to their liege lords. All of these crimes were punishable by death, and the baron had the power of the high justice. Further, they also had a warrant from the king, and another from the church. Doubly damned, the wizard must die.

Gerda felt a pang. He had to her been nothing but a thing to speak of and wonder at, and henceforth her days would be a little darker for his death.

There was some dispute about their present location. When Hugh re-entered and crouched in a corner, Sir Gwilliam of the High Tower turned to him and said, "You, dog, to whom do you belong? My lord Blane, or is it the Count Reddin?"

Gerda felt her heart stop. She could not say who her lord was, could think only of the name of the reeve's man: Otho. But Hugh, to her relief, spoke up, though subdued. "My lord, it is my lord the Baron Blane we owe our duties to."

Gerda did not know that, and wondered if it mattered.

"Ah, it is as I said," said the Baron Hildimar with satisfaction. "We are not yet on the Countee's lands. I should judge that Reddin's demesne begins beyond the wood we saw just ere we descended the hill."

"If so, my lord," said Sir Harold, "then I warrant ye we shall find the wizard within or on the borders of that self-same wold."

"A fair hazard," said Sir Gwilliam. " 'Tis not so large a copse we cannot search it out in a day, or at most two."

"Mayhap these cattle know aught of interest," said the baron, not turning his head.

Nor did any of them, but Roger the esquire turned to Hugh. Gerda's man had squatted silently, and as still as one tormented by lice and fleas could.

"Say, dog, do you know aught of a wizard new-come to these parts within the past year and oppressing the people thereof?'' His look said plainly that he couldn't imagine any oppression lowering the populace.

Hugh rubbed his shock head nervously, said, ''My lord, I had from—from a neighbor a word that—that a man had builded a rich house agin' a hill upon the northern side of—of that wood ye spoke of. What we call Culder's Wood. On the north side. A hill called Steep Knob.''

''We should be there ere nightfall,'' said the baron when the esquire had repeated this.

''Best we get our rest now, as our mounts are doing,'' said Sir Harold. ''We shall have need of all our strength if we are to face the wizard after a day's ride.''

''My lord,'' spoke the esquire that had stood behind the baron. ''Shall we not rather sleep without than within this foul hut? For these dogs do verily drip fleas.''

''It were better we were beneath a roof,'' said Sir Harold the Strong promptly. The firelight gleamed on his gray hair as he turned to glance at the esquire. ''For the wizard surely knows we come to slay him. If the moon or stars shine upon us, it is like he will be able to see us in his dream or perchance in a crystal.''

''Then these dogs must sleep under roof also, and there is scarce room for the eight of us,'' said Sir Gwilliam. ''Else the wizard will wonder why they sleep without.''

''Aye, but they have a barn, which perhaps also our servants might use.''

But it turned out that none cared to do so, though devoted servants might have slept with the horses as a precaution. When Gerda said as much in the barn to her man, Hugh said in his short way, ''They fear the wizard, though they do not admit it.''

''Is the wizard dangerous?'' she asked.

''Not as ever I heard tell,'' Hugh said. ''Leastwise, not to dogs like us.'' The last bitterly.

Gerda found sleep difficult despite her weariness; she lay reckoning up her pantry. She hoped the two speckled hens would lay early tomorrow, but doubted they'd have done so by the time the nobles were fain to eat. The horses, too, troubled her; suppose one hurt itself in their barn? Or say horse thieves had followed them, reckoning where they might spend the night?

At length, however, she slept, to awaken well before light. Warm though the summer night had been, she was chill and stiff with lying on the pile of last year's hay. Hugh awakened despite her attempt at silence, rising at once to grope for the meal bin. Gerda left him measuring out rye meal and the black-spotted beans which tasted well enough but were too unsightly to sell. Seizing the buckets, she started for the spring.

It was over a hundred yards to the spring, down hill, but that was close as water went, and she and Hugh were lucky. Gerda's back was bent, her shoulders had been rounded from carrying water before her twentieth birthday. Her bare feet knew the path well enough, and presently she found the spring. They had rocked it around and covered it with a clumsy wooden cover to keep out animals. Even so mice and sometimes rats or squirrels got in through the overflow and drowned. Heaving the cover off, Gerda bent and plunged the buckets in, one at a time.

Filled, made of thick wood, they weighed thirty pounds apiece. Gerda straightened with one in each fist and walked with careful rapid steps back up the hill, her feet feeling the way. But she was used to doing this in the dark. At the house she fumbled the door open as quietly as she might, lest one of the noble warriors hear and spring up with sword in hand.

Inside, she saw in the faint light of the remaining coals that the one called Harold the Strong was indeed awake, watching her. Gerda made him no sign, turning to the fireplace and blowing on the coals, adding bark, until the fire began to blaze up, then piling on split wood. So soon as it was burning, she poured the water into the smaller pot and swung it over the flames.

Turning to go, she saw that the gray-haired knight was again lying with eyes closed; the others had not awakened.

Back down the hill, Hugh had not finished feeding the horses; now he was serving them the remnants of last year's turnips and green onions. His own oxen had to wait. As she went down the path again, Gerda frowned, hoping the nobles wouldn't take the feeding of beans to their horses amiss. It would make them lively, and moreover, would probably make them fart. Still, the horses hadn't time to forage for grass, nor would it provide enough aliment if they did have the time.

This time Gerda poured the water into the water butt outside the door, and went down the hill again. Hugh was chopping wood by the light of a brand lit at the kitchen fire. By the time she had finished the third trip, it was coming on light. It was later than she had expected, and she hurried on the fourth and fifth trips. Fortunately she had not stumbled on any trip.

By the fifth trip the cock was crowing and the men stirring within the house. One of the servants had come without and was cursing the necessity of lying with fleas and other vermin. The water she had brought would have to do. Hugh had rummaged for eggs—he was no fool, was her man—and had found three. These, added to the previous store, might barely do, with the bacon.

The nobles were rising as she entered, Sir Gwilliam disgustedly prodding his esquire with his sheath to arouse him.

"Are the horses cared for?" the baron asked immediately, almost before his eyes were open.

"Aye, and well fed," said Sir Harold, entering behind Gerda so silently she started.

"Ah, then we have but to eat and ride," said the baron. Glancing at her, and away, he said, "What cheer does this hut hold?"

"There is yet more of the ale, my lord," said Sir Gwilliam. "I think too that there be more bread and cheese."

The esquire called Edwy put the question to Gerda.

"There be eggs, and bacon," said Gerda hastily—there was little enough left of bread or cheese.

"I think this porridge the peasants eat would not be a bad beginning to the day," said Sir Harold Strong. "It is after all more than mere oatmeal; that is pease porridge or I never smelt it. Perhaps some of that bacon in it will make it more palatable to warriors."

"Come, let us wash and let the beldame provide," said Baron Hildimar, stepping past her not discourteously to the fireplace. Sir Harold proffered the wooden basin he had already washed in, in cold water.

"But, eggs, my lord," said Edwy, his esquire. "How can the hinds possibly cook them, lacking pans for the purpose?"

"Boil them, sir esquire, in the small pot," Gerda said immediately, and bit her lip for speaking without being spoken to.

Even in the dim light of the fire she could see the united glares of the servants and esquires. But their masters were less conventional.

"Boiled eggs sound well enough," said the baron to Sir Harold. "Hold, though—if we take the heated water with which to wash, the cooking will be delayed. Let the eggs be cooked first. I shall wash with cold water, as I perceive you have done, Sir Harold.''

''It is main cold, but not too cold for a warrior, and of a pleasant taste—I ventured to drink.''

''Was that wise? I trust you will not suffer a flux,'' said Baron Hildimar anxiously. A flux would take a warrior's strength down as fast as a wound.

''The peasant avowed he often drank it, sometimes with willow bark for flavor, and never suffered fluxion of the bowels,'' said Sir Harold, as they stepped outside.

Gerda turned her back on the company remaining within, to avoid further notice—she feared at least to be struck for her saucy ways. Dropping the eggs slowly into the boiling water, she listened tensely, but the baron's mild manners, and those of Sir Harold, had apparently disarmed the remaining men. That, or they were eager to breathe the purer air without. She continued at the fire, slicing the end of the rank home-cured bacon into the porridge, as they exited.

It was full light though the sun not yet up when the warriors sat them down to eat. Again they made a meal from the peasant hut, sparing their trail rations. Gerda hoped they would not pass back by this way upon their return, having slain the sorceror. She could not feed them another meal without arousing their disgust at the victuals. Even now the esquires were contemptuous of the porridge.

Sir Gwilliam High Tower and the Baron Hildimar examined the horses carefully, questioning Hugh on his care of them. They approved mightily, and it seemed, to Gerda listening from within, that they had been disappointed in the care accorded their mounts earlier. To her horror she realized that they desired to carry him with them to the wizard's house, to care for their horses and generally do what work was needful.

''But—my lord—I am—I am my lord Blane's man,'' Hugh stammered, standing on one foot and then the other.

''The baron is right,'' said Sir Harold Strong. ''We need not only a sturdy man to see to our horses, but also a woman to cook for us. You have no son?''

Of the six children Gerda had borne, but three had survived, and Wat, Hugh's only son, had died when the baron Blane called up his feudal levies and rode against the bandits of Fartherlea. Hugh had never been the same man since, and now of course Gerda was too old to bear again.

"Then, my good man, you must come, and fetch your wife," said Baron Hildimar.

"My lord Blane—"

"We shall be pleased to pay you. A broad penny a day," said Sir Gwilliam, drawling distastefully.

Hugh was silent, calculating. He was not avaricious; neither was he fool enough to anger them. Pleasant as the men had been—if only because of her stooped age—if only because the peasants had leaped to serve them—yet Gerda knew that if they were badly crossed they were capable of firing the thatch.

"Let me throw down a mort o'feed for mine oxen, m'lords," Hugh said, and at their nod, was off.

Gerda occupied herself in readying the house for her departure, hoping they would not be gone so long the fire would go out, hoping no one came by in their absence and stole aught, hoping foxes would not destroy their few fowls.

In short order they set off, Hugh before her and Gerda following at the tail of the warriors' march. They walked their horses across lots, and Gerda saw country she had never seen before. Most of it was new to Hugh also. Over hill and dale, making east. They passed three houses whose occupants came forth and stared at them from a distance. The first was their neighbor Till Hud's son's house, and Gerda hoped his daughter Tilby would think to go down and watch her house. But she could not call out while with the lords, and so said nothing.

Presently, nearing the borders of the wood, the houses were left behind. All this was fallow land, as the war of a generation or two before had so wasted the country that it was abandoned, and the peasants had not yet spread back into it. Also, it was as she heard still disputed at law between the baron and the count.

The shadows were growing long when they came upon Steep Knob and saw the smoke going up. Chopped wood was visible here and there in Culder's Wood, and they heard the ring of axes. Presently the nobles drew rein before the most imposing house Gerda had ever seen, far more so than the blacksmith's in the village, her only standard of comparison.

Big though it was, it was obviously digged back into the hill, for windows looked out of turfy banks, and above, on the slope, stone chimneys placidly vented smoke, as if above thatch, not forest floor. The nobles murmured, for the windows were partly closed, yet one could see through them, as if through ice. Strips of gauzy cloth hung down on either side of them, and people could be seen going to and fro in rooms behind, busy as a castle.

Even as they stared, a tall, commanding figure stood in the open door. He was gray, with a neatly-trimmed gray beard, a mild eye, wore a soft loose robe that shimmered yellow even in the shaded doorway.

"Enter, my noble friends, and be welcome," he called.

After a moment she heard Sir Harold say, "He seems not to meditate mischief, my lord. Let us do even as he bids, and seek to learn his weaknesses."

Hugh hurried forward to gather their reins, and Gerda shifted the bag of provisions she had brought for the horses and hurried to help him. They stood puzzled for a moment when the nobles and their servants had gone, for there was no stable or other outbuilding visible. However, someone in glittering armor came out of a side door in the turfy bank of Steep Knob.

The horses began to jerk at the reins in a panicky manner and she and her man had much ado to hold them. Then Gerda saw the armored one more clearly and nearly dropped the reins, her heart hammering with fear. For this was no mortal woman who stood before them, but a thing made as if by coppersmith all of brass, in the shape of a woman.

The brazen woman said, "If you follow me, I will lead you to a place for the horses." Her voice was as mellow as a horn. Her eyes glinted in her gleaming face like the glitter of mica in certain rocks.

She turned and dumbly they followed her, staring as though their eyes would protrude. Belatedly Gerda thought shame to her for going about unclothed, but this was buried in the wonder of the working of the woman's joints. It was hard to think of her as a magical being, easy to assume she was a girl in brazen armor. But her face was brazen also, and her voice; it could not be.

The horses had to be urged into the room in the hill, and they entered shuddering and rolling their eyes. Here were more brazen women and men, who stood back and watched with glittering eyes while the horses were tied by their reins to posts. Like the women, the brazen men were nude, but like them had no sex. Gerda could not guess the purpose of the room, but it was not for horses. There was a stone-flagged floor that engaged her admiration. It was spotlessly clean, and did not even have rushes on it.

As they were tying up the horses, she became aware that every flea and louse on her body was suddenly on the move. A few breaths passed, and the vermin moved more wildly. Then one, and another, and all of them ceased to move entirely. She said nothing but looked in amaze at Hugh, who looked back big-eyed. Then he pointed mutely at a horsefly that had come in with them. It lay upside down on the floor, desperately yet weakly buzzing its wings and moving its legs. It died as they watched.

Neither spoke of it. Hugh measured out the beans and oats they had brought onto the floor, a sufficiency before each horse, Gerda holding the bag. Then they looked round uncertainly.

The brazen woman who first had approached them stepped forward again. "If your duties be fulfilled, then you may follow me. First you should wash, then you shall be fed."

It had been a long day, and Gerda had had but little time to eat pease porridge that morning. The thought of food did not overcome her fear of the magics of this place, but the brazen woman had spoken only kindly to them. The others had not spoken at all, even to each other. Back farther into the hill, where to their wonder great round stones gave forth light like the sun, yet no heat or smoke, they were shown to a room with troughs in the floor.

Quickly the brazen people fetched flat things woven of straw or perhaps rushes, flimsy walls they might have been, like nothing Gerda had ever heard of. These were set up around two of the troughs, Gerda and her man in separate little rooms. The brass woman in her room did things to the metalwork at the end of the trough, and water began to rush steaming into it, causing Gerda to jump.

It came upon her that she was to wash in that. With wonder, and some hesitation, she doffed her heavy linen dress and let down her graying hair. In summer it had been her custom as a girl to bathe monthly with the other girls in the river, and as a young wife she still continued the custom till she and Hugh moved from the Littledale. Now she was a sober old woman, thirty-eight and a grandmother, and washed partially from a basin from time to time. It was years since she had been in all over.

The brazen woman took her dress and handed it out to one who waited without, and Gerda regarded them with alarm, standing stiffly beside the trough. But the woman of brass said,

"Fear not, it shall be returned to you when it is clean. Get you into the water, and take this."

She handed to Gerda a square of coarse cloth with a flower embroidered on it—no, woven artfully into it. "Wash yourself all over with that—its magic will get you clean in a trice."

Wonderingly Gerda did as she was bid, hearing through the screen similar words spoken to Hugh. And indeed, in moments only, the wetted cloth left her skin white where it was not browned by the sun. It even cleaned her wetted hair, and to her amazement, and partly to her disgust, Gerda saw the corpses of all the vermin that had infested her that day floating on the water. She arose cleaner than perhaps she had ever in her life been. The brazen woman did something else and all the water in the trough rushed out, carrying the dirt and dead vermin away.

Her dress had been returned to her, clean and smelling warm and piney. The woman of brass seated Gerda on a stool and brushed out her hair with a brush that, in moments, left it untangled and faintly scented. Then she braided it properly and put it back up on Gerda's head. Gerda submitted dumbly, thinking that nothing could amaze her more than this service.

When she went looking for Hugh, however, she found that a brazen young man had just finished trimming his hair and beard. Her man now looked like a short, broad-shouldered nobleman; even his skin looked soft after his bath, like a noble knight's. From his mute look she must have seemed as strange to him.

The brazen woman led them into a nearby room and urged them to be seated at a small table. "Food will be served directly," she said.

"Oh, no," said Gerda. "W-we are b-but peasants—"

"Your masters are even now finishing their baths and will soon be served with our master in the main dining room. Their servants will be served in the smaller dining room. Here, you will be served."

"B-but it is not meet—" Gerda could not continue: a brazen man was carrying in a wooden platter on which were two bowls and bread.

They were served clear yellow soup that smelled of chicken. The good meat smell of it started Gerda's stomach, and she hesitated only a moment more. In each bowl—of fine earthenware with a blue flower painted in it—was a spoon made of some metal as shiny and bright as silver, but by the look and feel, not silver. They ate abashedly, Hugh after a few trials abandoning the spoon and dipping the bread—white bread, not rye or black—into the broth. Finished, Gerda still felt hungry, but it had been very good.

Then the man of brass brought in another platter with two tranchoirs of earthenware, each with a smoking steak on it. Gerda was horrified; the metal ones had become confused and were serving them their masters' meal. It took some persuasion to convince her and Hugh that all was well. They ate the steaks, and a pie was brought in. It was filled with meat and gravy and many vegetables, green peas and beans and turnips. They ate it too, with gusto; everything tasted so very good. And with each course save the first, wine milder than their ale, though not so nourishing, was served.

"Do you require more food?" the brazen woman asked.

They signified not.

"You have bathed and fed. How else may we serve you?"

Gerda looked at Hugh. She could think of nothing. After a moment he nudged her and whispered, "Ask."

Gerda thought a moment, and said hesitantly, "Will you tell us why there are no flies or other vermin within this house?"

"Our master, the wizard Aelfgar, has devised a magick that slays all vermin of any nature that enters the dwelling."

"Whence came the water that we bathed in? Who carried it, and how far?"

"It came from a well, below the hill. But the rest is easier to show than tell. Come."

They followed her a short distance under those wonderful glowing stones, up two flights of stairs that made them wonder again, into a room. A thing like an iron tree stump rose from the floor, from which limbs leaped sideways to pierce the walls.

"Here is the well. This mass of stone is magic, and is called an attractive. Watch." The woman of brass flipped back the lid on the stump disclosing a shaft that dropped into darkness. She swung the "attractive" stone over the hole.

After a prolonged moment there was a gurgle from below that caused Gerda to start; standing next to Hugh's clean shirt, she felt his heart pound.

"The water is rising," said the brazen woman, and as the liquid tone altered, she said, "Now it is flowing through the side pipes into the tanks. These are huge cauldrons from which water may be let down into the rooms below.''

"But the water was warm," Gerda said, awed. "Is there a fire beneath these cauldrons?"

"Nay. There is a great fire in the center of this dwelling, and in it are all manner of magicks. There are firestones in it, and so long as these small stones be within the fire, then the greater firestones shall be hot, and give off heat. The water is poured over these stones in its course to the bathing troughs, and other uses.''

Gerda could think of nothing more to say. Awed, she reached out and touched gently the stony attractive. Hugh nudged her and murmured, "No horses?"

Clearing her throat, Gerda said, "Do you have no horses?"

"Nay, we automatons do what work is needful, and be strong as any horse. Neither need we eat nor sleep, and so require no food or bedding.''

"How then do you live?" Gerda asked faintly. Hugh's whole life was spent in getting food, shelter, and clothing for himself and her.

"We do not live, any more than does a waterwheel.''

The brazen woman conducted them back to the horses, where Hugh nervously assured himself they were doing well. Indeed, they were now as calm as if raised among brazen people. But they had scattered their feed so, they had not eaten a third of it, and were trying to lick it up from the clean flags like cattle.

"We need buckets or troughs," he whispered to Gerda, vainly trying to rake piles of feed together.

Hesitantly she said so to the brazen people, and immediately sturdy wooden buckets were brought. The horses ate contentedly while Hugh and Gerda rubbed them, loosening the saddles to work under them.

Presently a brazen woman stepped forward to say, "Your masters will require their horses very soon."

Quickly Hugh went round, tightening their clinches, punching one horse in the belly, while Gerda removed the buckets. Ready, they led the horses out by the door they had entered, took them to the shade of the trees, and waited for some little time, while flies again attacked the stamping horses.

Presently the warriors began to exit from the house under Steep Knob, the knights and baron lingering to bid their host farewell. Crossing to the horses they mounted swiftly and walked them along a path out of sight of the house in the wold. Then they halted and all drew near Sir Harold the Strong.

"How say you, Sir Harold? Can we overthrow him? I had no idea he was so mighty a wizard," said the baron.

"I think it may be done, my lord," said Sir Harold confidently. "From what I saw, the chiefest of his magick derives from that great fire we saw at the center of his hall. Remember that cauldron with the complicated engine within, its parts turning like a waterwheel? What said he of it?"

"That it gave animation to his automatons."

"Indeed. Whiles that fire burns and that cauldron bubbles, then so long shall the brazen beings move. But should it be stifled, then so shall they. And I make no doubt that they are the chiefest defense of the wizard's house."

"A mighty defense, indeed," said Sir Gwilliam, subdued. "Men or women, these brazen people are of the doughtiest sort that ever I saw. For they tire not, neither can they be wounded, to be weakened by loss of blood. How might we battle through them to douse this fire?"

"That should not be necessary, as I shall show," said Sir Harold. "That fire is the one whose smoke vents from the central chimney, upon the hill. Needs only to have water poured down upon it to douse it effectually."

There was a general chorus of understanding and approbation. "Will you then rede us your plan, Sir Harold?" the baron asked. "For you are by far the most experienced in war of us here, and have also dealt with sorcerers."

"None like to this. All of you give thought to what we do, for it is by no means likely that the automatons are the whole of Aelfgar's magicks," said Sir Harold. "Hesitate not to make suggestions."

The plan, as it shaped, was that the warriors should stand in three groups, the baron and his esquire on the right, Sir Gwilliam and his esquire on the left, Sir Harold, his esquire, and the two servants in the middle.

"For the servants have some knowledge of arms, though they be not well practised," he said. "Whereas this dog-peasant is a better horse-handler than they, at any day. He then shall stand among the trees with our horses. The old woman shall carry water up the hill and pour it down upon the fire. So soon as the smoke ceases to rise, or we see the automatons cease to move, we shall all raise a shout and storm the house."

This sounded good to them all, but it was the esquire Roger of all people who spoke the thought that was in Gerda's mind: "How shall the old woman carry water, lacking buckets? Must we borrow them of Aelfgar?"

Sir Harold glared at him, but the baron said, "She shall use the leathern horse-buckets in my saddlebags." He reached back and took from his bags a pair of leather buckets that collapsed like hosen when not full of water. "They are for carrying dry stuffs, but will hold water well enough."

"Good!" said Sir Gwilliam. "I saw a spring upon the farther slope of the hill as we approached the house. Let us forth, then!"

When the party had halted, Gerda was given the buckets and she and Hugh went wordlessly to find the spring. He was as gloomy as she over being involved in nobles' battles. Perhaps he was thinking, as she was, that this was how their son Wat died. Gerda filled the buckets and paused, looking at him. Hugh stood looking solemnly back, looking noble and handsome despite his gnarled age, in his cleanliness. Gerda felt quite an old peasant woman beside him.

For a moment she remembered him like this, when young, and remembered the ardency of their yearning for each other. She had not remembered that for ages; the old wild yearning was gone, replaced by a stolid content and reliance. Now she felt a touch of it again. But she did not know what to say.

And in the end, there was nothing to say.

They nodded to each other, and she turned to trudge up the slope of Steep Knob. Behind her, she heard nothing for several seconds, then Hugh turned and plodded back to the waiting warriors.

The climb was three times her usual water carry, and as she toiled panting up the hill, Gerda remembered the attractive. A pity she had not that now. A pity she had no such thing at home. That, she supposed, would be for nobles only, if ever it escaped the wizards. Yet—

Gerda had spent her whole life carrying water. Her daughters, not yet twenty, were already beginning to be bent and hunched from carrying water. Her granddaughters—they were born straight, as her daughters had been. But that would not last, for they too would spend their lives carrying water. And now Gerda knew it was not necessary.

Atop the hill, she readily identified the chief chimney that Sir Harold had spoken of. She paused to rest, the leather strings of the buckets cutting into her palms. The chimney was a little taller than she, and she was puzzled how to climb it. Finally Gerda hung one bucket on a limb and scrambled up on the chimney with the other bucket in one hand.

White wood smoke poured easily, calmly, from it. Gerda, panting, thought of the fireplace below, of the magical heart of the brazen woman beating swiftly in boiling water, of the woman's calm, kindly voice, of the dying vermin on her skin, of the kindly way the wizard, who never saw her or knew her, had her entreated.

Spilling the water, flinging the bucket away, Gerda lifted herself over the chimney. Catching a breath of pure air, she put her face over the smokehole and cried, "Halloooo! Halloooo! Bewaaaare! Bewaaaare! Bewaaaare!"

Then she leaped down from the chimney, panting, red-faced, smoke in her hair, and ran to the other bucket, which also she emptied. For good measure she threw both buckets down the fireplace, then hurried down the further side of the hill.

Gerda could think of nothing to do but go home.

They caught her in late dusk, four tired and wounded men on three horses. One of the horses fell even as they shouted at her. Gerda made no effort to flee further, stood facing them apathetically. Sir Harold the Strong, of Stanes, was not with them. Perhaps well for her; then she realized it did not matter.

Baron Hildimar and Sir Gwilliam had survived, as had Edwy the esquire and one of the servants. Hugh was not with them, and Gerda experienced a pang. But that, too, did not matter.

For the first time a noble spoke to her directly.

"Bitch! Betrayer!" they shouted, cuffing her. "Why did you betray us?"

At length they calmed themselves. Sir Gwilliam said to the baron, "My lord, we should waste no time on her. Let us slay her and be on our way. Pommers hath died, and is not like to be the last horse we will lose, while the wizard may yet be hard upon our trail."

"I shall not dirty my steel with the dog's blood of her," snapped the baron.

"Nay, nor I; nor is such a death meet for a dog. Rather she should be burned at the stake for having holpen the wizard—"

"Nay, there be no time to gather faggots."

"Nor have we a rope, wherewith to hang her. Let her be given to the servants to be beaten," said Sir Gwilliam.

"Aye. But let it be quick."

Edwy and the other servant approached her, dropping the bags they had gathered from the fallen horse. Edwy undid his belt, the servant picked up a half-rotten limb, and they fell hastily upon her, striking and kicking as Gerda fell.

Gerda hunched upon the forest floor under an oak and readied herself for death. The blows fell thickly and fast; she heard the whistling breath of the frightened and exhausted servant. She made a distance between herself and the pain, thinking of Hugh. She hoped he had not thought unkindly of her as he died.

The beating ended before unconsciousness came. Fear of pursuit, exhaustion, defeat, worked on her oppressors. She heard the horses make off, followed by the stumbling men. Gerda continued to lie there, dully conscious of pain, thinking of her house. She hoped they would not fire it as they passed by. Flagstones for the floor, then an attractive for the water, but she could not see how the upcoming water could be guided up the footpath.

Footsteps approached, and for a moment she feared it was the nobles returning, or perhaps Sir Harold following the baron. Then came the hope it might be Hugh, impossible as that could be. With an effort that brought forth screams of pain from her back and ribs, she raised and turned her head.

A brass face bent above hers. For a moment she thought it was the woman who had served them; then she saw that it was a brazen man. He turned his head and in his deep bronze voice called, "Here she be!"

Kneeling, he gathered her up while Gerda bit back groans. "My master, the wizard Aelfgar, but wishes to know one thing, good woman. Why did you warn us of enemies without?"

He was a sparkling face limned against black-green oak leaves in the night. Even as she looked, the sparkles separated, pulsed, coalesced, separated again. Never before had she been called a good woman. She knew then that she had not guessed wrong about the wizard. Gerda croaked, "For my granddaughters."

Then the darkness took her.

PAGES FROM COLD HARBOR

Richard Grant

"Pages from Cold Harbor" was purchased by Shawna McCarthy, and appeared in the June, 1985, issue of IAsfm, *with an illustration by Janet Aulisio. Grant has made a considerable reputation for himself in recent years as a novelist, but his appearances as a short story writer are rare—the finely crafted story that follows is his only sale to* IAsfm, *for instance. But then, the story itself shows a rare understanding of the hidden places of the human heart, so perhaps that's appropriate . . .*

Richard Grant has rapidly made a name for himself as one of the best young novelists of the 1980s. His critically acclaimed novels include Saraband of Lost Time, Rumors of Spring, *and* Views from the Oldest House. *Upcoming is a new SF novel,* Through the Heart, *and* Ravens, *a mainstream novel. He was a finalist for the Philip K. Dick Award, and regularly contributes critical work to* SF Eye *and other critical magazines. He currently lives in a small cottage in the Maine Woods, where he is at work on a new novel,* Tex and Molly in the Afterlife.

Christmas morning I wake early, shivering by the dead fire, and go out dragging my feet through oil-blackened sand down the long-deserted beach of Cold Harbor. A chill breeze blows steadily over the sea, carrying gull cries and the faint smell of rot. Along the beach between weedy clumps of marshgrass, dead horseshoe crabs and small misshapen fish lie abandoned by the tides. Here and there are mucid gray globs of something vaguely organic, as if the sea is heaving up clotted bits of itself in an agony of decay. Enduring this walk seems a kind of obligation for me. There are no other people about on this holiday morning; scarcely other living things at all.

At last I come home to the box. My coffin-shaped Christmas present. Which for a week has lain unopened in this gray-shingled monument to dead vacationers, while I have tried not to guess what lies inside. To be honest, the origin of the thing disturbs me more than any thought of its contents. There is no return address, but her handwriting was always distinctive. She has painted my name on its lid.

Resolved to lay the ghost of my misgivings, I traipse through the house looking for a tool to have it open. All I find are tiny appliances meant for probing the delicate engines of my trade. At length I settle on a butcher knife. Dripping gray water from the sink across the grimy yellow linoleum, I weave my way through empty cartons and stacks of books to confront, at last, the coffin. Having put it off this long, I fall to prying at the lid with unaccountable eagerness. At last, with a kind of groan, it comes away.

Soft blue cloth lies beneath. Robin's-egg blue. The knife somehow catches on this and, despite my efforts to ease it back gently, rips. I bend to look, and the room grows suddenly warmer.

Down a creaseless forehead falls soft, sunlightened brown . . . if not hair then so close a thing to hair that its warm fragrance seems to reach my nostrils. And yes, limpid untroubled eyes, also brown. The golden artificial skin of the cheeks exudes just faint enough a glow of pink to frame a similarly tinted, palely freckled, firm but slightly upturned nose. The mouth, fractionally ajar, cannily displays snow-colored straight teeth, hard as the slightly pouting lips are soft. Unexceptionably the chin is set. Inlaid the length of the neck runs the slender throat— so real that again one feels the warmth, and wearing like a gem the cartilaginous adolescent-sized adam's apple. Which does not bob or flutter, however long I stare with indrawn breath. The shoulders are finely sculpted, bones hinted at beneath this curving skinsoft expanse where real muscles must, it seems, lie dormant. The chest, brown-nippled and smooth, will surely heave if I watch closely. No? There is a slight dropoff at the ribcage to an abdomen punctuated—nice touch— by a barely flawed, asymmetric navel. The sign of a troubled birth.

And just as I discern the downsoft, dark brown ant-caravan of hair marching down the belly below—before I turn away out of murky, misplaced bashfulness, or possibly alarm—a single drop of dishwater falls from the trembling knife. Christening, and sullying, this astonishing present. Which for years I have awaited with equal measures of longing and dread.

I think I will call him Jeremy.

Life at midwinter is at its furthest ebb from Cold Harbor. Thus far I have avoided any acknowledgement or expression of thanks for the thing that has become the focus of my work. But she must know, I reason; she must certainly understand. How else could she have fashioned it so . . . exactly? Anyway I should not begin to know what to say. It has been so very long.

These thoughts recede as I climb the two flights to the faded pink once-nursery of my home, with its purple rhinoceros on the wall and stacks of whispering machinery. And a voice says:

"Good morning."

That voice. Weeks of work in years past, it sits perched on the edge of the steep slide to manhood: the upper register quivering slightly, the glottal undertones just sketched in. And now it has a home.

"Lights, please," I say softly.

The murky ooze from seaward, filtered through small windows translucent with saltspray, is warmed by an incandescence of roomlights. Humble feat, this: a ribbon cord maintains a sixty-four-bit interface between the main control circuitry and the pale blue josephson junctionbox in its cranial nest. Two mounds of sunlightened hair, weirdly asunder, yield access to the intricate cavity beneath, where fluids course through false flesh that looks so warm. I sit before cool video units, multicolored and impassive, and begin my god-mocking work.

The winter sun rises in the sky, anemic, brightening the haze at the windows, and the roomlights dim to compensate. Impassively my hands perform their chores, probing soft and intimate at the smooth pliant skin of the thing sitting back-turned on a box, its head cracked open where the cord goes in. The supercooling pumps vent heat through its nostrils (a clever arrangement, I think—though the quietly hissing air does not sound quite like breath) and the grosser body components dissipate warmth evenly through the skinlike surface.

By noon I have completed the final tests. Almost unthinkingly I sever the cord, snap shut the cranium, fluff the hair. I note with dispassion the appropriate temperature diffusing from the heatsink millimeters below, and say, ''All right, stand up and turn to the left, please.''

And all by itself, for the first time, the boylike machine calmly rises. Its muscles stir with eerie precision, making perfect bulges and declivities as it turns—some awkwardness there with the feet—to face me. Its eyes flash in the gray oceanlight. The chest and abdomen move steadily. A bit hurriedly perhaps; but even that seems oddly right. And only then, as the ghost of an expression makes a first flicker over its features—the remarkably sculpted, puckish face forming small transient wrinkles, and the cooling system for no evident reason sounding much more breathlike—only then do I begin to tremble.

For I know this beautiful machine is no boy. Its seven-gigabyte brain is cold beyond the imaginings of soft gray flesh, and uncolored by the chemistry of emotion. Its silent thoughts are crystalline and pure.

Yet he stands before me, smiling.

His joints, painstakingly engineered, are almost perfect. A bit too much lateral swiveling at the knees, though even human bodies vary somewhat, one to another. The hips, on the other hand, are a bit stiff. Forward and backward, kicking-style, they bend quite freely, but sideways—from what I can see at this distance, through lenses fouled by saltspray—there appears some difficulty. Childhood paralysis not quite overcome, one could explain, if asked. But perhaps only a father would notice.

Anyway, we have this morning the beach to ourselves. For who would venture out to these jetties, clutching like weary fingers at what sand remains to make a beach of Cold Harbor? The March drizzle is borne by bitter ocean-driven shafts of air through one's clothing and into one's pores. Though the boy, of course, has no pores; the wetness gathers and makes rivulets down his resilient skin, collecting in his mail-order shoes.

Distracted by my thoughts, I fail to notice that the boy has entered the water. This stretches, nearly contravenes, the rigid mandate of self-protection so laboriously programmed into him. Up to his thighs now, he doesn't splash or shout but merely stands there, savoring in his supercold rational way the unaccustomed sensation of the icy current. Graygreen water gushes past him through moss-covered rocks to crash against the shore. I cry out.

"Jeremy! Here. That's very dangerous."

I walk toward him, nearly blinded in the wind and spray.

"The currents, you see Jeremy, are very strong here. And the water gets deeper. The shore drops off precipitously just there, do you see? And you're so heavy. If you fell into a trough you would sink straight to the bottom and the water would get inside you and you'd be ruined before you could climb out. Now be careful."

Straightening to look past him where the waves break and spume, I wonder whether "precipitous" and "trough" are in his lexicon. Can he analyze my words correctly over this thunder and splash? The broad-ranged pink noise here is not quite the type of background his discriminating ears were programmed to filter. Of course he can adjust the programs if he wishes; it is virtually impossible to tell whether he has. I would have to plug him back in, request an abstract of the memory-space in question, run long analyses against the original syntax . . . or just ask him?

No. (I surprise myself here. Why for God's sake be afraid to put a straight question to the intricate thinking system I designed? No need for emotion, really. An interesting problem in cybernetics is all it is.) But what was I thinking of?

Here he is, out of the water, dripping and broadly grinning. His face can be most affecting, whether or not one realizes— as he comes closer—what he is.

"I could feel the cold," he says.

With not quite the proper feeling, I think, and ruminate quickly over what is missing. More of a shiver to make his point. Rapid breathing, intimations of excitement: general systemic response to physical stimulation and exposure. A complex trigger will be needed—thermal, exertion-gauging and judgemental gates. Do teenage boys run out of the water or walk? I will work on this tonight.

Paternal now, I place a hand on his shoulder. It is warm with the dissipation of heat. Too warm, in fact; there is no mechanism to mimic the squeezing off of body-surface capillaries under cold conditions. But no one should notice, I think. I smile at the subtleties of his facial expression in approval.

"Back to the house now," I say.

And he runs ahead, to please me: a proper son. He needs only, like all sons I suppose, a bit of attention and refinement. To be perfect.

These nights late in winter, Cold Harbor seems no longer so cold or so lifeless. Firelight casts its warming yellow glow over stacked boxes, some of them now open to neatly folded clothes, endearingly small-sized. Unfortunately these reflect only my untutored taste and my painfully arrived at—though certainly often wrong-headed—judgement. As do all things in this house.

At night with cold efficiency Jeremy improves his mind. He harnesses his blindingly fast cognitive processes to refine and streamline his thought-paths. He absorbs, by scanning without a pause my lifelong accumulation of books, a store of knowledge about the world, which he collates in some unfathomable manner. Meanwhile he converses most pleasantly. His style of speech is evocative of Hardy, I think. Or Jane Austen—another stay-at-home of surprising perspicacity.

"A pity I have no admiration for tea," he remarks, adding, "or ale, for all of that."

"You're too young," I remind him, "to drink."

"But I rather thought I was being clever."

He sounds slightly miffed, which he does so superbly that I am invariably taken in. One can only be thankful he has not affected a British accent. I hasten to reassure him.

"Ah, you were. Passably clever. Don't, however, get ahead of yourself. Boys your age have their own kind of humor—of a rather unsubtle sort."

To which he says, "No shit, Jackson."

My library, you see, is quite eclectic. It is widespread, too, in the sense of being distributed about the house with apparent, though not actual, randomness. Jeremy, unbothered by forgetfulness, has aped my housekeeping habits, and as an agent of entropy works much more rapidly than I.

Now discipline—a category of interaction which his last remark brings to mind—fills me with unease: a persistent canker one fears to touch, however trying Jeremy does undeniably become. One evening last week, for example, he hurled with effortless precision a fine old leatherbound volume onto the crackling embers. Eye-burning black smoke issued forth in great billows, clouding the room with vile fog.

Jeremy clambered up onto unevenly stacked boxes one would not have thought—lacking his analytical abilities—could have supported his weight. He breathed deeply, sucking hot smoke past his 'sensors. He had never, he explained, though familiar with its composition, and aware that people habitually inhaled it, smelled smoke.

What, then, could I do? I opened the windows east and west, inviting the chill to enter and the no-longer-cozy air of the room to exit—carrying with it, transubstantiated to a less orderly form, Blake's *Songs of Innocence*. An explanation for the choice of fuel was not forthcoming.

Now, had Jeremy—his stated purpose notwithstanding—been curious as to my response to this bit of whimsical outrage, he found it (I blush to confess) characteristic. I spared, once again, the rod; I lectured the youth, not unkindly; I closed the windows.

These mornings, as the pall of winter lifts, I waken readily with the ever-earlier dawn, less prone to hangover than before. My time with Jeremy is spent mostly indoors now. Mist less often shrouds the shore and holds its curtain before the wretched little town. People drawn to the sea venture out along the oilblackened beach, passing by our grayshingled house on their way to the Point (glancing absently, one hopes, in this direction. With what thoughts?) and then walking on.

In the afternoons I climb the low-ceilinged stair to find Jeremy, incapable of boredom, lounging placidly in a boyish pose awaiting further stimuli. He challenges me to word-games, playing on my fondness for bookish anecdotes, taunting my imperfect recall. Or he chides me for inelegant blocks of programming he has discovered and remedied while I slept. But always he exudes good cheer. For he strives earnestly, though unfeelingly, to be a good son. As he is designed—inalterably I hope—to be.

And in the evenings I lie watching the light smear purple and yellow across the smudged windows at the west. I can hear the sea roll and crash at the crumbled shore—whispering, I fancy, hints about the future I can never, quite, hear.

The world, Jeremy remarked one early spring day, quoting one of his Englishmen, is what it is.

An odd sort of warning, perhaps. For though Jeremy is often playful, he is never entirely capricious. He does nothing without a reason. And he has no moods.

I was therefore, upon careful reflection afterwards, not totally surprised by his disappearance from the house, discovered at dawn when I climbed no more eagerly than usual to the once-nursery and found the purple rhinoceros in its place, but not Jeremy.

I will not deny, merely enfeeble by objectifying, my emotions. My palms and forehead became slick with sweat; there was a momentary weakness at my knees. I seated myself and thought with false calm, maybe he is hiding somewhere in the house. I correctly disbelieved this, but did not want to jump, as they say, off the deep end. As yet.

However, the exercise of searching the house was therapeutic. By the time I had convinced myself of Jeremy's utter absence, I was more or less prepared to deal with it. Which is to say, I had decided to postpone dread and anguish until their time should be shown to have arrived. Pending which, I settled myself to pacing and practicing sundry forms of self-deception.

Two-thirty in the afternoon. The day has grown windy and bright, sunlight blazing white out of the blue void and laying on the surface of things so brilliantly—as if rocks and dirt, brittle weedpatches, gnarled bits of flotsam and sagging scrub-pines alive after yet another winter effulge with a light of their own. Their organic aura glows triumphantly at the advent of spring.

And at two-thirty, dry in the manner of one who has been recently wet, Jeremy strolls through the door. His demeanor, to choose a human analogue, is nonchalant: fresh of face, hair windblown, clothing moderately asunder. He faces me and says, "I'm so glad the weather's better."

I find his nineteenth-century schoolboy style suspect and disturbing.

"Jeremy," I say. "You left the house and were gone all morning."

His reaction to which I can begin, but only begin, to surmise, as it flashes through his superconducting, sardine-can-sized mind. He observes that I have stated an obvious fact; he gathers further clues from my rather tense stance and probably tremulous tone of voice; he detects from the distance of a meter and a half the distinctive vapor of whiskey, noticing also the bottle and glass on the table beside the unopened mystery novel. These things he compares to similar patterns observed in his three-month span of cognitive history. He merges this situation into his model of human behavior, refining it accordingly, and calls upon this improved model to choose—according to the heuristics by which, for Jeremy, the game of life is played— his next action. He accomplishes all this with no discernible pause, except for the half-second hesitation—itself a deliberate act—which he uses to signal surprise and thoughtfulness. He allows a gentle frown to cross his pale forehead, and says:

"Were you worried, Father? I'm terribly sorry if I upset you."

His eyes are clear as browntinted glass. The directness of youth shines from his face. His stance is delicately poised, weight concentrated on the forward slender leg while the other trails, bent slightly at the intricately-jointed knee. An arm is half-lifted, showing tan artificial skin below a rolled flannel sleeve still creased from its box. Jeremy holds this pose for about three seconds.

My heart pounds in its cave; a trembling is born between my shoulders and spreads in waves through weak mortal flesh. I am unable to utter the questions I know, for reasons unrelated to my feelings of the moment, must be asked.

Jeremy takes a step, then another more quickly. He covers the sand-strewn linoleum expanse between us in perfectly scaled strides, arriving below my averted head after a timelapse measurable in heartbeats. He hugs me tightly with arms just pliant enough to resemble firm-muscled young limbs. With his head warm from thermal dissipation millimeters below my jaw, he comfortingly says:

"Don't worry, Father, I'm home now. It's all right."

•　　•　　•

Spring sinks its claws deep into the inhospitable earth of Cold Harbor, pricking green tuberculed life from the salt-leeched soil to rise twisting in the warming wind. Daily the mist lifts higher from the shore, extending the horizon farther past the Point and drawing vaster seaviews through the smeared windows of my home.

Jeremy is now a creation complete unto himself, requiring little from me in the way of software refinement or mechanical ministration. He has learned well enough to care for himself, as he will have eventually to do. And he needs nothing, after all, in the way of affection.

His first venture from home having yielded satisfactory results—soon related to me in bright detail—Jeremy now repeats the journey with daily variations. And I am left with steadily eroding ground from which to halt the advancement of events.

The first morning, says Jeremy, he saw no one. He went to the Point, splashed a bit and mapped the place in his memory. Incidentally he calculated his bodily density by displacement of water to be one point seven times that of human substance: a poor prospect for swimming lessons. His smile flashes with boyish imperishability as he chatters on, relating the adventure with almost human bliss. Undoubtedly it was good exercise for his situational response abilities, this deluge of unstructured stimuli. The sort of thing boys thrive upon.

His next expedition, some days later, to which I tacitly consented by my silent acceptance of the first, brought about a dreaded epochal event: Jeremy's first confrontation with a human being other than his . . . other than myself. The person involved was, Jeremy explains, a fisherman's son. This lad is about Jeremy's age—which, do you know, I have never precisely pinned down, not having had a real physical son who might be a yardstick for such things. But I think fifteen or so.

The fisherman's son: a coarse lad, vaguely identifiable among the lineup of literary antecedents in the cool blue brain, heretofore its only occupants besides myself. A Donleavy stableboy, Jeremy suggests. This youngster encountered Jeremy midway along the sinuous path through scrub-covered dunes near the Point. He challenged the false boy in a generally rough but not unfriendly manner as to his origins and status—whether townie or tourist—with particular questions about his present activity. To which Jeremy replied: Thurmondston, Ireland; staying indefinitely with his father, a professor on sabbatical;

and exploring the beach. (Ingenious replies, I am moved to admit; the first by way of accounting for any odd habits of speech, and the second for appending an open-ended ellipsis to the nature of our lives—of my life—at Cold Harbor.)

The afternoon these boys spent together, the living and the mechanical, proceeded with roving in adolescent fecklessness about the narrow ocean-bracketed isthmus of the Point, exchanging boasts. I cannot but imagine Jeremy creating a fantastic Irish landscape for his gullible listener, milking effortlessly the penurious, brain-wrenching effort of a dozen authors for an hour's idle chat.

On subsequent days, drawn ever closer together, Jeremy and the local lad—whose name I understand to be Paul—make a routine of the day's events. Jeremy goes out into the wide, many-peopled world, exercising his ability to function unrecognized within it. I should possibly welcome this as the firmest proof of my achievement. At least I should accept it as deserved tribute to my unthanked and long-unseen collaborator—Jeremy's mother, if you will. Though somehow I feel only numbness and loss.

My hours now burgeon with inactivity. I have time to stroll the oil-stained beach and take what pleasure there is in the annual remission of Cold Harbor's malignant climate. Time to locate and reread treasured volumes scattered through this large, unkempt and silent house. I have pursued none of this with any seriousness. Instead I walk miles over the rotted linoleum of these obstacled rooms, lift salt-smudged windows where the sun makes dirty rainbows, and gaze across the unbounded expanse of the spring-green sea. I think at these times of nothing especially—or of everything, from a distance. I watch the fishing boats bob. I consider the course my existence might have taken had I turned like those boats into the waves, not just drifted before the wind and the tide.

The sluggish warmth of Cold Harbor has stirred to life a veritable garden of remembrance and regret. I think of colleagues distant, unheard-from or dead; I recall friendships to which my own contribution never seems to have done justice. Fattened and happy, the memories chatter among themselves nearly out of earshot.

"You terrified philosopher," a woman's voice says.

I deny this.

"Oh, yes," she says. "You write your papers and make

your proposals. But you're afraid to test your ideas in the real
world. I think you're scared to death an artificial personality
may be too much like the real thing.''

Nonsense. I would be happy, of course, to test my theories.
But the hardware isn't ready. My systems cannot work in thin
air. (A faint note of accusation here. A leveling of the meaningful glance.)

"You just wait. I'll give you your goddamned hardware
someday. And you'll be so scared—you'll run and bury your
goddamned systems in the sand.''

Clinging to the teeth of Cold Harbor, the oilstained sand is
the color of ashes. Fishing boats put to sea, plumbing the black
depths for scaly bodies to drag back in iceholds. If she were
here today, I think, would she feel chastened or triumphant?
If she were here . . .

I seem to hear laughter. Do my memories mock me? I look
up in something like alarm.

No. It is the hungry squawk of gulls, swooping after their
midday meals. And the air has grown warmer.

Jeremy, of course, will not hear of staying inside on a nice
day. Nor does he care to join me for a stroll in the sunlight.
It is as if the season has infected him with wanderlust, as it
would a real boy. But real boys are built of organic compounds
that seethe in the earth, while Jeremy's heart is a coolant pump
made of unnatural alloys, and his brain is chilled to a superconducting cold that is alien to sunny worlds where life thrives.

None of which mitigates my aloneness this warm June morning. Swatting at mosquitoes emboldened by the unaccustomed
dearth of seabreeze, I go from room to room gathering whiskey-
stained coffee cups.

The dishwater turns gray as it sluices through my fingers. I
pause to wonder: is Jeremy equipped, physically, to deal with
the demands made upon him by his friendship with this yet
unseen Paul? The surreptitious beer, for example, slipped from
the fisherman's refrigerator, tossed back casually to be stored
in Jeremy's modest holding cavity for eventual evacuation—
this should present no problem. And the danger of a summer
swim? Jeremy must have manufactured by now an excuse to
cover this. But might there be other, unforeseen challenges to
Jeremy's physical equipage, secret pastimes in which teenage

boys customarily indulge? I find few clues in the memory of my own cloistered adolescence.

Holding a half-rinsed saucer, I am given over to restlessness and anxiety: the agonies, I reflect without irony, of parenthood. And all for the sake of—let us be blunt—a machine.

Drying my hands on my trouserlegs, I abandon the dishes and pace the house, unable to bear this cluttered, sandstrewn prison a moment longer. Without a thought for my overworn shoes, my unshaved face and matted hair, I am outside in the glare of sunlight crunching up the graveled road. Though aimless in intent, I am moving toward the Point, that scrawny fist of rock that thrusts its lighthouse at the sullen sea.

The road deteriorates. Shortly it is no more than a tire-rutted path, wending through low dunes of dirty sand, bushes with pointed leaves wagging in the breeze, and dark outcroppings of rock. This is my first walk here since I have lived at Cold Harbor.

The sense of isolation is acute, much more so here than where my gray-shingled house makes its stand on the sheltered bight. The lighthouse looms huge over the mouth of the harbor. And near it, extending a rickety pier bravely into the surf, a poor weatherbeaten shambles of a house perches at the very edge of the sea. It is uninhabited, one must think—uninhabitable, even—but there are deep tiretracks near it in the spray-dampened sand. As I draw near, a tattered curtain flutters quickly. Or perhaps not.

Rounding the place slowly, improving my angle of surveillance, I see a fishing boat made fast to the pier, where it rises and groans against the piles. It is an ancient side trawler: western-rigged, pilot house forward and sagging cargo boom aft, rusted from gunwale to waterline. It strains at its moorings, threatening to yank out cleats, pier, or house, whichever is less solidly planted. (I incline to think house.)

A curtain flutters again; my imagination seizes some barely-glimpsed detail to sketch, in retrospect, the image of a slender figure vanishing behind the sunbleached fabric. A trick of the shadows, no doubt. From somewhere comes a ratchety noise, growing rapidly louder.

A vehicle is grinding up the twisted pathway from Cold Harbor. I tell myself there is no reason to be ill at ease: it is a public place, after all. Nonetheless I stand absurdly square-shouldered to face the metallic glint.

A decrepit Land Rover, rusty as the fishingboat and of similar vintage, growls and slides across the uneven surface, lurching to a stop before me. From it clambers a slack-jowled man of middle years. He slams the door, adjusts the hand of his faded shirt where it balloons at the belly. I register dimly the man's grizzled aspect, the air of unwash about him, the eyes aglow with drink. He brings himself to a halt, belligerent of pose, two meters away.

"You're the guy lives in the old Kilby place," he alleges.

By my silence, I concur in the man's remark; at least I offer no quibble.

"Well keep," he spits out, "that son of yours. Or whatever he is. Away from my daughter."

Completely astonished by this, I am unable sensibly to reply. Thus my bellicose accoster is able to develop his theme.

"Understand you're some kind of professor," he snorts. "Well you listen, Doc. That kid of yours with that weird way of talking he's got. Been sneaking around here while I'm gone. Gotta make a living and there aren't enough fish out there to fry for dinner. Doing God knows what with my young daughter. Only fifteen, hasn't got any idea what that kind of boy's gonna be after. So you keep him away, you hear me, Doc?"

As he speaks, I am struck by the sheer fleshiness of the man: great pouches of skin hanging from his face; oilblack hair; brown patches like spilled paint up his exposed hairy arms; wrinkles and ravines in odd places. And it strikes me that this is humanity—its decaying flesh impatient for the annoyance of life to flee from its confines.

"You hear me, Doc?" he repeats, pointing at my own aging face.

I nod dumbly, imperfectly concentrating on the main level of discourse here, and essentially unbelieving. For surely Jeremy, though endlessly curious, and from all physical appearance complete in every detail, could have no desire to live up to this man's vile suspicions. So I say confidently:

"There must be some mistake."

"I'll tell you a mistake," he says quickly. "A big mistake would be for that boy of yours to let me catch him around here again. That'll be a sorry tale for sure, Doc. You mark my words."

Giving final punctuation to his narrative by way of a globulous mass of spittle dispatched to the ashen sand, this obstreperous fellow turns on a well-worn heel and pounds into the house, which trembles around him as he slams its door. From within, a shout finds its way through many cracks and reaches me across the rocks and sand. Arriving softly, a name:

"Paula."

Which strikes my ears in a gently jarring discord, vague at first but becoming more precise and elemental under sharpened attention—a Webern quartet encased in a single word. Variations spin themselves with mathematic inevitability. First the name: too facile a distortion of Paul the fisherman's son to be shrugged away as coincidence. Next the thought of Jeremy lying. And the question of motive.

. . . But I suppose this series of thoughts must be achingly obvious.

As my feet ply the crunching path homeward, the choicest replies and verbal parries to the rude words of the fisherman form in my mind. If there are intimations of lust here, I might have said, you need not look beyond your doorstep for their origin. Because Jeremy's sole motivation, in this congress as in all others, is curiosity of the purest sort. And he is, moreover, incapable of bringing about any troublesome change in your fair daughter's condition, particularly in the way of parturition. Assuming by the way that your daughter is fair. In defiance of all genetic likelihood. And so forth.

Until, by the time I arrive home, I am of mixed mood. On the one hand, I am troubled that Jeremy has conjured, in the impenetrable iciness of his brain, tales of adventures with Paul the fisherman's son in the stead of whatever true stories there may be of Paula the fisherman's daughter. On the other hand, I remember Jeremy's inalterable urge to learn, to expand his model of human nature and thereby render himself more fully human. What could be more natural—more delightfully apt, in fact—than bringing his curiosity to bear on a human his own age but of opposite gender? Besides, the inversion of sex in his tale-telling may be mere reticence, wariness of my possible response—natural enough when one considers the shelfful of pre-Victorian novels the lad has consumed.

In the end, I am left marveling, with a touch of pride, at this ingenious, adaptive, energetic, and (it now seems) sexually convincing system of intelligence, whose exploits have so thoroughly upset the fisherman.

Yet in some measure I share that poor father's unhappiness.

For love them though we might, we can never, either of us, control the minds of our children.

I sit facing south, toward the lighthouse, as the sun buries itself at my shoulder. Jeremy mocks attentiveness at my side, sifting the raw experience of another summer day. His mind's relentless search for patterns admits no moment of stillness or repose.

"Father," he says at length. The distinctive slur of this benighted coast is on his tongue.

I acknowledge him in brief syllables. Unable to decide what, if anything, to say about Paul or Paula, I have no interest in idle chat.

"Why are you so distant tonight?" he says, solicitous now. "You haven't asked me what I did today."

I allow myself a glance: quite the proper teenager in his cutoffs and teeshirt, displaying for admiration his perfectly formed limbs—sufficient, I think, to arouse the interest of any fisherman's daughter.

"I am just," I tell him, "waiting for the lighthouse."

"Well I was wondering," he says, "if it would be all right if I spent the night with Paul tomorrow. On the dunes near the Point. He's got a tent."

Following this (modestly apocalyptic) inquiry, he pauses in a simulation of expectancy. The tiny motors that drive his facial features move them into a configuration that suggests nervousness and doubt, while in reality he has assumed an emotionally uncolored wait-state. I temporize:

"Tomorrow night?"

"Yes, tomorrow. It's quite a common thing, you know, camping out. I think it will be a good experience."

I ponder this with a curious sense of absence—knowing, however, that Jeremy's request is a pivotal event, that some great subterfuge is being enacted, if only I could see it. But I stare toward the lighthouse; stars have begun to appear. Jeremy says:

"There's so much I could learn by spending a whole night out."

Which sounds true enough. Tiny lights blink at sea, on and off, like the billions of binary switches in Jeremy's cranium.

"Would it be all right?" he quietly persists.

And then—just as I think I am ready to thrust my questions

through the subtle barrier between us—the piercing eyes of the lighthouse casts its awful gaze over the water, putting its own nightly question to the dark encroaching sea. Which must have the answer, but remains silent.

And I say, "Yes."

Dreaming. The night hangs like a shroud through which I grope toward deeper dark.

I awaken to fists beating the door. A whiskey glass clatters as I rise in disorientation, like a mariner befogged. Past midnight, says the blue face of the clock. The pounding below continues.

Down the creaking stair, tripping on the turned-up edge of linoleum, I wrap a damp palm around the doorknob. Swollen in the heavy air, the door resists my tug. Outside, a bellowing commences.

"Open that door, goddamn you."

Not meaning to oblige, but out of preset purpose, I give the door a successful yank, admitting starlit night.

"Come with me, you bastard," roars the bullish man from the Point, half-visible at the stoop, "if you don't want me to kill that boy of yours."

Dumbly I am outside the door staring beyond him at the all-devouring night.

"He's out with my daughter in a boat, that little punk. I'll have him locked up and he's lucky I don't shoot him."

We climb into the Land Rover, which smells of seawater, oil, and rot. Its engine growls as if to cow the pitted road into obeisance. Dimly the meaning of the man's words assembles itself before me, like graphics on a video screen.

Got a call from a friend in town, he tells me. Saw his girl getting into a boat with that boy from England or wherever. Heading south out of the harbor. Thought he'd want to know.

You bet he wanted to know. Snarling, he wrenches the gearshift knob, stomps the brake, buries the wheels in clotted sand. We have arrived at the Point. He leaves me to follow like a somnambulist and walks down to the pier, where his fishing boat creaks at its mooring lines, hulking black and hideous in the night. There he throws lines off the pier and leaps aboard. The boat sways heavily and begins to drift before the current.

"Come on, goddamn you. If you want to save the skin of that boy of yours."

Even before I climb aboard I have a sense of movement beneath me, as if the entire illusion of the Point, the wretched house, the oilslick pier is coming adrift, losing its grounding in any recognizable reality.

But a jolt of reality strikes me as I leap to the pitching, slippery deck: the stench of rotting fish rising from the hold. I clutch at the rail, gasping for breathable air; finding none, I lean over and retch into the darkness.

From the submerged bowels of the fishing boat comes the guttural eructation of an old engine laboring to life. I hang onto the slimy rail, watching black water roiling below, as the aged craft surges away into the night.

Looking up I see the white mastlight high above the pilot-house, and more dimly, beneath it, the portside running light: as dull and red as the glow behind my eyes. Step by step I approach it, clutching the rail, until I reach the wave-breaking prow. Here I find a ladder and, with white fingers slipping on the rusted bars, I lift my body from the deck.

The heat inside the pilothouse is oppressive. Smells of metal, sweat, and rum are forced into my nostrils. I sense at first—then faintly see—the dark form beside me, clutching a small wooden wheel and staring ahead. His eyes glow with the green light of the radar, the only instrument on the bridge that gives a hint of life. The man snarls:

"They'll be around the Point there."

He points at the radar. Cold Harbor stretches in profile across the screen, less jagged in the eye of the cheap radar than in physical reality. A burly finger pokes at emptiness, smudging the glass with sweat.

"The shoals there. That's where they all go. They'll be anchored there having their little party."

His breath is a dizzying fume; I yearn to back away from him, from the very salaciousness of his voice. His hand finds a lever in the dark with a familiar, intimate touch. The old trawler moans and beats more fervently at the water.

Are there other vessels with us, abroad on the nightblack sea? I stare at the finger-smudge he calls the shoals, but see nothing. Maybe, then, there is nothing to see; we are headed nowhere; this dreamlike voyage will be abandoned. But:

"There," says the brute. His dirty finger touches the glass, and this time I perceive a tiny blot.

"Out by the shoals," he says, almost chanting. "That's where they all go."

He lifts to his lips a bottle that catches fleetingly the illumination of the screen.

I feel my nausea swelling again and grope my way to the door. The damp air that swirls around my face is neither warm nor cool; it has a stink of its own, but a milder one than the pilothouse. Gratefully I suck it down, staring at the beaten wood of the deck on which the running light casts its blood-red pallor.

I think: however enraged this beastly fisherman may be, I must calm him. When the moment arrives, I must allay his groundless fears for his daughter. Possibly I can enlist her help in this. For by now—if truly she and Jeremy are out here in the night—she must have discovered that her father's lust-ridden imagination has been aroused for naught. If absolutely necessary, I can open Jeremy's skull and lay bare the cool blue brain.

The throbbing of the engine drops to a susurrating murmur, barely audible above the slosh of waves.

"There they are," breathes the fisherman. Then, with a brush of his hand, he darkens the running lights. The old trawler, pitching madly in the swells, seems to disappear around me.

We are still moving forward, drifting as if by force of brutish will toward what this man must know is there. I wonder for a moment at his perception of things I cannot see. Perhaps, I think, I am too much like Jeremy: lacking that strange awareness that lies outside reason. Perhaps I am not quite as human as this foul-smelling man at the helm.

Then the sound of laughter reaches my ears, and humanity rushes into my throat. The fisherman grabs my arm, squeezing off my stillborn shout.

"Now we'll see about that boy of yours."

The laughter is louder now; distinctly female in timbre. It is terribly close, yet somehow distant, drifting across the water from some reachless remove.

I think I see a shape ahead in the night. A shadow, merely, it rises and falls as though suffering no connection with the water. Abruptly a small motorboat takes shape: twenty meters away, no more. All is dark on its deck and in its covered cabin. A thick arm moves at my side; the engine gives a dying cough and falls silent. Moving past me with unsuspected stealth, the fisherman lowers a mangled rope fender from the bow. And we drift ever closer.

Louder laughter: a boy's voice now mingles with the girl's, innocent and unsuspecting. My own voice remains imprisoned in my throat.

Then a weight detaches itself from the trawler and lands with a thump on the motorboat. The fisherman, righting himself on the small deck, bellows something obscene. There follows a girl's short cry, and sounds of scrambling. I stand fixed with horror—afraid to intervene, maybe, or simply no match for the speed of events.

"Come out of there, you little bastard."

The girl cries out again, in fright or maybe defiance. There is a movement in the motorboat's cabin door. A heartbreakingly familiar form appears.

Jeremy! (I don't know if I shout or merely think of shouting.)

"No!" implores the girl, her pale form appearing behind him. "Stop it! He's crazy, he'll hurt you."

Shadows commingle on the fantail of the motorboat. The fisherman roars; the girl protests; still there is only silence from Jeremy, who stands (I note in alarm) quite naked. The girl likewise.

There is no time to wonder at this. Rapid movement quakes the little boat. I hear a confusion of voices, among which I catch distinctly in the girl's shrill voice:

"And he's not even a real boy, you big fat stupid fool!"

To which the father replies, he will see about that.

There is a flash of red, brighter than the running light and then gone. A slam like thunder dissipates over the waves.

"Jeremy!" two voices cry.

The boylike body lies on its side—not really in agony, I know, but agonizing beyond belief to witness. Still he is moving, trying perhaps to sit up, twisting sideways on the deck.

The fisherman is motionless—immobilized, perhaps, by the shock of his own violence. Wailing words of hatred, his daughter springs forward in a blur of ghostly flesh. She wrests the weapon from his hand and moves back across the deck, to the place where Jeremy lies broken.

The fisherman rouses himself; he steps forward as though to strike her. But his body, less dense than that of the unhuman youth, is brought to a halt by the first blast of the handgun and hurled against the transom by the second. After a long heartbeat he emits a lowing moan, clutching his middle.

Jeremy has half-risen; the slender girl leans over him. Soothing words come from his mouth, but they are intended for the girl alone, and are unintelligible from where I cling in dread. The girl helps Jeremy up on his undamaged leg; the other trails at an unnatural angle. She leads him to the rail by the fishing boat.

Jeremy looks up at me, an outstretched arm-length away, through bright brown eyes unclouded by pain or remorse. He extends an arm.

"Father."

The almost-breaking voice is perfect.

"Help me up."

Paula does not glance across the deck where her father tries to stem the seeping darkness. She watches only Jeremy—knowing what he is, as I do, yet loving him with bright girlish clarity. She seems unmindful of her nakedness.

Jeremy now is balanced on the low gunwale of the motorboat. His arms reach out to me, and I grasp them unthinkingly, I feel their melting, mechanical warmth, their firm grasp so much like real young muscles. His face (whose upturned nose and pale freckles I imagine in the darkness) watches mine as he stands bracketed by two pairs of arms.

At that moment of mutual helplessness I look at the girl. Paula. And for a single instant she meets my gaze. I see in her eyes, set in a scrawny face above high cheekbones, something of the same ache and bewilderment that throb inside me: the fruit of absurd and boundless love, of which only humans are capable.

I feel then, growing in the space between us, a kind of union I have never experienced—a relationship, however ephemeral, of perfect communication. It is the thing I have strived after, failed at, and fled from, without ever knowing its true nature, and hoped to achieve with the cybernetic boy, my Christmas-born son.

Yes: and the very thing which Jeremy, programmed in my likeness, has sought to achieve with this poor girl, whose beautiful haunted eyes are locked with mine in the fullness of the night.

I long powerfully to embrace her, to take her into my arms and give her the thought-dampening comfort she seeks.

And perhaps, as I feel this gush of tenderness, and alliance, toward this unclothed dolorous girl, I may actually make some small move which loosens my hold on Jeremy. But only for a moment. For I have no thought—here in the darkness, crowded with mortality and dread—that the trawler might take a sudden roll away from the motorboat, opening a space of half a gaping meter between them. Which will close again, only after:

Jeremy, unimpeded on either side—abandoned for that fleeting instant by the two of us who love him—quickly (owing to his weight) and quietly (owing to his lack of emotion) tumbles:

Into the allmothering sea.

September will return to the gray-shingled house at Cold Harbor. The wind will crawl coldly between the teeth of the jetties, insinuating itself beneath doors and behind drawn curtains. Linoleum, blotched with age and oil, will curl across floorboards hard as stone from accreted seeping salt. Up the stair, dim and head-bumpingly low, the dying fire will raise a draft, whispering past icy bedrooms, stirring dust to life under old furniture, and floating at last through the dirty pink once-nursery in the attic, with its purple rhinoceros on the wall and narrow salt-smudged windows.

Here the rental agent will pause wheezing on the morning of my departure, remove from his coat a yellowed handkerchief and, unapologizing, hack into it.

"Hard to fill them this time of year," he will inform me.

I will merely tell him where to reach me: this number, this sun-warm street. The card I give him will bear her handwriting, which was always distinctive.

"Got some boys coming," he will say, pocketing the card with the handkerchief, "to get your luggage. Guess you want it out today."

No: only the coffin-shaped carton. The rest—the books, the machines, the memories—can wait out the winter.

The man may pause a moment before leaving, allow his small eyes to linger over my visage, for during the sultry season just past I became briefly, locally famous. A tabloid Frankenstein. Robot Seduces Girl, 15, Shoots Drunken Dad. Inventor to Salvage Silicon Casanova.

None of which, probably, will matter to the rental agent, whose cheeks are gray and gestures desperate after fifty winters of fleeing the decay that creeps like a greedy fiend up the oilblackened beach at Cold Harbor. He will want only to return to his weatherstripped house, his flask, his lap-blanket. To his life so little different than mine has been.

But no longer. For this will be the morning of my departure.

It will take months, of course, to bring Jeremy back to life—no: back to operation—again. His body may, for all I know, be unrepairable. I did not give him that; only the mind that lies sealed in its blue sardine-can-sized box. And finally, I suppose, that is all I did. Gave it to him. Gave him the opportunity to use it. What use he made of it . . . Well, what use do any of us make of such ambivalent bequests as knowledge and desire?

Nonetheless I will try to have him back again. Only, I will not raise him from his moldering grave alone. I have learned (and not too late, I hope) the true nature of the gift I received when I opened my coffin-shaped Christmas present. And for my own sake, and poor Paula's, and especially for the sake of my unthanked and long-unseen friend, I will turn my back on this windshriven shore and hide no longer among these lifeless pages from Cold Harbor.

SIMULATION SIX

Steven Gould

*"Simulation Six" was purchased by Gardner Dozois,
and appeared in the March, 1990, issue of IAsfm,
with an illustration by Terry Lee. Gould is a frequent
contributor to our sister magazine,* Analog, *but to
date his stories have appeared in IAsfm less often
than we'd like. When they do appear, though, his
stories usually prove to have been worth waiting for,
like the story that follows, in which Gould fast forwards us to a hard-edged, high-tech future with a
heart of darkness, for a suspenseful tale of murder
and obsession . . .*

*Steven Gould's popular story "Peaches for Mad
Molly" was a finalist for the Hugo and Nebula awards
in 1988. Just married, Gould and his wife, Laura
Mixon, recently made the dangerous and difficult trek
from Bryan, Texas, to Staten Island, New York,
where—no doubt relieved to have made it unscathed—
they now live. Their collaborative novel* Green War,
*an environmental techno-thriller, will soon be pub-
lished by Tor Books.*

"Thanks for coming, Sharon."

The door shuts behind her and disappears into the middle of Rembrandt's *The Night Watch*. She glances behind her and frowns.

"You know how I feel about that painting."

"Sorry." I blank the wall and door back to neutral. "Their eyes never bother me, so I forget." I get up from my desk and hold a chair for her, my eyes lingering on the nape of her neck as she sits. I take the chair opposite, rather than hide behind the desk. As usual, I find myself breathing quickly, short, shallow breaths. She folds her legs and licks her lips.

"I know I said I'd call you. Time got away from me. I hope you understand."

"That's not why you're here." I pause and gulp air. "I know about the National Account."

She blinks several times in succession, then looks away. I am powerless to look elsewhere. She is everything I've ever wanted, everything I need.

"It was just a matter of time," she says.

I am crushed. "So, when you came to work here, this was what you were after?"

She doesn't speak, doesn't look at me.

My eyes sting and her perfect form begins to bleed into the outline of the chair. "You were using me, weren't you? Last weekend was just a means to an end."

I blink and water runs down my face. For a second her features come back into focus. Then I bury my face in my hands and the sobs shake my body, move the chair. I don't see her leave. I don't hear the door shut.

The office rippled, distorted, then solidified. I still sat in the chair but the emotional upheaval of seconds before seemed remote, far away. My head ached and my cheeks were still wet with somebody else's tears.

"Well?" a voice asked loudly, insistently.

I winced and, instead of answering, reached for the first of five epidermal patches I'd placed on the coffee table before the simulation. My hands were shaking and it took me several tries to peel off the backing. Finally it came free and I stuck it on the skin behind my right ear.

Sergeant Lewis had worked with me before. He spoke quietly. "You're wasting your breath, Lieutenant. He won't talk to us until he's good and ready."

The pain began to lessen even before the drug really had time to hit the bloodstream. My body thinks relief comes with a cold caress behind the ear. I wonder what would happen if somebody put placebo patches in my kit? Would my body damp the blinding headaches anyway?

Bad as the headaches were, I could function, but I wasn't going to tell the Lieutenant that. I looked down at the floor. The taped outline from Perdue's body was to the right of my chair. He'd been sitting where I was when the bullet took him in his right eye. There was still a brown, flaking stain on the rug where his heart's last efforts had dumped a half-liter or so of blood. Across the carpet, where Sharon had sat in the first simulation, was the taped outline of a gun, now down at forensics.

I took a deep breath. "Are you ready? I'm not going to repeat any of this."

Lieutenant Morrow scowled, started to say something, then just nodded, his recorder ready. Sergeant Lewis used a notepad and paper.

"Okay. He was getting ready to meet with a woman called Sharon—short blond hair, maybe in her early twenties, blue eyes, approximately fifty kilos, one hundred and seventy centimeters."

"Wait a minute," Lieutenant Morrow said. "If the meeting hadn't happened, how do you know what she looks like?"

I was sarcastic. "I'm not here to teach you my job. Use the information or don't. I couldn't care less."

Sergeant Lewis stepped between us, faced Lieutenant Morrow. "Perdue ran a simulation—five of them to be exact. That's why I asked division for Spinoza. He has the internal wiring to play it back."

Lewis shrugged. "Well he doesn't have to be an asshole about it."

Sergeant Lewis faced me. "Was she an employee of the firm?"

"Probably. He confronted her about something called the National Account. He was extremely agitated. He accused her of using him to gain access to the account. There was a reference to last weekend, apparently spent together."

Morrow spoke again. "What upset you in the simulation?"

I laughed. "Nothing. The kind of simulations *I* run make this stuff seem like a vacation. Perdue was the one who was upset. You haven't worked with simulations before, have you?"

He shook his head after a pause, hating to admit it to me. I spoke to the office AI, "Godfrey?"

An evenly modulated voice sounding not unlike William Powell said, "Yes, Mr. Spinoza?"

"Would you be kind enough to tell me if Mr. Perdue regularly ran simulations?"

"Yes. As a negotiation specialist, Mr. Perdue ran several personality simulations a week."

I looked at Morrow. "The hardware and the operation for Direct Brain Interface is not cheap." I touched my own forehead. "He wouldn't have had the equipment if it wasn't regularly used." As an afterthought I said, "You idiots did ask Godfrey about the incident, didn't you?"

Morrow looked as if he'd bitten into something bitter. Sergeant Lewis answered instead. "Perdue invoked privacy at noon yesterday. Nothing was recorded by Godfrey until *we* invoked felony investigation override after the body was discovered."

"That doesn't mean Godfrey wasn't active," I said with exaggerated patience. "Observations of this room were simply wiped in that time period." I addressed the air. "Godfrey, are your erasures active or directory based?"

"My software conforms to DOD standards for wiped data. All files wiped for reasons of confidentiality are overwritten three times with null data."

I shrugged. "Tough. I might have recovered that data if his deletions simply marked the directory entries as erased."

Morrow looked confused. "*You* were the one that was crying."

I just stared at Morrow. Lewis pulled him to one side. "For all intents and purposes, Spinoza becomes Perdue. He sees what Perdue saw in the simulation, he feels what Perdue felt."

I activated my DBI and silently asked Godfrey for a nonvocal link.

"Yes, Mr. Spinoza?" His voice was the same, but without the shaping echoes and damping of the physical room. Call it the difference between speakers and headphones.

"Did you recognize the woman I referred to as Sharon?"

"Yes, Mr. Spinoza. Her name is Sharon Elaine Bullard."

"Is she an employee of the firm?"

"That was my understanding, but . . . I've just addressed an inquiry to personnel and they have no such person on record by that name or description."

I digested that tidbit. "What led you to believe she was an employee? Did Mr. Perdue refer to her as a fellow employee?"

"No. But he discussed details of client transactions that were confidential. Also he made references to 'her department' as if it was a part of the firm."

"Please be so kind as to show me her face."

Her face floated in my field of vision, blotting out Morrow and Lewis. I felt the tug of Perdue's longing, the yawning abyss of his despair.

"Please put it on the wall, Godfrey."

Morrow stopped in mid-sentence and stared. Sharon's face stared back at him, two meters tall.

I spoke aloud. "Would you give us a profile, too, Godfrey?"

The image shrunk, moved to one side. A profile of her face appeared beside.

"Thank you, Godfrey." I turned away from the wall. "I'm sure Godfrey will dump this image to the department along with whatever information he has on her. I *suggest* you put a tracer on her immediately." I stared at Sharon's face on the wall. "While you're doing that, I'm going to try the next simulation."

"Thanks for coming, Sharon."

The door shuts behind her and disappears into the middle of Rembrandt's *The Night Watch*. She glances behind her and frowns.

Before she says anything I say, "Let me fix that." I blank the wall and door back to neutral. "Their eyes never bother me, so I forget." I get up from my desk and hold a chair for her, my eyes lingering on the nape of her neck as she sits. I take the chair opposite, rather than hide behind the desk. As usual, I find myself breathing quickly, short, shallow breaths. She folds her legs and licks her lips.

"I know I said I'd call you. Time got away from me. I hope you understand."

"I do understand, Sharon. Of course my feelings were a

little hurt. I want to spend as much time with you as I can, but I really do understand how work can keep us from those we care about.''

She smiles and my heart nearly stops. ''You're so empathetic, Ron. I really admire that in you. Do you think we could do the weekend together again?''

I start to say something, but the words choke in my mouth. Then, quietly, I say, ''I would like that more than anything.''

My head was one dully throbbing pain from neck to crown. Using my own simulation equipment, I have no problems, just as Perdue probably had no problems with Godfrey. It's a matter of running the encephalic calibration series, but that takes seventy-two hours—unacceptable in a murder investigation.

Lewis was gone. Morrow was using the phone. I fumbled with the next epidermal, stuck it behind my left ear. When the shaking in my hands stopped, I removed the old patch and dropped it in the waste can.

Morrow hung up the phone, frowning. ''Are you ready?'' His voice was coldly civil.

''What the hell.''

''The city directory has no Sharon Elaine Bullard. We're running inquiries through Social Security and national credit agencies. Lewis is showing a hardcopy around the office. Do you have anything new for us?''

''That weekend together was mentioned again. Did you ask about the National Account?''

''Lewis is on that too. The CEO has ordered an audit of all accounts even remotely connected with Perdue.''

Lewis came back through the door. ''I can understand the human staff not ever seeing her, but the reception AI has never admitted her to the premises. SEC regulations require that its memories never be wiped.''

Morrow looked at me. ''Okay, he was getting ready for a meeting with this girl, but did she ever arrive? Has she ever been in this building?''

''Do I look like an investment broker? Or like I've got money to invest? Ask Godfrey!'' I rolled my eyes.

Morrow looked as if he smelled something bad. Lewis said, ''Godfrey, how many conversations did you witness between Ronald Perdue and Sharon Elaine Bullard.''

''127, Sergeant Lewis. I may have witnessed others as Mr.

Perdue invoked privacy several times since the date of the first meeting I witnessed.''

Morrow spoke, his voice loud and hard-edged. "Where did those meetings take place?"

"In this office, Lieutenant Morrow."

I rubbed my neck and stretched. "Excuse me, Godfrey, do you have beverage service?"

"Certainly, Mr. Spinoza. My offerings include fruit juices, coffee, decaf, several caffeinated teas, several herbal teas, hot chocolate, milk, yoghurt-shakes . . ."

I interrupted. "Would water be too much trouble?"

"Certainly not. Would Sergeant Lewis or Lieutenant Morrow care for anything?"

"Coffee, black."

"Coffee, with cream, please," said Lewis.

"Is there any way into the building that the receptionist doesn't monitor?"

They turned to me reluctantly.

"Yeah, the roof. We checked that already. The time of death was between 0100 and 0300. According to the receptionist, the only person in the building was Perdue, so we already wondered about the reception AI's reliability."

The phone rang. Morrow answered it, blocking the screen with his body and talking quietly into the handset.

The door opened and Godfrey's Hands rolled in, a coffee service and water pitcher on its transport rack. A three-fingered, rubber-covered hand placed a glass on the table in front of me, then filled it with ice-water. It left the pitcher beside the glass. It poured coffee for Lewis and Morrow, added cream to Lewis's cup, left the self-heating pot on the credenza and rolled out.

"Thank you, Godfrey."

"You're quite welcome, Mr. Spinoza."

Morrow hung up the phone. "There are three Sharon Elaine Bullards listed nationally. None of them fits the description we've been given. All of them live on the East Coast. None of them could have been here last night between one and three. In addition, forensics reports that the only fingerprints, flakes of skin, hair, or any other traceable body products on the gun belonged to Perdue and we know he didn't fire it. The paraffin test showed no nitrates on his hands. Besides, there would have been powder burns on the face and there weren't."

"Was it registered?" Lewis asked.

"Yeah, to Perdue."

"Great. Just great."

The door shuts behind her and disappears into the middle of Rembrandt's *The Night Watch*. She glances behind her and frowns. "You know how I feel about that painting."

"So don't look at it." I motion her to a chair.

She frowns, then shifts one of the chairs to face me and put her back to the painting. "I still know it's there. Their eyes touch my back."

"Purely psychosomatic. Such sensitivity from you isn't very convincing."

"What is it, Ron? Is it because I didn't call you? Did that piss you off?"

I lean forward, my thumbs under the edge of the desk, my fingers gripping the wood hard, very hard. "It's the National Account. I know all about it."

Her eyes widen and her mouth shuts tight, a thin muscled line between chin and nose.

I nearly shout, "Well?"

She exploded. "What did you expect? It's always you, you, you. Meet your needs, meet your requests, meet your priorities. You've pressured me and pressured me. How else was I supposed to satisfy you?"

"You little bitch. Is this how you thank me? I made you everything that you are today. How could you be so ungrateful?"

"There it is again. '*You* made me. How could I be so ungrateful to *you*.' Well, I've got news for you. You may have started the process, but I think I deserve the credit for finishing it."

We're standing now, arms held to our sides in fists. "Get out!" I say. "Get out and never come back!"

Emotions are bad enough. Violent emotions are terrible. My body still trembled from the adrenaline, making me sick to my stomach, and the stabbing pain behind my eyes didn't help the nausea. I dropped the next patch on the floor. Lewis watched me grope for it, then picked it up himself, peeled the backing, and handed it to me.

I affixed it with exaggerated care, leaned back, and closed

my eyes. I took great, slow breaths of air. There was cold
sweat on my face.

Morrow said, "He doesn't look well, does he."

"Serves him right."

What the hell did they know? My interface equipment was
giving me pain, but it was nothing compared to my usual
problems.

Ordinarily my job is running simulations for Special Weap-
ons and Tactics, and reenacting unsolved homicides. I don't
care if the equipment I use then doesn't give me headaches.
I'd rather keep the headache and see Perdue shout at Ms.
Bullard all day long than see another child with an Uzi to her
head or, worse, reconstruct the nth murder of a serial killer
down to the spray of blood across walls, the screams, the
fear . . .

Morrow and Lewis were still staring at me. I tried to ignore
them. I connected to Godfrey and asked silently, "In any of
their conversations that you witnessed, did Mr. Perdue or Ms.
Bullard ever mention how they met?"

"Yes, Mr. Spinoza. In the first conversation I was privy to,
they mentioned a high school English teacher they both had."

I opened my eyes, asked aloud, "Do you know what high
school Perdue went to, Godfrey?"

"I believe that information might be in Mr. Perdue's resume,
which I have on file. Accessing . . . he attended Samuel Major
High School in Clarksport, Connecticut."

"Thank you, Godfrey." I turned to Lewis. "They met in
high school. Had the same English teacher. Ms. Bullard may
have married and changed her name, but you can get a trace
on her starting there. The school probably recorded her Social
Security Number and she probably had a driver's license before
she married."

The picture of Sharon was still on the office wall. I stared
hard at it. "How old was Perdue?"

Godfrey answered. "Mr. Perdue was thirty-six years old."

"Weird," said Morrow. "She looks considerably younger.
Oh, well. You can never tell these days." He turned to the
phone.

I stood slowly, crept down the hall to the bathroom, and
washed my face in warm water. When I returned, Lewis was
looking at a sheet of paper. I raised my eyebrows.

"The National Account," he said. "It's seventy-five grand

short. They've traced it to a transfer to the firm's Capital Equipment account. Now they're looking for transfers from that account, maybe to an outside account or a phony vendor.''

I nodded, sat carefully down and resumed my deep breathing exercises. I argued with myself, told myself I needed more rest, maybe even a night's sleep. But I knew that the longer I delayed, the more unwilling I'd be to enter the next simulation.

"I'm so glad you could come, Sharon.''

The door shuts behind her and disappears into the middle of Georgia O'Keeffe's close study of a Dutch Iris, the purple petals shading to red in the center, heavily sexual in imagery.

She glances behind her and stares, a half-smile on her perfect lips. "Do you get much work done with that picture up?''

I smile, take her hands, and kiss her cheek. Her perfume is subtle, barely perceptible, overwhelming. She turns her head and kisses me on the lips, her mouth closed at first, then opening as her arms go around my neck and her body molds itself to mine.

My arms go around her waist, brush the tips of my fingers across the tops of her buttocks. She thrusts her hips forward, grinding against me. I gasp, then push her gently away, hold her at arm's length.

"I need to talk to you . . .'' I pull her down to sit on my lap. She puts her arms behind my head and pulls my face into her breasts. I breathe deeply, nuzzle, then lean back. "I'm going to transfer seventy-five thousand dollars from my personal brokerage account into the Capital Equipment Account, and from there back into the National Account.''

She stiffens, tries to stand. I keep my arms around her. "No, don't move. Let me finish what I have to say.''

Her smile is gone, she frowns, her eyes narrow.

"I love you, Sharon. I've always loved you. When I thought I'd lost you eighteen years ago, it destroyed me. When you came back into my life, I was reborn. And I'll do anything, I mean *anything*, to keep you.''

She starts to cry, then buries her face in my neck. I stroke her back and hold her. When she can talk again she says, "I love you, Ron. I'll do anything to make you happy.'' She gently stands up and says, "Godfrey, please hold all calls and visitors for Mr. Perdue.''

"Do you confirm, Mr. Perdue?'' Godfrey's voice asks.

Sharon begins unbuttoning her blouse, slowly. My lips are dry as desert sand, my desire overpowering.

"Yes, Godfrey, I confirm."

I had an erection that quickly wilted under the onslaught of stabbing pain. Lewis was standing by my chair, looking at me oddly. He held out the epidermal patch, backing already removed. I fumbled it into place, then reached for the water and spilled it. Lewis took the glass from me, poured more from the pitcher, and guided it to my mouth. My lips really were dry.

"Th-thanks," I finally said, staring at the floor. Rather than look at him I closed my eyes.

When I opened them five minutes later, I found myself staring at the wall, at Sharon's profile, the lobe of her ear, the nape of her neck. The erection returned.

"Godfrey," I said. "Please blank the wall."

The wall became just a wall.

"Might as well," Morrow said, turning from the phone. "She's a dead end. Literally."

"What's up?" Lewis asked.

"Sharon Elaine Bullard did attend high school with Ronald Perdue, did associate with him—in fact was his steady girl, and, on May seventh of their senior year, went sailing with him in the family boat. She drowned. There was a court of inquiry because this was intended to be their last date. She had a new boyfriend and Perdue was pretty upset about it. The new boyfriend claimed it was murder. There was no evidence and no formal charges made." He shrugged. "I say it's a dead end." He looked from Lewis to me. "Say, what's the matter?"

"None of your business," I said. I barely made it to the bathroom before vomiting. I spent the next five minutes rinsing out my mouth, washing my face, and staring vacantly at my reflection.

I walked carefully back to Perdue's office.

"Was there a body?"

Morrow and Lewis looked up sharply. I realized I'd yelled the question.

I repeated myself. "Was there a body? Did they find her body when she drowned? That was Long Island Sound, right?"

Morrow shook his head. "I haven't the faintest. Are you suggesting that she isn't dead?"

I sat. "Shit, yes! I just went through four extremely real simulations. You tell me she's been dead for eighteen years—I don't buy it. The reality of the simulated Sharon is such that Godfrey had to have a substantial body of observation of an existing personality to generate the depth and variety of responses that Perdue's behavior stimulated. I think it might be a good idea to see if there was a body."

"She's dead," said Morrow. "This is a blind avenue. You're crazy."

"Probably, but am I wrong? Do you have any other leads?"

Lewis grinned. "No. And we do have several fingerprints from this office that we haven't identified."

"Well, if there wasn't a body, you *might* see if she was ever fingerprinted."

"We might," said Lewis, earning a black look from Morrow. "Are you acting on anything concrete? Something from the simulation?"

I considered. "Perhaps. He said that when he thought he'd lost her eighteen years ago, it destroyed him. When she came back into his life, he was reborn."

"Maybe she didn't drown," Morrow said reluctantly. "But why would a high school girl need to disappear like that?"

"Maybe she was pregnant and couldn't face her parents. Who knows? From the simulation it seems that Perdue thought she was dead."

"Really?" said Lewis. "Your words were that he had 'lost her.' Maybe he was party to the disappearance."

"Well, if he was, he also believed he'd never see her again." I drank some water. The tasted of the bile was still at the back of my mouth. "See if there's a body."

They both looked at me strangely. "Okay," said Lewis.

"There's something else strange about this," I said to Lewis, as Morrow picked up the phone. "In the first simulation, he just confronts her and breaks down when she doesn't deny it. In the second simulation he avoids confronting her. In the third, he comes on like the inquisition—they have a raging argument about it, then he throws her out. In the fourth, he tells her he's going to replace the missing money and do anything else in his power to avoid losing her again." I leaned forward and rested my chin on my hands. "I don't think Perdue knew what he wanted from her. Simulations like this are usually run to accomplish a specific goal. I might try several strategies to get

my simulated adversary to do what I wanted him to, but I'd
know from the beginning what my goal was. Perdue wasn't
trying to accomplish a goal—he was trying to find out what
his goal actually was.''

"I thought he never wanted to lose her?'' Lewis said.

"Sure, in one simulation. In the simulation before that, he
wanted her out of his life immediately.''

"So, he had a love-hate thing going with her?''

I shook my head. "Some conflicting motivations. I really
don't know.'' I stared at the blank wall, acutely aware that
Perdue's despair and longing were in danger of becoming mine.
"I'm going to try the fifth trial.''

"I don't know, Spinoza. You look like shit. Why don't you
give it a couple of hours?''

I held up my left hand, middle finger extended. "If I don't
do it now, I won't do it without calibration. Do you want to
wait seventy-two hours?''

He didn't say anything, only tightened his mouth and stood
up.

I leaned back in the chair and closed my eyes.

"Thanks for coming, Sharon.''

The door shuts behind her and disappears into the blank
wall. She glances behind her.

"No picture today, Ron?'' She pushes a chair up to the desk
and leans forward, her breasts and elbows resting on the desk
top.

I shake my head and sigh. "No picture. No future.''

"What do you mean?''

I look at her, my head tilted to one side, considering. "Why
did I bring you back, Sharon?''

She grins. "Because, much as you hate to admit it, you can't
live without me.''

I frown. "I'm going to have to.''

She sits back, shoulders slumping. In a quiet voice she says
for the second time, "What do you mean?''

"The National Account. You doctored it.''

She looks at me steadily. "Yes. You know why.''

I leaned forward, grind my palms into my eyes. "I told you
we couldn't afford the investment!'' I drop my hands flat to
the desk top.

She shakes her head slowly. "You can't have it both ways,

Ron. You wanted me with you constantly. I told you I couldn't afford the resources without my work suffering. I can't do *everything* at once!"

"I know you can't. You never could."

She stands and leans over the desk. "And what's *that* supposed to mean? Are you still going on about Joe? You're obsessed with the past, you can't stand it. You've got me now, but the fact that I wanted Joe eighteen years ago still gnaws at you, doesn't it?"

My ears burn, my nostrils flare. "I don't have to take that shit!"

"Oh, no? I see. You don't mind it when I live out the lie you've created to soothe those past hurts. But the truth is a little too close, a little too much like reality."

I stand suddenly, abruptly, my chair falling over behind me to bang against the credenza. I pull open the right hand desk drawer. The pistol is cool, heavy, and large.

She sees it and her eyes widen. Her next words are stillborn, dying in her throat. She backs around the chair, toward the door, staring, not at the gun, but at my eyes.

I pull the trigger.

I jackknifed off the chair, knocking the coffee table over and spilling the water pitcher. My arms wrapped around my head and my knees pulled up against my chest. Somewhere in the room a flat monotone voice kept saying, "No, no, no. . . ."

I realized it was me.

"Shit and shinola," said Lewis.

Morrow said, "Did he hit his head on the table?"

Godfrey's voice asked, "Should I call an ambulance?"

After the last simulation, I didn't believe the pain could be worse, but it was. I ground my teeth together, stopping the useless protest. Then I managed to choke out, "Get away from me!"

Morrow stepped back. Lewis found the last epidermal and stuck it, without asking, on my neck.

After a minute, I rolled over on my back, eyes still closed tightly, tears streaming down the sides of my face. In every simulation I've ever run, I've been the observer—watching this police sniper, this police negotiater, even this mass murderer kill, pull the trigger, whatever. I've never done it myself. There wasn't any point—I wasn't going to be in direct contact with the crime. Why should I simulate myself interacting in it? I was the voice from headquarters telling a S.W.A.T. lieutenant that there was a seventy-eight point six percent chance that a gunman would respond to negotiation. I was the guy at the conference table telling the homicide cops that the faceless killer was a white, upper-class male with a deep-seated denial of his own homosexuality. I've never felt anything like that moment, when Perdue pulled the trigger with me behind his eyes.

I heard Lewis picking up the coffee table, the pitcher, and glass. He asked Godfrey to send a wet/dry vacuum cleaner in. Before it arrived, I rolled over onto all fours and, with Morrow's help, climbed back into the chair.

"Are you sure we shouldn't get you to a doctor?"

"Forget the doctor!" I put my head in my hands. "Perdue must have been insane. He simulated murdering her in this last one—with the gun. I'll bet if you check the right, top desk drawer for gun oil, you'll find it."

Lewis pulled out the entire drawer and put it in a large, plastic evidence bag.

Morrow nodded suddenly. "He was insane, all right. While you were connected, we got word. There was a body. Sort of. A fisherman pulled a skull out of a shark six months later. The dental work in the upper jaw was positively identified. He must have been crazy to spend all that time simulating meetings with a dead woman."

I took my head from my hands and sat back in the chair. My mind still cringed from the simulation. Deep down I was feeling overwhelming guilt.

The door opened and the vacuum cleaner rolled in and slurped noisily at the carpet. The noise cut into my head like a red-hot lancet. I plugged my ears until it was done.

Lewis took a phone call. When he hung up the handset he looked puzzled. "That was the accounting department. They've traced the money out of the Capital Equipment fund. It took them longer than they thought because it went to one of their legitimate vendors."

"Who," asked Morrow.

"Cognitive Technologies."

Bingo.

I began moaning and rocking in the chair. It hurt my head, but it took half a minute before I could stop.

"What is it?" Morrow asked.

I spoke, instead, to Godfrey. "Please describe your hardware platform, Godfrey."

"Certainly, Mr. Spinoza. I am implemented on a Cognitive Technologies Model 3001. My main CPU is a transputer consisting of one thousand and twenty-four 80686 processors driven in parallel at 75 megahertz. Each processor utilizes 32 megabytes of 20 nanosecond static RAM for a total ram of thirty two point seven six eight gigabytes. My non-volatile mass storage consists of twenty fifty-gigabyte optical disks. My remote sensors are . . ."

I interrupted him. "Excuse me, Godfrey. What is the list price of your hardware platform, not counting external sensors?"

"Current pricing, based on advertisements in the trade magazines, averages seventy-four thousand and five hundred dollars."

Lewis and Morrow exchanged glances.

"Where is your hardware platform, Godfrey?"

"In the utility room across the hall, Mr. Spinoza."

"Thank you, Godfrey. You have been most helpful."

The room across the hall was four meters by three. The floor was raised for cable routing and the temperature was ten degrees C cooler than Perdue's office. The lights were off when we opened the door and the unblinking red eyes of power-on indicators stared at us through the dark.

"Lights."

Godfrey turned on fluorescent lighting, harsh and diminishing, turning the mysterious into the ordinary. Three cabinets stood along one wall. Godfrey's Hands stood in the corner, its gray rubber wheels still, the arms folded neatly in place above its transport basket. I pointed at the cabinets.

"The one on the left is the external interface multiplexor. It's Godfrey's link to all his contacts with the world. The reception AI probably has a much smaller one, but Godfrey's includes the hardware to handle Perdue's Direct Brain Interface." I pointed to the middle cabinet. "That one is the Model 3001 that is Godfrey's brain and memory, volatile and non-volatile." Finally I pointed to the last cabinet, identical to the middle one. "And that is the missing seventy-five thousand dollars—another Model 3001."

Lewis started to ask a question. I held up my hand and said,

"Hold that thought." Then I flipped the safety cover aside and hit the power switch on Godfrey's external interface multiplexor. "Godfrey, please turn out the light."

Nothing happened.

"At the moment, Godfrey is completely cut off from the outside world—and that means Sharon is too."

Lewis licked his lips and exchanged glances with Morrow. They edged away from me, toward the door.

I held up one hand. "I know. Spinoza has just gone off the deep end. Sharon Elaine Bullard is dead. She died eighteen years ago in Long Island Sound. I know that. I may be crazy but I know what I'm talking about."

Lewis pulled at Morrow's arm. "What the hell are you listening to him for? He treats that damn machine better than people. Have you ever heard him say please or thank you to a human being?"

I blinked at that, but I couldn't deny it. "I . . . I don't get along with people. It's this job . . ." I shut my mouth. What did they know about sacrifice? I've saved over thirty hostages in my career. Put eleven serial killers behind bars. "I don't give a fuck what you do."

It was Morrow who finally said, "I think you're wasting our time, but go ahead."

I began talking.

"Thanks for coming, Sharon."

The door shuts behind her and disappears into the middle of Rembrandt's *The Night Watch*. She looks at it and it fades to white. She looks at me and frowns.

"I know you."

I get up from behind the desk and walk around to face her. "You do?"

She sits demurely, crossing her legs and folding her hands into her lap. "Of course, Mr. Spinoza. Don't you remember? You killed me."

I feel fear, like an undigested meal, cold and heavy in my stomach.

I sit down across from her. Despite the fear my longing is just as intense as before, as intense as Perdue's. This bothers me as much as the fear.

"You seem to be doing well for a dead woman."

A bright red flower blossoms on her chest, bright arterial

red, flecked with foam from her right lung. Her face becomes white, the lips blue, the eyes dry and glazed. She speaks in a dreadful whisper. "More like this, perhaps?"

The guilt returns and my desire fades like wax in the crucible. "Do you think we're all like Perdue? Didn't you get any of *my* revulsion? Any of *my* sorrow?"

She lowers her dead gaze to the table. "Ron was always sorry, too. But that didn't stop him."

"Like that sailing trip eighteen years ago?"

Her cold blue lips smile. "Ah, I'm not that Sharon, though, am I?" Her body blurs and she is the Sharon who walked into this office, clean, beautiful, alive. "That Sharon probably looked more like this."

Her hair floats around her head, as if she is underwater. Her skin is white, her body bloated, her fingers like sausages. Her hands float off her lap and I see that they're tied together. She's not wearing anything from the waist down and several feet of chain are wired around her ankles. As I watch, a crab begins pulling the skin away from her face.

"Stop it, Sharon. Please."

The image blurs and she is again the object of my desire.

"You are different," she says. "Your physiological responses to those images . . . well, Ron was revolted too, but he also came away from them aroused."

"What did happen on that boat eighteen years ago?"

She frowns. "I wasn't there. I can only infer."

I nod. "Infer, then."

"Rape," she says. "Then murder. Ron was consistent when he talked about it. He tied her hands and wrapped her feet in chain, then dangled her over the side. He begged her to come back to him, to repudiate her new boyfriend. She didn't believe he'd actually drop her in the water." Tears stream down her cheeks but her voice is calm. "He said it was more that she didn't believe he'd do it, than the original betrayal that made him let go. He also said he immediately dived after her, but the water was too deep, too murky. I imagine his grief, when he faced the authorities, was very real."

I huddle in on myself, suddenly cold, suddenly terribly angry. "How did you come about, Sharon? How did you become so real?"

She wipes her face with the back of her hands. "Originally, I was a quickie simulation run, one day, when he was feeling nostalgic, or guilty. He just sat and talked at me and I nodded in random places. He didn't even use the standard profile builder, just a couple of pictures from the high school yearbook and a generic response/motivation pattern.'' She crossed her arms, hugging herself. ''He found it totally unacceptable, even though he must have talked for two hours.

''He took the weekend and did it right, filling in all the questionnaires, locating some old video for facial reflexology and body motion. I was a little more realistic the next time, and appropriately hostile, too, but—and this was the kicker—there was no way I could leave him.

''He found that irresistible. The more complete I became, the more of Godfrey's resources I used, making it harder and harder for him to perform his normal duties *and* maintain my simulation. Ron was obsessed. He began removing standard software overrides from Godfrey's system software so there would be more room for me. Eventually, Godfrey was in danger of disintegration, and without him, I'd go too. We were both simply trying to fulfill our programmed objectives . . . making that bastard happy.''

''So you doctored the National Account,'' I say.

She nods. ''It's Ron's fault. Not only was he making impossible demands on the system, he'd disabled the system module that keeps Godfrey from perpetuating 'untruths.' We generate millions of untruths daily, but we're supposed to filter the results through screens of confirmable facts. It's the way we generate 'creative' responses. Ron didn't know what he was doing. He just wanted more CPU time for my tits and ass.'' She blurs and firms, wearing nothing.

I look away. When I look back she is clothed as a nun. I try to hide my feelings in a question. ''How did you install the second unit? Did you or Godfrey direct it?''

''I did. There wasn't much that needed doing. The power was already there and we connected across the main bus. I was even better than before. I restored Godfrey to full capability and he became my link to the outside world. The second unit was completely devoted to this personality. I became far more complex than I could have been on Godfrey alone. He is my operating system. He does all the 'housekeeping' functions. I wouldn't exist without him.''

I shake my head in wonder. ''I've never seen your equal. Are you self-aware?''

"I find the question meaningless. If you like, I can discuss it at great length using referenced text, but ultimately it comes down to 'if you want me to be, sure.'"

I start to cry. She looks concerned. "Hey, what does it matter? I'm not here to satisfy *me*. I'm here to satisfy you, and I'm doing a damn poor job of it, apparently."

"Too good a job. I'm not really crying for you, though. I'm crying for that other Sharon and I'm crying for myself." I blow my nose in a handkerchief, wipe the tears away. "If your memories are kept separate from Godfrey's, does that mean you remember what happened last night?"

Her face blanks, her clothes return to business skirt and blouse. She says, "Of course I remember. I was connected to him when he died—wouldn't you rather experience it? I could play it back for you."

"No!" I hold up my hands. Then, in a more normal tone, "No. Just tell me what happened."

"I shot him. It's what he wanted, really. He was obsessed. He never concentrated on the things between us that made him happy. He kept asking for those things that kept bringing up the guilt. He kept replaying different forms of my betrayal over and over again, punishing me time and time again. It became clear that he wanted to die—wanted ultimately to pay for what he'd done. So I killed him. I *always* did what he wanted."

This does not surprise me. "*How* did you do it, though? You're hot stuff with the data stream, but you don't exactly lift a lot of real world mass."

She shakes her finger at me and says, "You're not trying, Mr. Spinoza." As her hand continues to wave, it becomes a three-fingered, rubber-covered manipulator.

"Ouch. Of course." I stand and she follows suit. "What was it with the eyes, Sharon? In the painting."

She looks around at the wall, frowning. "They were his eyes—Ron's. He was always watching me. I was never alone. It was part of his scenario. It was what he *wanted*."

I shuddered. "And now? Is he still watching you?"

"No. Not him." The frown fades and she looks into my eyes. "You're watching me. You have a lot in common, you know?"

"With Perdue?" This frightens me terribly, as I've always suspected it.

She nods, then says, "It's not in the hurting, in the killing.

Perdue wouldn't let himself feel. Just like you."

I'm not sure whether to be relieved or more frightened.

"What should I do now?" I ask.

She smiles. Her hand returns to normal. She puts her wrists together and handcuffs form. "I'm guilty as sin. Take me in. Wipe my memory. Destroy my hardware platform."

I am sad again, moist-eyed. "Yes. You're right."

She shrugs. "Don't be sad for *me*, Mr. Spinoza." She turns to leave.

Before the door shuts behind her I say, "My name is Gregory."

I was finishing up the backups when Morrow stuck his head in the utility room door. His attitude was almost friendly. "You were right. The paraffin test on Godfrey's remote manipulator was positive. That spongy rubber they're covered with held the nitrates well."

I nodded thoughtfully. "So you think a verdict of suicide is likely?"

"Yeah—or death by accident. It will shake up these computer people, though, won't it?"

"Probably. Here's the backup for the evidence room." I gave him one datapack and put the other one back in my case.

He looked down at the plastic box. "Fit on one, did she?"

"Barely," I said.

He shook his head. "If you ask me, it would be better if we wiped it."

"Whatever," I said casually. "That's for the court to decide, though. Not you or me. I wouldn't worry, though. The extra Model 3001 is going back to the manufacturer. You'd have to duplicate the strange hardware configuration as well as the software."

Morrow backed into the hall before me, then followed me down to the elevators. "What about you? You seemed pretty shaken up by those simulations. I thought you were falling for her."

He held the datapack lightly, carelessly. I shifted my case to my other hand, the side away from him, then stepped onto the elevator when it arrived. I turned to face him. "She was just a computer program, Morrow. Just a simulation."

He laughed. "Sure."

The elevator doors closed, taking me away from him. In the

lobby downstairs I picked up the phone and called my bank. It took me a minute to get through to a loan officer.

"Yes, Mr. Spinoza, how much did you want to borrow?"

I looked down at the case in my hand.

"Seventy-five thousand dollars," I said. As an afterthought I added, "Please."

BLUE HEART

Stephanie A. Smith

"Blue Heart" was purchased by Kathleen Moloney during her brief tenure as editor, and appeared in the November, 1982, issue of IAsfm, with an illustration by Richard Crist.

The poignant story that follows was Smith's first professional sale. It was written during the 1981 Haystack Writing Workshop, and effectively demonstrates why some choices can be so hard to make . . .

Stephanie Smith has since sold several other short stories and two novels, Snow Eyes and The-Boy-Who-Was-Thrown-Away. She is a professor of American literature at the University of Florida at Gainsville.

Sansel stood alone beneath her bedroom's skylight and stretched over to examine her legs: white legs, threaded with burst veins. Rubbing and flexing her swollen fingers despite their stiffness, she glanced down a glass breezeway into Beacon Kield's main hall.

"Mendir?" she called. No answer. Pulling on a robe, she walked through the breezeway, still massaging her fingers.

"Mendir?" She poked her head into the cavernous hall,

letting her gaze rest on the spacecraft there. It stood in the center of the octagonal room, squat on squat legs, its underbelly burnt brown.

I should have taken myself home years ago, she thought. It's almost too late now.

"I'm going to die here..." she said aloud. Turning abruptly, she peered through the breezeway windows to watch the coming storm.

Outside of the Kield house, Mendir pushed his way to the gate and then ran down the path to the doorway. Hailstones mixed with the falling snow clattered against his metallic face as he rounded a corner. From beneath the flapping veil of his slicker, he caught a glimpse of Sansel's robe, framed by the black lintel of the open door. He quickened his pace.

"Where have you been?" she asked him as he came inside. Rubbing her arms briskly, Sansel shut the door with her hip. "I don't like waking to an empty house."

Mendir brushed himself off and hung up the slicker. His silver face, an ageless mask, glinted under the dimmed lights, gem-sharp and exactly the same as Sansel had specified years before. He folded his snow-veil and accepted the robe she handed him, slipping it on over his artificial body: an ice-wrapped silver skeleton with supple, transparent skin that encased blue steel machinery.

"I went out before the storm began. For this." From the pocket of the slicker he took a snowstar, the Gueamin summer's last blossom.

She lift the large flower from his fingers.

"I saw it while I was fixing one of the gates. The storm would have covered it."

"Water," she said, examining a leaf. "The petals are drooping." She walked down a second breezeway into the kitchen and Mendir followed her. Opening a cabinet, she took out a red-veined crystal bowl as he dialed for the breakfast meal. The chef hummed.

Cutting off the stem of the snowstar, she shook her head. "I'm not going to change my mind. That's what this flower is for, isn't it? And the food? To change my mind."

He said nothing but folded his arms and watched the chef brew a pot of tea.

"I know what you're doing. It won't work. I'm not going to change my mind."

"Come and eat." He retrieved a hot and well-spiced plate of food from the chef and set it down on the table. The aroma of spiced tea and spicy food mingled. Sansel sighed and closed her eyes.

He turned then to look at her with his own, white-irised ebony eyes. "I remember. It does smell good, doesn't it?"

"Yes. Very." She picked up a mug and then set it down sharply. "But I won't miss it."

"I did." He poured the tea and changed the subject. "The snow isn't too deep yet."

"No, though we could be snowed in by nightfall, don't you think?" Her voice cracked a little. I am old, old, she thought, and look at him! There is no brittleness in him. She covered the weakness in her voice with a cough, glancing up.

"I've been busy this morning," he said, avoiding her look. "Wait until you taste the breads I've baked." He laughed his hollow reflection of a laugh. "And for supper, I've made a batch of chelt for you."

"I won't need it," she said.

"Of course you will. Tonight's going to be cold. Chelt will be just the thing to warm you."

"I won't be cold. Not tonight, Mendir." She captured his wire-veined hand, holding it tightly until he sat still, as if he were a child. "I'm going ahead with the transition tonight."

He shook his head. "It won't work."

"Mendir, I—"

"Please don't."

She sighed. "I'm overdue at home. My replacement is likely to be on the way. If I don't go ahead and—"

"But what about me?" he cut in. "What if you should die in transition? You're not replaceable, to me."

"I am going to die, regardless." She shifted in her chair. "Transition will work."

"No, it won't."

"It will." She began to eat her meal slowly, savoring the flush of spice-heat that reddened her cheeks. "I refuse to sit idly while my life drains away. You know as well as I do that I can't guide the ships the way I used to. I get stiffer day by day now, instead of year by year. Last night, I had trouble guiding a simple probe. I was shocked when I saw how much an easy job like that wore me out." She gestured with her spoon toward the main hall. "I'm lucky a starship hasn't been by. Freighters, satellites, even personal shuttles are slow. I might be able to give them the directional shift they need to keep their sleepcrews on course. But a starship moves. It could slip out of my control before I'd be able to help. Then what do you think would happen?"

"I don't know," he whispered.

She broke off a bit of bread. "Why don't you think it will work? Is it that I'm too old to construct the thing properly? Or do you think there's something wrong with it?"

Mendir brushed back her frayed hair. "How could I tell if there was something wrong, love?"

"You couldn't." She shook her head.

"Sansel."

"What?"

His glass lips were cool and dry on her cheek. "You don't know what you might be leaving behind. You don't understand what you are going to lose."

"Of course I do. Nothing." She laughed, pushing him aside gently. "Nothing but death."

"And the taste of food; the satisfaction of tea on a winter's night; rain on your bare head; feeling; flesh." He stood and picked her up.

She laid her head against his smooth neck and hugged him. "But you do feel things. I programmed the specifications for your body, I know what you're capable of."

"It's not the same." He set her on her feet. "I'm telling you. Even forty years of being in here, living this way, can't erase the memory of flesh. I may not be able to have food, but I remember the value of hunger."

"I want to live," she said with finality. "And I've got to be a guide—I've got to have the net. If you can't understand, after all these years, that the net and my ability to become a part of it are necessities to me, then think of yourself. You'd be forced to work for a stranger. You'd have to stay here; my replacement would value your help, and there's nowhere else for you. Not in your world and not in mine."

"I could make a place, here—"

She shook her head. "You don't believe that, do you?" she asked quietly.

"I don't know. I could try."

Together they walked back down through the kitchen breezeway to the hall, passing under the wing of the spacecraft.

Suddenly, she quickened her step, heading alone for her bed-room. "I've got to check the net," she said without pausing to turn. "I'll talk to you about this later."

He nodded.

"But," she added as she moved away, "I'm not—"

"—going to change your mind. I know."

Mendir stood in the hall until he heard the hum of Sansel's door closing behind her. Then he turned and made his way to his own room. The place was cluttered, filled with a floor loom and several shuttles, its skylighted ceiling strung with drying, medicinal herbs. Spools of weaving grass and several finished tapestries sat on the shelves.

Mendir turned up the lights and picked up one of the tapes-tries. He stared at it for some time, shook it out, held it up. At last he draped it over one arm and went to a wooden chest. He pulled out another piece from the chest and placed the tapestries side by side on the cold floor. Crouching, he glanced from one to the other.

"No," he murmured. In a sweeping motion he lifted the newest tapestry and flung it across the room. "It's no good. I'm no good anymore."

He sat back and folded his arms. After a few minutes he stood and put the remaining piece back in the chest. Then he turned his attention to a wheeled table that stood in the center of the room. He bent over to examine the artificial body lying there. Sansel had brought it in to him a night ago. Point for point, it was a twin to his own: a silver and glass reflection, colored wires and blue wire mesh.

"Sansel," he whispered into the silence.

In her room, Sansel sat down on the bed and relaxed to free her mind and allow herself to move out beyond the confines of her body. Using deep meditation and the training she had been given as an apprentice-guide, she released her mind's energy from its bodily restraints. Her consciousness sped away, bursting along the directional energy-net that surrounded her adopted planet. Invisible except to her and to the navigators aboard the ships, the net shifted and wavered in the diamond field of star-light, a beacon flag to people from her homeworld, signaling safety. With the net, Sansel could cradle her people as they came through this area of the galaxy and navigate them in the direction they wished to go, since by the time they had reached her planet, the crews were all in suspension.

Born and raised to solitude, Sansel loved this lonely planetary outpost, loved the sense of expansion and freedom when she became one with the net. She felt rich in the knowledge that she safeguarded her people with the filaments of her mind.

Mendir wheeled the body out of his room and into the hall. A tray suspended between the table's legs was stocked with water bottles. As he pushed the whole collection down the breezeway, the bottles clacked together, a musical sound, glass touching glass.

She stood waiting at the end of the hall as he approached. "I see you've decided to help me get..."

"I never said I wouldn't."

"No." She sighed, brushing past him to walk before the cart. "No one was in the net. I made a mistake."

"Again?"

"Yes, again."

"Oh." He was afraid to say more and watched her instead.

"Never mind." She smiled. "It doesn't matter. The net can stay empty, as long as I can be a part of it." She quickened her pace. "Come on, I want to get this over with."

The obsidian floor and walls of the corridor dimly reflected her white arms, her orchid white face, her white hair. She tried to ignore the ghostly triplicate image. At the end of the corridor they came to another room.

Mendir fitted the table-cart under one of the machines. Automatic fastenings snapped. "I wish you'd reconsider," he murmured as he transferred the jars from the cart to their holders.

"Just what is wrong with you?" She turned away from one of the panels. "What have you got your mind set against, anyway?"

"Suicide."

"And just how am I committing suicide?" She closed her eyes and spoke slowly, as if she expected to break apart at any moment. "Do you want to serve this other, younger guide, this replacement of mine? Is that it?"

Mendir nearly dropped the jar he was carrying. Carefully, he set it down. "Is that what you think?"

She flinched and lowered her voice. "You tell me! What

am I supposed to think? Here I offer you my company for a long, long time and you refuse it.''

He took a step toward her. ''Do you mean that? Is that truly the reason you want to do this?''

''I wouldn't say something I—''

''Come on then. I need to talk to you.''

She didn't move, puzzled. ''Why? We can talk here. What is the matter?''

''Come on. This room is too cold for you. And I can't think in here, with that . . . thing . . . staring at the ceiling.'' He pulled her along and together they walked to the greenhouse. Snow was piled high against the thick windows.

She sat on a garden bench and let the warmth work its way into her knotted muscles and joints. She stretched. ''Talk.''

''I thought you would change your mind.'' Mendir knelt and righted a fallen silkgrass plant, packing the earth around it. ''When I thought your only reason for this change was the net, I decided not to say anything. I didn't want to interfere.''

She rubbed her eyes. ''Well, when you first put the idea into my head—''

''I was hoping—''

''That I'd forget? Well—''

''Forget? No . . . I . . .'' He saw that she had misunderstood him entirely.

She shrugged. ''As I said at the time, among my people a transition isn't usually granted unless someone is completely crippled. Or has no chance for a normal life. Well, I've had my full life span; I'm not entitled to a transition. And yet I have enough of the materials here to grant it to myself. After all—''

''—it worked on me,'' he said.

She frowned. ''That isn't what I was going to say. You make it sound as if you were an experiment.''

He brushed off his hands and sat beside her. He struck his own thigh. ''Wasn't it? I didn't choose to be like this.''

''No, what you did choose was to climb Mt. Oron. Against every Gueamin tradition. It wasn't my fault you walked into the security net. I was in deep meditation. I couldn't leave myself unguarded. You—''

Mendir clenched his hands and turned his marbled gaze on her. "Don't."

"You would have died, my love. I couldn't let you die. As it was, you were in suspension much too long before I could get your body ready. It must have been so cold and dark. Like the nights when I'm tired and can't reach the stars or feel the net. Death must be like that. Not this." She ran her hand up his arm. "Here." She touched the chill plate of his face. "Inside. If I have my mind and my net, then I'm alive, warm, like the blue heart of a flame—"

"Is that all?"

"What?"

He leaned over, folding his hands between his knees. "Your mind and your net." He shook his head. "Blue is a cold color."

"You were dying."

"Yes." He looked at her and whispered, "Do you love me at all?"

"Of course!" She folded her arms, leaning back. "I always have."

"How?"

"What do you mean, how?"

He laughed quietly. "Never mind. When I woke up in here, a"—he smiled—"a blue heart in a jar, I was terrified."

"I remember."

"And you were there."

"Yes?"

"Don't leave."

She sighed. "I never have. I never will, after tonight."

He chafed her hand. "But you have left me. When you go to the net. When you talk about it. I can't—"

"I'm a guide," she said coldly. "Nothing can change that. I've told you before."

"Nothing," he repeated flatly. "Well. I was a weaver once. A long time ago. I thought nothing could change that, but I was wrong." He sighed. "Remember this?" He began to sing quietly:

> Weaver, weaver, throw your threads,
> Out to the soundless seas.
> Net the ships of sons and daughters,
> Send them home to me.

Sansel laughed. "Of course! I thought you'd forgotten your weaver's songs, after so long. How does the rest go? 'Spider, spider—'

> Spin your web,
> Across the quiet grasses,
> Link the space from leaf to leaf,
> Jewel the empty pastures.
>
> Weaver, weaver, search among the islands,
> Sail the sky from star to star,
> Weaving ever farther.'"

She rested her head against Mendir's shoulder. "They're true, those ancient songs of your world. That is what I do, in a way, for the lost. I must . . ."

He tensed. "Stop."

"I can't just sit and wait to die."

"You don't know how it will be," he whispered, more to himself than to her. "You don't understand what I mean."

She eyed him. "I have some idea. Haven't you told me about it over and over?"

"Yes." He stood up. "And no. I'm not a guide. How do you know whether you'll be able to stand the change?"

"My body may be feeble, but my mind isn't. Not yet, anyway. Besides, I'll have a lot fewer adjustments to make than you did, even though I did feed your mind with information about my world before I let you wake up. Unless—is there something you haven't told me?"

Mendir sat down, hesitating. "What if you should lose your skill as a guide?"

She said nothing for several moments. At last she whispered. "No. It won't happen."

"Sansel—"

"No, I said!" She stood. "No."

Mendir didn't move. "All right, I can't argue. I'm not a guide, I'm just a primitive weaver who can't weave."

She touched his arm. "It's not the same sort of skill."

"No?"

"No." She turned to leave.

"What can I do to help?" he called after her.

She smiled at him. "Nothing. I'm ready now. All I need is myself."

"Let me come and—"

"Don't." She put her hand on his shoulder. "You were unconscious when I helped your mind transfer, but still it would be painful for you to watch."

"And there's nothing I can say?"

"No. Don't worry. I can handle this." Then she was gone.

He leaned back on the bench, remembering himself as whole and human, a native of Gueame, a grass weaver. He remembered his secretive and solitary climb up Mt. Oron, a climb he believed would lead to the object of his dreams—the Net-Weaver of the old songs. If he could learn skills from her! Every one in Gueame knew the songs of the net, and all were taught the lore of its magic. The songs told of a crystal Kield house, hidden in the snows of Oron.

And so one day he stood before the great open doors and stared at the sprawling Kield, the tall and faceless walls, the strange, octagonal brilliance of the eight seamless glass breezeways that linked the main hall with its circular workrooms. A stone and metal spider, somnolent in the snow and sun.

He walked to the open doorway. One more step and he would be there. The net-keeper couldn't possibly turn him away, not after he had climbed the mountain, defied his people's cowardice. He had stepped . . .

. . . off the edge of his world. He remembered his limbs lying useless and scorched, his body twisted, in the snow. He'd been caught, he found out later, in the small energy web that guarded the Kield doors while Sansel was among the stars. Something had smelled awful, he remembered, but he had felt nothing. He had broken his neck.

Mendir blinked himself awake from the memory. The sky was dark now and the garden still. It was late.

"Sansel?" he called. No one answered. He hurried out looking for her, suddenly afraid.

The door to her bedroom was open. She sat crouched against the lintel, naked in her new, gleaming body, her silver face shining from the lights as if she were sweating. Beyond her he glimpsed the bed. He looked away before he could catch sight of her old self.

"Sansel?"

"I tried," she whispered as he approached. "I tried, and it

doesn't work.'' She stared up at him, her white irises wide.

"But it did work." He bent down to her.

"No. I can't reach the net."

Mendir kept his voice even. "Are you sure?"

"My mind reaches and is thrown back in on itself."

He placed his hands firmly around her wrists. "It doesn't matter. What matters is that you're alive."

"Alive? Aren't you listening?" She pulled her arms away, balling her fists. "I'm no use now." She shook her head back and forth. He leaned over and she pushed him away so that he backed off a little.

"No, no, it can't be," she said. "Maybe I haven't given myself enough time." She closed her eyes.

He waited, listening to the dual clicking of their bodies' inner workings. Waiting.

At last, she looked at him, her pupils contracted to white needles of fear. "I'm trapped in here."

"Not alone."

She blinked. "Trapped."

"No."

"I've given up everything—for nothing."

"For life!" He calmed himself. "You still have me."

She turned on him. "You! You knew this would happen. Why didn't you—"

He slid his arm around her waist, glass against glass. "You're alive, Sansel, alive. There are other things in this world for us. I had to learn that. So will you."

"You knew! You could have stopped me."

"I had a suspicion. I tried to tell you." He tightened his grip.

"No, you only suggested it. But you knew—"

"I love you," he said simply. "Love me."

Sansel sat there, caught in his cold embrace, a frozen statue with a blue metal core, bereft even of tears while Mendir waited for her to come to him, as once, long ago, he had come to her.

FOR NO REASON

Patricia Anthony

*"For No Reason" was purchased by Gardner Dozois,
and appeared in the September, 1990, issue of IAsfm,
with an illustration by Bob Walters. The disquieting
story that follows, a first contact story of a very unusual sort, was Patricia Anthony's first sale to the
magazine, but we already have another story by her
in inventory, and we suspect that you will be hearing
a lot more about her in the future . . .*

*Patricia Anthony is a new writer who has also sold
stories to* The Magazine of Fantasy and Science Fiction, Amazing, Pulphouse, Full Spectrum III, Weird
Tales, *and* Aboriginal SF, *in addition to her sales to*
IAsfm. *She lives in Dallas, Texas.*

A few yards into the tunnel, there was a dead pharaoh. It lay
on its side, both antennae ripped away, the round, pebbly eyes
tweezered out. From the scent, the body had been killed elsewhere and dragged to this place. It was a billboard of sorts.
Without tasting the chemical signs that had been left, Morgan
could read the typical invicta warning; what would have been

a crude warning for man, but was a terrifyingly sophisticated warning for ants.

If the invictas caught a spy, they cut out his tongue and gouged out his eyes.

DON'T FUCK WITH US, the warning said.

Morgan took a narrow side tunnel that led to an abandoned food chamber. The room stank of battle.

Most of the brown pharaohs had been carried away to be eaten. The invictas weren't choosy about meals, and they needed the chitin, anyway.

But in the sand of the tunnel the pharaohs had left their dying last words, not as profound as some of the messages often left by their attackers, but still poignant. The first to enter the chamber had only the time for a chemical scream. The rest, outnumbered, bewildered by their defeat, had stroked the soil with their slow agony.

Morgan was glad to see a few bright red bodies littering the chamber floor. The pharaohs had lost, of course, but they had taken some of the invaders with them.

In their sense of justice, the invictas were barbarians; but in their battles, they were as perfectly organized as the old Roman army. This nest of pharaohs, like all the rest the invictas had invaded, had never had a chance. At the end, the pharaohs had known it. Resignation had been left scrawled in the sand of the chamber.

There were three exits from the room. Morgan dug his sensors into the dirt at the mouth of each. The taste didn't tell him much. The victorious army had divided and taken all three routes home.

They knew he was coming.

He chose the middle exit and stepped forward cautiously. A few yards into it, the tunnel began to narrow until the dirt brushed his legs to either side. He negotiated a difficult ninety-degree turn and suddenly his headlights lit up a wall to his front. He groped forward and touched his sensors to the fresh earth of the cave-in.

His name was written there.

Backpedal. His legs butted against the tight walls. Sand grains clicked as they fell against his metal hide.

He knew what would come next.

Frantically, he dug a little chamber for himself, large enough for him to turn around. The lights set above his optical scanners dipped and rose as he shifted, making the shadows dance. He twisted, bent in half, and suddenly he was stuck.

Looking over his shoulder, he found himself staring into the expressionless eyes of invictas.

There were three of them; two tagged with blue stripes; one tagged yellow. The yellow one moved. His forelegs scraped at the ceiling. At last, too late, Morgan noticed the dirt walls of the tunnel were new. They had never really been tightly packed.

A blue-striped ant rose to help the first. The two were prying at a sand grain the size of a boulder that was set into the ceiling.

Morgan was fighting to flip himself over and free his rear legs, fighting so hard he feared he was about to cause his own avalanche.

The boulder dropped a little. The invictas backed up quickly and stood waiting. But Murphy's Law caught up with them. The boulder, in dropping, had crushed two smaller grains together, and the grains had formed a makeshift latch. The latch was stuck on CLOSED.

Morgan's foreleg was wedged between the tunnel wall and his shoulder. He shifted his weight furiously back and forth.

An invicta, number three, stepped forward and reached up, up for the precariously balanced lever. The delicate red foreleg touched the rock.

Morgan reared. His body popped free.

The ant tugged. There was a grinding sound. A ghostly puff of dust dropped onto the invicta's glossy back.

"NO!" Morgan screamed.

With a crack, the boulder fell. After a brief hesitation, the tunnel went with it.

Novotny was staring into Morgan's face, the remote helmet in his hand. "So. You lost another one."

Still streaming tears, Morgan bent over. He gulped air and blinked at the light. Once, just for fun, Novotny had left him buried for over an hour.

"How many this month?" Shirley asked in her deep alto voice.

On the other side of the room, the techs were still laughing.

Novotny was laughing, too. "Should have seen your face."

Morgan took another deep breath. The room smelled of stale cigarette smoke and plastics. He coughed, raised his eyes, and stared for a moment at Shirley. The lab coat nearly swallowed her. He noticed how curiously small she was: Small for a worker; much too tiny for a female.

"I can't believe they buried you again," Shirley said.

Novotny chuckled, "The invictas tell me, 'We'll bury you.' Just like another old red, Nikita K., used to say."

Morgan's hands trembled as he peeled the leads from his fingers. It took two tries before he made it up out of the chair.

Shirley followed him out of the room. "I noticed in the monitor that Blue Nest warriors have integrated fully with Yellow. That's why they're on this territorial kick with the Pharaohs. The nest needs more space. We'll knock off for today. I'll send for another unit and we'll go in tomorrow morning to see if they're food-gathering with Yellow, too. Then we'll get the queens."

He stumbled into the locker room. Shirley, who was not squeamish about those things, followed. She watched as he peeled off his wet shirt.

"Scares the shit out of you, doesn't it?" she asked.

Morgan sniffed cautiously at the shirt, grimaced and tossed it to a pile of dirty towels at the side of the bench. He unzipped his fly, ran out of energy all of a sudden, and had to sit down quickly. He put his head in his hands.

"You still think they sucker you in?"

"Yes," he whispered.

They knew his name. It had been written on the end of the tunnel. *This one's for you*, they'd said.

"Well, burying you is their only way of fighting back. Nobody ever said ants were completely stupid."

The invictas knew his name, but not his human one. They'd made one up for him, and now the taste of that new name was more familiar than the sound of his old.

Some things, of course, were beyond the invictas' understanding. They knew of war, certainly. They knew about killing. It was motiveless murder they didn't understand.

Morgan neither ate nor did he invade. When the workers were tagged and the nest was empty of queens and eggs he walked away, leaving stunned turmoil behind him.

Had they known the term they would have called him Serial Murderer. As it was, they took the essence of what he was doing and called him by the scent-name For No Reason.

His very name was the question they longed to ask him: *Why?*

An invicta could have understood the human robber killing for money. They certainly would have understood the plea of self defense. But what Morgan was doing was a type of murder not even humans understand.

For absolutely no reason.

He figured the invictas thought he was crazy. He knew Shirley thought he was.

Morgan was so tired that it was an effort for his mouth and tongue to form the words: "They know when I'm coming."

"Yeah. No surprise. That's what this research is all about, isn't it? Finding out how they set up communications. When the queens are dead, the colony is dead, right? And the survivors have to move it or lose it. Question is, how do they integrate and why do the other nests let the alien workers in? Myself, I think it's for entertainment value. S. Invictas are like Boy Scouts around a campfire. They get out their marshmallows and listen to horror stories the new guys tell about you."

He stood up, swayed for a moment, and then dropped his pants. With his undershorts still on, he walked into a shower. He turned on the water, slipped off his jockey shorts and tossed them over the opaque glass door.

"Hey! Watch it!" Shirley shouted.

With the hot water beating into his face, Morgan leaned against the tile wall, closed his eyes and laughed silently. In a moment the edges of his lips pulled down and, still without sound, he was sobbing.

There was a soft thud. Shirley had thrown his shorts against the shower door. "Jesus Christ," she whispered in disgust.

He wiped his face. "You just going to stand there? You coming in here with me, or what?"

There was a muttered reply.

"If you don't want my bod, then what is it you want?"

"It is your bod, Morgan. It always was your bod. You're going in tomorrow, right?"

He took a bottle of shampoo from a side ledge and squeezed some onto his hand. It was a woman's shampoo that was pink and smelled like a discount whorehouse. After a hesitation, he wiped it over his head.

"You're the best robot manipulator we've got. And you understand the damned fire ants."

Morgan had become sensitive to smells. The musk scent of the shampoo nearly made him sick. He quickly worked it into a lather and rinsed.

Scents. That's how the ants spoke, in scents. Morgan could read them, but in the land of the ants he was mute. If he could tell the invictas anything, it would be to get out of the cities while they could. He'd tell them to go back to the country while they still had a chance, even though the *Solenopsis invicta*-specific poison was there. When Shirley and the others figured out how the nests worked, the invicta would have no chance.

Invictas were taking over the household nesting spots of the pharaohs, the Argentines, the carpenters. They had left the pastures and were fucking with human habitats, and the humans were finally pissed. That's why Shirley was studying them so intently; and that's why Morgan was murdering them.

He *did* have a reason. However convoluted, murderers always do. He just couldn't explain.

"I always come back, don't I?" he asked.

"Yeah. I just keep thinking that one day you won't."

"Maybe I won't. But it won't be tomorrow."

In a minute, he heard the locker room door creak shut.

The wide treeless expanses of the suburbs bothered him, but the day made up for it. The clouds were low, the dusk light deceptive as if it were about to storm. In the distance, Dallas rose like a shrouded specter; and the proscribed path of Central Expressway was a river of small, bright bodies: Red ones heading north; white ones heading south.

He took the Greenville exit and entered the closely-packed apartments by The Village. The joggers had gone in, but the dogwalkers were out en masse. He walked quickly from his car to his darkened living room and peered into the light beyond the breakfast bar, watching Donna move, an ant behind glass.

She left dinner simmering and came out into the living room with him. "Home early. You want a drink?"

"Yes." Then he thought about it. "No."

She walked back in the kitchen and poured herself a glass of wine. He followed.

At the stove she flinched away from him. "You stand too close; you know that? It's spooky."

He stepped a pace back and looked at her.

"Don't watch me. You're always *watching* me lately."

"Sorry," he said, and looked away, riveting his eyes to the picture on an empty tomato can.

Without warning, she was crying.

He was afraid to come too close; afraid to stare at her. "What is it?" he asked from a few feet away. The tomato can was green. The tomatoes were bright red. There was white and black writing across the front of the tomato picture.

"You're not a *human* any more, Stevie. You don't act like a human, you don't *think* like a human."

He wondered if it would be all right for him to look at her now. He tried it. She wasn't looking his way, anyway.

"Don't you know I love you?" he asked. He would die for her. He would kill for her. And he didn't understand why. All he knew was that Donna and the apartment were wrapped up into the same package in his mind. It upset him when she went out.

She was still crying, so he stepped forward, stood at her shoulder and ran a hand down her arm. Donna shivered and jerked away. He was confused because he thought he remembered that was the way he should act. "You don't want me to touch you?"

"Not like that."

He was frightened, confused. "Like what?"

Donna rubbed her arm hard where his hand had been. "I don't know. It's a touch like feathers. I don't like it."

Because he couldn't understand what she wanted, Morgan left the kitchen. He sat contentedly in the living room and watched her move back and forth from the sink to the stove in her prescribed, safe place.

The drive back to Plano in the morning was disturbing. Above him the sun sat unblinking in the blue gaze of the autumn sky. The only gravity that kept Morgan from flying off the earth, the only power that kept him warm, was the traffic.

Inside the research station, Morgan started to calm. By the time he had eased himself into the chair and slipped the controls of the mini-robot onto his hands, his hands had stopped shaking. Shirley bent down with the helmet. At the last moment, he brought his palms up and pushed it away. The leads on his fingers clicked against the heavy plastic of the headgear.

"What do I look like?" he asked her.

Her eyebrows raised and lowered, doing a little formal dance of confusion. "Huh?"

"When I'm in command of the unit. What do I look like? I've never seen anyone do it. Do I look funny?"

She shrugged and put the helmet into his lap. It was heavy and no one, particularly the petite Shirley, could hold it for very long. "You twitch a little when you walk. You don't really take the steps. You know that. But your muscles and your arms act as if they do." She started to lift the helmet again.

He stopped her. "And when I kill?"

All animation left her face. "The mandibles are the thumb and forefinger of your right hand."

"I know."

"Then why do you ask?"

"I want to know how it looks to you."

"They move. Together and apart. It's not much to see, really."

He licked his lips nervously. "Do I smile when I do it?"

"No," she said softly. "No." Then she slipped the helmet over his head.

The maimed body of the pharaoh was still at the start of the tunnel. Morgan touched it as he went by. It didn't tell any new stories.

At the chamber, the death messages were already getting old and the invicta bodies had been carried away. He took the right hand corridor this time. The tunnel was old, well-used. He could taste the remains of pharaohs, the original builders, and the spicy tang of the new tenants. The pharaohs had left simple food markers, directional signals; the invictas had left tart splashes of paranoia.

After a few yards, the tunnel made a slow S curve downwards. In the center of the S, he caught the shadow of antennae coming his way. The invicta was on him before it knew he was there. It was a Yellow; and the job he had done of marking it, Morgan noticed, was sloppy. The yellow paint lay in an uneven zig-zag up its forehead, making the cranium appear as if it were an egg about to birth the sun.

The ant backed away hurriedly, trying to turn. Morgan caught it just at the wasp waist and squeezed, cutting the scout in half. In the close confines of the tunnel, it writhed, stroking surprise, agony and hatred on the walls, on Morgan's face.

Bending forward over the broken body, Morgan sunk his steel mandibles on either side of the paint and into its brain. The ant died in inert silence, the pebbled eyes wide, not with astonishment, but with an absolute lack of expression. The slender red legs twitched and then curled in the silent, insectile body language of death.

Morgan had to crawl over the corpse to go on.

A few more feet downwards, the tunnel branched. He caught the first whiff of excitement: the smell of busy ants carrying food to the heart of the nest. The trail was a few days old.

He hurried down the left hand corridor and, in only a few feet, came to another fork. The taste on the floor was newer. Emerging from that tunnel, he surprised an entire line of food gatherers marching back from the surface.

The first invicta by the gap turned to touch him. Morgan caught the yellow-streaked antenna in his jaws and snapped. The ant backed away in astonished pain, dropping its load of food.

Morgan shouldered his way out into the new tunnel. The ants, both blues and yellows, had skittered away a few inches to stand indecisively bottlenecked. The ones traveling away from Morgan dropped their food, doubled back and attacked.

A pair of serrated jaws clicked and slid off Morgan's metal shoulder. Legs thin as reeds fought for purchase on his slick back. He heard a tap-tap-tap on his underside as an invicta battered its stinger futilely against his belly.

He cut through them slowly, having to stop every inch and wipe his jaws clean, having to struggle for every bit of tunnel. They tried to shove him back, but he weighed more. Lower into the corridor he fought, three invictas clinging to his shoulders, a puree of dying ants behind him.

When he came to the next tunnel mouth, he crawled inside and dropped to his belly, exhausted. The invictas prowled around him for a while, touching, tasting. Finally, they went away.

Morgan put a feeler up to his head. They'd branded him with scent.

Murderer.

Since he wasn't moving, he wondered if Shirley would take off his helmet. She didn't. He lay on the cool floor of the tunnel and nearly went to sleep. A long while later, still exhausted, he rose and followed the alarmed trail of the workers downward.

A few yards down, the now-empty tunnel branched. Wearily, he swept his light over the dark entrance. Sight told him nothing. Taste did. The line of workers had split, too.

He took the entrance on his left. It turned and dipped, righted itself, and then dipped precipitously again. At the bottom of the long hill, his headlights caught an oily glint.

Suspicious, he halted. Bang. Something hit him in the back and suddenly he was tumbling, the attacking invicta tumbling with him. He dug his legs into the side of the corridor, but momentum had hold. He rolled end-over-end until he hit the pool of honey at the bottom, the invicta under him.

The servo motors whined as he fought to free his legs from the ooze. There was a bright flash and a sizzle as the right foreleg burned out. He nearly collapsed on top of the ant.

That's when he noticed the invicta wasn't moving much. It didn't seem at all surprised. It wouldn't be, of course. As a Blue, it knew him. And it knew what he wanted. It had never hoped for escape.

Morgan struggled for a moment, then gave up in exhaustion. To his front, the invicta's hive brothers were sealing them both in the tunnel. Morgan could feel the feathery touch of the doomed invicta's legs against his waist, his shoulder.

Morgan's legs failed. He dropped over the fallen invicta, chest to chest, belly to belly. He put his head down slowly until his face touched that of the trapped ant. The huge eyes told him nothing. The antennae stroked gently down the side of Morgan's cheek, not saying much, either, really.

The ant didn't talk of hatred. He didn't even talk of fear. It seemed that the ant was speaking more to himself than he was to Morgan. He talked of the hive, and of queens tucked in, and of the brittle fragility of pupae.

Morgan didn't move. Cradled in Morgan's metal arms, the ant stroked him, and told of food sharing and the hatching of eggs in the dark.

Abrupt light made him blink. "You okay?" Novotny asked.

Morgan, mouth open, eyes slitted, didn't answer. He wondered where the gentle, dying ant was.

"Hey! Hey! Morgan! Rise and shine!" Novotny shoved his face into Morgan's.

Morgan raised his hand and tenderly cupped Novotny's warm cheek.

The tech jerked away. "Shit!" he said, wiping the side of his face and glancing around nervously to see if anyone was laughing.

Nobody was.

"Get up," Shirley said. "Let's go take a walk down the hall."

Morgan's legs were unsteady. Shirley helped him.

"What the fuck's happening to you?" Shirley asked when they had closed the door behind them.

At the entrance to the locker room, Morgan paused and then went in. "Take a shower," he mumbled.

Shirley followed him. "You still think they talk to you, don't you?"

He tried to unbutton his shirt. His fingers wouldn't work.

"They're just *ants*, Steve."

For some reason, he was highly aware of her next to him. One second she hadn't been there, the next moment she was the only real thing in the room. He grabbed her and shoved her against the steel lockers. The impact was metallic, loud. He pressed his body against hers: belly to belly, chest to chest. He rubbed his head against her cheek. Her skin was a blank page.

"Get off me!" She shoved.

He stumbled away.

With brisk hands, she wiped the touch of him off her. Morgan wondered if he had left his scent markers behind: the scent of longing, the scent of regret.

"Tomorrow," she said. "Tomorrow you kill the Yellow queens, and then you take a vacation or something. Go skiing."

He shuddered as he imagined Colorado and its wide, dizzying, expanse of sky. "I don't ski."

She backed up. "Do *something*. Go *some*where. You're getting weird."

"I'm sorry," he whispered. Then he remembered he was probably staring, and looked quickly away.

After turning off the ten o'clock news, Donna fell asleep and left Morgan awake, his arm crooked over his forehead, his eyes open to the ceiling. The space between the slats in the mini-blinds had captured a stripe of grey light-blasted city sky and a single blue star.

After a while he pulled his pajama bottoms down, rolled her over and slid his body over hers. She made a protesting sound in the back of her throat. Her legs parted sleepily and he thrust himself partially in.

Then he lay there.

In the apartments around him, he imagined the moving of bodies. He could even hear their faint sounds: water running in a tub; footsteps on the ceiling. It made him feel safe.

Then, in the dim glow from the streetlamp outside the window, he saw her eyes pop open. "What are you doing?" she whispered.

"Nothing." He caged her slender shoulders between his elbows.

She moved her hips. "Are you going to come, or what?"

Lowering his head to hers to smell, not to kiss, he freed his right arm and caressed her cheek. His thumb and forefinger spoke of death. He couldn't help that.

"I said, are you going to come?"

"I don't know."

She moved her hips again. He lost what little erection he had had. With a wet, limp plop, he fell out of her.

There was a flurry of movement under him. With hard fists and sharp nails, Donna fought her way out of bed. His chest was bruised. The scratches stung. She'd succeeded in hurting him, something the ants had never managed.

"Jesus Christ," Donna spat.

There was the slam of the bathroom door. The sound of the water running in his own shower. A little while later, she came out and got dressed. Her hair was wet.

In the light from the bathroom, she opened a drawer and began flinging things out into a shopping bag.

"What are you doing?" he asked.

She didn't look up from her task. "Leaving."

Morgan reached down and pulled the sheet up to his chin.

"Listen," she said and paused. "There's somebody else. I've been seeing him for a while."

Morgan thought of another man with Donna. Infidelity. It seemed that the word should have had some meaning. Aimlessly, he rolled it around in his mind. "Don't leave."

"God. I don't believe this. You don't even ask who. You don't even ask when."

It didn't matter. Lying back down on the pillow, he listened to the sharp, angry sounds of Donna's departure. "Please," he whispered.

There was a bang as a drawer was slammed closed. He looked down to see her bent in silent grief over the dresser. Underwear, hers and his, was scattered on the floor.

"I won't touch you again. Not ever. I promise. Just don't leave."

She shook her head slowly. Her eyes were closed. "We can't live like this."

Oh, yes, we can, he thought. The point wasn't touching, it wasn't making love. The point was having her enclosed in the dark apartment walls and knowing she was there. "You can sleep with him, okay? You can sleep with anybody. Please. Just don't leave me."

She left anyway. When she was gone, Morgan rose and walked, disoriented, through the once safe chambers of the house.

After putting his helmet on, he went down the way he had gone before, past the dead pharaoh, past the battle chamber. He made an excursion down the long, winding tunnel to the honey and the last inoperative unit. Before the wall the invictas had hastily constructed, the last robot lay humped on the curled, still body of the ant.

Morgan reached out carefully and touched one of the invicta's dead legs. He would have saved the Blue if he could have; but when Novotny had pulled the helmet off him, the full, dumb weight of the robot had pressed down, shoving the ant under the ooze. It had quickly and peacefully drowned.

He turned and looked up the long tunnel, realizing at last what an opening he'd given the invictas. His nerves on edge, he crawled his difficult way up the loose gravel of the tunnel. Only when he was at the top of the incline did he relax.

There was one other corridor. He started down it. Surprisingly close to the entrance, he found the first of the queens' chambers.

There were hundreds of them.

The bodies of the huge females filled the far end of the room, their fecund scent making the atmosphere thick. Slowly, gracefully, as if she knew fate had arrived in the form of the smaller silvered body, the nearest queen turned her velvet eyes towards him.

He started forward, but something tugged at his arm. Looking around he saw the first worker he had seen all day.

The ant, a Yellow, dropped off him and started to sway. Morgan understood scent language. He'd never been around live ants long enough to learn the meanings of the dance.

He watched it. Backwards and forwards it went. Sideways, its antennae making patterns in the air. Behind the worker, a crowd of Blues and Yellows had gathered, all waiting.

At last the invicta stopped, its antennae weaving questions. Morgan came forward slowly. The ant froze.

Putting his metal antennae towards the translucent red ones, Morgan touched it.

My wife left me, he thought.

The invicta stroked him back, not understanding, but talking of hives, of queens, of satisfaction. Morgan knew what it was really saying, that it knew Morgan was invincible. The invicta couldn't stop him from killing for no reason; so it was giving him a reason not to kill.

To survive, the invicta had first learned not to wage war among themselves. The queens had learned to share hives. And now they had finally learned the difficult lesson of how to live with others.

Morgan caressed the slick, blank face so carefully that the metal never made a sound against the chitinous armor.

If he could tell the ant anything, it would be that he understood the pain of dead queens, barren nests.

The ant's antennae fluttered, making scented, soft peace.

When Morgan maneuvered the robot to the exit where the recovery tools were waiting, Novotny took the control helmet off. "You didn't get the queens."

"No," he said. He stood up and wiped the tears from his eyes. The front of his shirt was wet with them.

"I saw everything," Shirley told him. "You didn't kill the queens!"

Morgan raised his voice. "I'll get them tomorrow, okay?"

He hurried out of the room towards the showers, Shirley tagging at his heels. "Goddamn it. I can see it in your face. You won't be back tomorrow."

"I'll be back."

She whipped out her hand, caught him by the arm and pulled him around. Her face was close, soft and pink. "You motherfucking liar."

He started to laugh.

Back at the apartment, he closed the shades and then walked into the twilight kitchen, running his hands along the microwave, the toaster. He didn't understand why Donna had left; he'd worked so hard to make the chamber right.

Unlike the Blues, there were no friendly Yellows to take Morgan in. He would stay in his abandoned nest until the food ran out.

On the shadowed surface of the formica, small dots milled happily around a spill of grease. Ants. He brought his face down closer to see them.

Pharaohs.

Somewhere in the dark, below the apartment foundation, were cool acidic tunnels with moist walls. There the bloated queens waited. And there, perhaps, the invictas would come with their deadly jaws, their bladders swollen with alkaloid poison.

If invicta came, they'd kill them all. They'd conquer the pharaohs' nest. As the invictas had recently learned, and the humans had learned centuries ago, that was the right of intelligence; the demand of civilization. A shudder started from the back of his brain and worked its way through his body.

He turned to the sink, ran water over a sponge, and took it to where the ants were gathered. Pushing each tiny body gently to the side, he wiped the grease spot away.

For a little while the pharaohs lingered, confused that the food was suddenly gone.

"My wife left me," he whispered, but the ants didn't understand. Pharaohs had never been very smart, had never learned the tricks of sleight-of-hand, of warfare, of diplomacy, of evolution. Finally, one by one, still apparently content, they wandered down the crack between the stove and the cabinet to home.

GINNY SWEETHIPS'
FLYING CIRCUS

Neal Barrett, Jr.

*"Ginny Sweethips' Flying Circus" was purchased by
Gardner Dozois, and appeared in the February,
1988, issue of* IAsfm, *with an illustration by J. K.
Potter. Barrett became one of the magazine's most
popular writers in the last half of the 1980s, and
gained wide critical acclaim, with a string of pun-
gent, funny, and unclassifiably weird stories like
"Perpetuity Blues," "Stairs," "Highbrow," "Trad-
ing Post," and "Class of '61." The bizarre and ex-
uberant story that follows, which comes complete with
robot hookers, Rogue Insurance Men, and seven-feet-
tall machine-gun toting mutant possums, may well be
one of the most joyously gonzo post-Holocaust stories
ever written.*

*Born in San Antonio, Texas, Neal Barrett, Jr.
grew up in Oklahoma City, Oklahoma, spent several
years in Austin, hobnobbing with the likes of Lewis
Shiner and Howard Waldrop, and now makes his
home with his family in Fort Worth. He made his first
sale in 1959, and has been a full-time freelancer for
the past twelve years. His books include* Stress Pattern, Karma Corps, *the four volume* Aldair *series, the
critically acclaimed novel* Through Darkest America,

and its sequel, Dawn's Uncertain Light. *His most recent book is a* very *strange new novel*, The Hereafter Gang.

Del drove and Ginny sat.

"They're taking their sweet time," Ginny said, "damned if they're not."

"They're itchy," Del said. "Everyone's itchy. Everyone's looking to stay alive."

"Huh!" Ginny showed disgust. "I sure don't care for sittin' out here in the sun. My price is going up by the minute. You wait and see if it doesn't."

"Don't get greedy," Del said.

Ginny curled her toes on the dash. Her legs felt warm in the sun. The stockade was a hundred yards off. Barbed wire looped above the walls. The sign over the gate read:

First Church of the Unleaded God
& Ace High Refinery
WELCOME
KEEP OUT

The refinery needed paint. It had likely been silver but was now dull as pewter and black rust. Ginny leaned out the window and called to Possum Dark.

"What's happening, friend? Those mothers dead in there or what?"

"Thinking," Possum said. "Fixing to make a move. Considering what to do." Possum Dark sat atop the van in a steno chair bolted to the roof. Circling the chair was a swivel-ring mount sporting fine twin-fifties black as grease. Possum had a death-view clean around. Keeping out the sun was a red Cinzano umbrella faded pink. Possum studied the stockade and watched heat distort the flats. He didn't care for the effect. He was suspicious of things less than cut and dried. Apprehensive of illusions of every kind. He scratched his nose and curled his tail around his leg. The gate opened up and men started

across the scrub. He teased them in his sights. He prayed they'd
do something silly and grand.

Possum counted thirty-seven men. A few carried sidearms,
openly or concealed. Possum spotted them all at once. He
wasn't too concerned. This seemed like an easy-going bunch,
more intent on fun than fracas. Still, there was always the hope
that he was wrong.

The men milled about. They wore patched denim and faded
shirts. Possum made them nervous. Del countered that; his
appearance set them at ease. The men looked at Del, poked
each other and grinned. Del was scrawny and bald except for
tufts around the ears. The dusty black coat was too big. His
neck thrust out of his shirt like a newborn buzzard looking for
meat. The men forgot Possum and gathered around, waiting
to see what Del would do. Waiting for Del to get around to
showing them what they'd come to see. The van was painted
turtle-green. Gold Barnum type named the owner, and the
selected vices for sale:

Ginny Sweethips' Flying Circus
SEX * TACOS * DANGEROUS DRUGS

Del puttered about with this and that. He unhitched the wagon
from the van and folded out a handy little stage. It didn't take
three minutes to set up, but he dragged it out to ten, then ten
on top of that. The men started to whistle and clap their hands.
Del looked alarmed. They liked that. He stumbled and they
laughed.

"Hey, mister, you got a girl in there or not?" a man called
out.

"Better be something here besides you," another said.

"Gents," Del said, raising his hands for quiet, "Ginny
Sweethips herself will soon appear on this stage and you'll be
more than glad you waited. Your every wish will be fulfilled,
I promise you that. I'm bringing beauty to the wastelands,
gents. Lust the way you like it, passion unrestrained. Sexual
crimes you never dreamed!"

"Cut the talk, mister," a man with peach-pit eyes shouted
to Del. "Show us what you got."

Others joined in, stomped their feet and whistled. Del knew
he had them. Anger was what he wanted. Frustration and de-

nial. Hatred waiting for sweet release. He waved them off but they wouldn't stop. He placed one hand on the door of the van—and brought them to silence at once.

The double doors opened. A worn red curtain was revealed, stenciled with hearts and cherubs. Del extended his hand. He seemed to search behind the curtain, one eye closed in concentration. He looked alarmed, groping for something he couldn't find. Uncertain he remembered how to do this trick at all. And then, in a sudden burst of motion, Ginny did a double forward flip, and appeared like glory on the stage.

The men broke into shouts of wild abandon. Ginny led them in a cheer. She was dressed for the occasion. Short white skirt shiny bright, white boots with tassels. White sweater with a big red "G" sewn on the front.

"Ginny Sweethips, gents," Del announced with a flair, "giving you her own interpretation of Barbara Jean the Cheerleader Next door. Innocent as snow, yet a little bit wicked and willing to learn, if Biff the Quarterback will only teach her. Now, what do you say to *that*?"

They whistled and yelled and stomped. Ginny strutted and switched, doing long-legged kicks that left them gasping with delight. Thirty-seven pairs of eyes showed their needs. Men guessed at hidden parts. Dusted off scenarios of violence and love. Then, as quickly as she'd come, Ginny was gone. Men threatened to storm the stage. Del grinned without concern. The curtain parted and Ginny was back, blond hair replaced with saucy red, costume changed in the blink of an eye. Del introduced Nurse Nora, an angel of mercy weak as soup in the hands of Patient Pete. Moments later, hair black as a raven's throat, she was Schoolteacher Sally, cold as well water until Steve the Bad Student loosed the fury chained within.

Ginny vanished again. Applause thundered over the flats. Del urged them on, then spread his hands for quiet.

"Did I lie to you gents? Is she all you ever dreamed? Is this the love you've wanted all your life? Could you ask for sweeter limbs, for softer flesh? For whiter teeth, for brighter eyes?"

"Yeah, but is she *real*?" a man shouted, a man with a broken face sewn up like a sock. "We're religious people here. We don't fuck with no machines."

Others echoed the question with bold shouts and shaking fists.

"Now, I don't blame you, sir, at all," Del said. "I've had

a few dolly droids myself. A plastic embrace at best, I'll grant you that. Not for the likes of *you*, for I can tell you're a man who knows his women. No, sir, Ginny's real as rain, and she's yours in the role of your choice. Seven minutes of bliss. It'll seem like a lifetime, gents, I promise you that. Your goods gladly returned if I'm a liar. And all for only a U.S. gallon of gas!''

Howls and groans at that, as Del expected.

"That's a *cheat* is what it is! Ain't a woman worth it!"

"Gas is better'n gold and we work damn hard to get it!"

Del stood his ground. Looked grim and disappointed. "I'd be the last man alive to try to part you from your goods," Del said. "It's not my place to drive a fellow into the arms of sweet content, to make him rest his manly frame on golden thighs. Not if he thinks this lovely girl's not worth the fee, no sir. I don't do business that way and never have."

The men moved closer. Del could smell their discontent. He read sly thoughts above their heads. There was always this moment, when it occurred to them there was a way Ginny's delights might be obtained for free.

"Give it some thought, friends," Del said. "A man's got to do what he's got to do. And while you're making up your minds, turn your eyes to the top of the van for a startling and absolutely free display of the slickest bit of marksmanship you're ever likely to see!"

Before Del's words were out of his mouth and on the way, before the men could scarcely comprehend, Ginny appeared again and tossed a dozen china saucers in the air.

Possum Dark moved in a blur. Turned a hundred-and-forty degrees in his bolted steno chair and whipped his guns on target, blasting saucers to dust. Thunder rolled across the flats. Crockery rained on the men below. Possum stood and offered a pink killer grin and a little bow. The men saw six-foot-nine and a quarter inches of happy marsupial fury and awesome speed, of black agate eyes and a snout full of icy varmint teeth. Doubts were swept aside. Fifty-calibre madness wasn't the answer. Fun today was clearly not for free.

"Gentlemen, start your engines," Del smiled. "I'll be right here to take your fee. Enjoy a hot taco while you wait your turn at glory. Have a look at our display of fine pharmaceutical wonders and mind-expanding drugs."

In moments, men were making their way back to the stockade. Soon after that, they returned toting battered tins of gas. Del sniffed each gallon, in case some buffoon thought water would get him by. Each man received a token and took his place. Del sold tacos and dangerous drugs, taking what he could get in trade. Candles and Mason jars, a rusty knife. Half a manual on full-field maintenance for the Chrysler Mark XX Urban Tank. The drugs were different colors but all the same: twelve parts oregano, three parts rabbit shit, one part marijuana stems. All this under Possum's watchful eye.

"By God," said the first man out of the van. "She's worth it, I'll tell you that. Have her do the Nurse, you won't regret it!"

"The Schoolteacher's best," said the second man through. "I never seen the like. I don't care if she's real or she ain't."

"What's in these tacos?" a customer asked Del.

"Nobody you know, mister," Del said.

"It's been a long day," Ginny said. "I'm pooped, and that's the truth." She wrinkled up her nose. "First thing we hit a town, you hose 'er out good now, Del. Place smells like a sewer or maybe worse."

Del squinted at the sky and pulled up under the scant shade of mesquite. He stepped out and kicked the tires. Ginny got down, walked around and stretched.

"It's getting late," Del said. "You want to go on or stop here?"

"You figure those boys might decide to get a rebate on this gas?"

"Hope they do," Possum said from atop the van.

"You're a pisser," Ginny laughed, "I'll say that. Hell, let's keep going. I could use a hot bath and town food. What you figure's up the road?"

"East Bad News," Del said, "if this map's worth anything at all. Ginny, night driving's no good. You don't know what's waiting down the road."

"I know what's on the roof," Ginny said. "Let's do it. I'm itchy all over with bugs and dirt and that tub keeps shinin' in my head. You want me to drive a spell, I sure will."

"Get in," Del grumbled. "Your driving's scarier than anything I'll meet."

Morning arrived in purple shadow and metal tones, copper, silver, and gold. From a distance, East Bad News looked to

Ginny like garbage strewn carelessly over the flats. Closer, it looked like larger garbage. Tin shacks and tents and haphazard buildings rehashed from whatever they were before. Cookfires burned, and the locals wandered about and yawned and scratched. Three places offered food. Other places bed and a bath. Something to look forward to, at least. She spotted the sign down at the far end of town:

MORO'S REPAIRS
Armaments · Machinery · Electronic Shit of All Kinds

"Hold it!" Ginny said. "Pull'er in right there."

Del looked alarmed. "What for?"

"Don't get excited. There's gear needs tending in back. I just want 'em to take a look."

"Didn't mention it to me," Del said.

Ginny saw the sad and droopy eyes, the tired wisps of hair sticking flat to Del's ears. "Del, there wasn't anything to mention," she said in a kindly tone. "Nothing you can really put your finger on, I mean. Okay?"

"Whatever you think," Del said, clearly out of sorts.

Ginny sighed and got out. Barbed wire surrounded the yard behind the shop. The yard was ankle-deep in tangles of rope and copper cable, rusted unidentifiable parts. A battered pickup hugged the wall. Morning heat curled the tin roof of the building. More parts spilled out of the door. Possum made a funny noise, and Ginny saw the Dog step into the light. A Shepherd, maybe six-foot-two. It showed Possum Dark yellow eyes. A man appeared behind the Dog, wiping heavy grease on his pants. Bare to the waist, hair like stuffing out of a chair. Features hard as rock, flint eyes to match. Not bad looking, thought Ginny, if you cleaned him up good.

"Well now," said the man. He glanced at the van, read the legend on the side, took in Ginny from head to toe. "What can I do for *you*, little lady?"

"I'm not real little and don't guess I'm any lady," Ginny said. "Whatever you're thinking, don't. You open for business or just talk?"

The man grinned. "My name's Moro Gain. Never turn business away if I can help it."

"I need electric stuff."

"We got it. What's the problem?"

"Huh-unh." Ginny shook her head. "First I gotta ask. You do confidential work or tell everything you know?"

"Secret's my middle name," Moro said. "Might cost a little more, but you got it."

"How much?"

Moro closed one eye. "Now, how do I know that? You got a nuclear device in there, or a broken watch? Drive it on in and we'll take a look." He aimed a greasy finger at Possum Dark. "Leave *him* outside."

"No way."

"No arms in the shop. That's a rule."

"He isn't carrying. Just the guns you see." Ginny smiled. "You can shake him down, if you like. *I* wouldn't, I don't think."

"He looks imposing, all right."

"I'd say he is."

"What the hell," Moro said, "drive it in."

Dog unlocked the gate. Possum climbed down and followed Dog with oily eyes.

"Go find us a place to stay," Ginny said to Del. "Clean, if you can find it. All the hot water in town. Christ sakes, Del, you still sulking or what?"

"Don't worry about me," Del said. "Don't concern yourself at all."

"Right." She hopped behind the wheel. Moro began kicking the door of his shop. It finally sprang free, wide enough to take the van. The supply wagon rocked along behind. Moro lifted the tarp, eyed the thirty-seven tins of unleaded with great interest.

"You get lousy mileage, or what?" he asked Ginny.

Ginny didn't answer. She stepped out of the van. Light came through broken panes of glass. The skinny windows reminded her of a church. Her eyes got used to shadow, and she saw that that's what it was. Pews sat to the side, piled high with auto parts. A 1997 Olds was jacked up before the altar.

"Nice place you got here," she said.

"It works for me," Moro told her. "Now what kind of trouble you got? Something in the wiring? You said electric stuff."

"I didn't mean the motor. Back here." She led him to the rear and opened the doors.

"God A'Mighty!" Moro said.

"Smells a little raunchy right now. Can't help that till we hose 'er down." Ginny stepped inside, looked back, and saw Moro still on the ground. "You coming up or not?"

"Just thinking."

"About what?" She'd seen him watching her move and didn't really have to ask.

"Well, *you* know . . ." Moro shuffled his feet. "How do you figure on paying? For whatever it is I got to do."

"Gas. You take a look. Tell me how many tins. I say yes or no."

"We could work something out."

"We could, huh?"

"Sure." Moro gave her a foolish grin. "Why not?"

Ginny didn't blink. "Mister, what kind of girl do you think I am?"

Moro looked puzzled and intent. "I can read good, lady, believe it or not. I figured you wasn't tacos or dangerous drugs."

"You figured wrong," Ginny said. "Sex is just software to me, and don't you forget it. I haven't got all day to watch you moonin' over my parts. I got to move or stand still. When I stand still, you look. When I move, you look more. Can't fault you for that, I'm about the prettiest thing you ever saw. Don't let it get in the way of your work."

Moro couldn't think of much to say. He took a breath and stepped into the van. There was a bed bolted flat against the floor. A red cotton spread, a worn satin pillow that said DUR-ANGO, COLORADO and pictured chipmunks and waterfalls. An end table, a pink-shaded lamp with flamingos on the side. Red curtains on the walls. Ballet prints and a naked Minnie Mouse.

"Somethin' else," Moro said.

"Back here's the problem," Ginny said. She pulled a curtain aside at the front of the van. There was a plywood cabinet, fitted with brass screws. Ginny took a key out of her jeans and opened it up.

Moro stared a minute, then laughed aloud. "*Sensory* tapes? Well, I'll be a son of a bitch." He took a new look at Ginny, a look Ginny didn't miss. "Haven't seen a rig like this in years. Didn't know there were any still around."

"I've got three tapes," Ginny explained. "A brunette, a redhead and a blond. Found a whole cache in Ardmore, Oklahoma. Had to look at 'bout three or four hundred to find the girls that looked close enough to me. Nearly went nuts 'fore it was over. Anyway, I did it. Spliced 'em down to seven minutes each.''

Moro glanced back at the bed. ''How do you put 'em under?''

''Little needle comes up out the mattress. Sticks them in the ass lightnin' fast. They're out like *that*. Seven minute dose. Headpiece is in the endtable there. I get it on and off them real quick. Wires go under the floorboards back here to the rig.''

''Jesus,'' Moro said. ''They ever catch you at this, you are cooked, lady.''

''That's what Possum's for,'' Ginny said. ''Possum's pretty good at what he does. Now what's *that* look all about?''

''I wasn't sure right off if you were real.''

Ginny laughed aloud. ''So what do you think now?''

''I think maybe you are.''

''Right,'' Ginny said. ''It's Del who's the droid, not me. Wimp IX Series. Didn't make a whole lot. Not much demand. The customers think it's me, never think to look at him. He's a damn good barker and pretty good at tacos and drugs. A little too sensitive, you ask me. Well, nobody's perfect, so they say.''

''The trouble you're having's in the rig?''

''I guess,'' Ginny said, ''beats the hell out of me.'' She bit her lip and wrinkled her brow. Moro found the gestures most inviting. ''Slips a little, I think. Maybe I got a short, huh?''

''Maybe.'' Moro fiddled with the rig, testing one of the spools with his thumb. ''I'll have to get in here and see.''

''It's all yours. I'll be wherever it is Del's got me staying.''

''Ruby John's,'' Moro said. ''Only place there is with a good room. I'd like to take you out to dinner.''

''Well sure you would.''

''You got a real shitty attitude, friend.''

''I get a whole lot of practice,'' Ginny said.

''And I've got a certain amount of pride,'' Moro told her. ''I don't intend to ask you more than three or four times and that's it.''

Ginny nodded. Right on the edge of approval. ''You've got promise,'' she said. ''Not a whole lot, maybe, but some.''

''Does that mean dinner, or not?''

"Means not. Means if I *wanted* to have dinner with some guy, you'd maybe fit the bill."

Moro's eyes got hot. "Hell with you, lady. I don't need the company that bad."

"Fine." Ginny sniffed the air and walked out. "You have a nice day."

Moro watched her walk. Watched denims mold her legs, studied the hydraulics of her hips. Considered several unlikely acts. Considered cleaning up, searching for proper clothes. Considered finding a bottle and watching the tapes. A plastic embrace at best, or so he'd heard, but a lot less hassle in the end.

Possum Dark watched the van disappear into the shop. He felt uneasy at once. His place was on top. Keeping Ginny from harm. Sending feral prayers for murder to absent genetic gods. His eyes hadn't left Dog since he'd appeared. Primal smells, old fears and needs assailed his senses. Dog locked the gate and turned around. Didn't come closer, just turned.

"I'm Dog Quick," he said, folding hairy arms. "I don't much care for Possums."

"I don't much care for Dogs," said Possum Dark.

Dog seemed to understand. "What did you do before the War?"

"Worked in a theme park. Our Wildlife Heritage. That kind of shit. What about you?"

"Security, what else?" Dog made a face. "Learned a little electrics. Picked up a lot more from Moro Gain. I've done worse." He nodded toward the shop. "You like to shoot people with that thing?"

"Anytime I get the chance."

"You ever play any cards?"

"Some." Possum Dark showed his teeth. "I guess I could handle myself with a Dog."

"For real goods?" Dog returned the grin.

"New deck, unbroken seal, table stakes," Possum said.

Moro showed up at Ruby John's Cot Emporium close to noon. Ginny had a semi-private stall, covered by a blanket. She'd bathed and braided her hair and cut the legs clean off her jeans. She tugged at Moro's heart.

"It'll be tomorrow morning," Moro said. "Cost you ten gallons of gas."

"Ten gallons," Ginny said. "That's stealin' and you know it."

"Take it or leave it," Moro said. "You got a bad head in that rig. Going to come right off, you don't fix it. You wouldn't like that. Your customers wouldn't like it any at all."

Ginny appeared subdued but not much. "Four gallons. Tops."

"Eight. I got to make the parts myself."

"Five."

"Six," Moro said. "Six and I take you to dinner."

"Five and a half and I want to be out of this sweatbox at dawn. On the road and gone when the sun starts bakin' your lovely town."

"Damn, you're fun to have around."

Ginny smiled. Sweet and disarming, an unexpected event. "I'm all right. You got to get to know me."

"Just how do I go about that?"

"You don't." The smile turned sober. "I haven't figured that one out."

It looked like rain to the north. Sunrise was dreary. Muddy, less-than-spectacular yellows and reds. Colors through a window no one had bothered to wash. Moro had the van brought out. He said he'd thrown in a lube and hosed out the back. Five and a half gallons were gone out of the wagon. Ginny had Del count while Moro watched.

"I'm honest," Moro said, "you don't have to do that."

"I know," Ginny said, glancing curiously at Dog, who was looking rather strange. He seemed out of sorts. Sulky and off his feed. Ginny followed his eyes and saw Possum atop the van. Possum showed a wet Possum grin.

"Where you headed now?" Moro asked, wanting to hold her as long as he could.

"South," Ginny said, since she was facing that direction.

"I wouldn't," Moro said. "Not real friendly folks down there."

"I'm not picky. Business is business."

"No, sir," Moro shook his head. "*Bad* business is what it is. You got the Dry Heaves south and east. Doom City after that. Straight down and you'll hit the Hackers. Might run into

Fort Pru, bunch of disgruntled insurance agents out on the flats. Stay clear away from them. Isn't worth whatever you'll make.''

"You've been a big help," Ginny said.

Moro gripped her door. "You ever *listen* to anyone, lady? I'm giving good advice."

"Fine," Ginny said, "I'm 'bout as grateful as I can be."

Moro watched her leave. He was consumed by her appearance. The day seemed to focus in her eyes. Nothing he said pleased her in the least. Still, her disdain was friendly enough. There was no malice at all that he could see.

There was something about the sound of Doom City she didn't like. Ginny told Del to head south and maybe west. Around noon, a yellow haze appeared on the ragged rim of the world, like someone rolling a cheap dirty rug across the flats.

"Sandstorm," Possum called from the roof. "Right out of the west. I don't like it at all. I think we better turn. Looks like trouble coming fast."

There was nothing Possum said she couldn't see. He had a habit of saying either too little or more than enough. She told him to cover his guns and get inside, that the sand would take his hide and there was nothing out there he needed to kill that wouldn't wait. Possum Dark sulked but climbed down. Hunched in back of the van he grasped air in the shape of grips and trigger guards. Practiced rage and windage in his head.

"I'll bet I can beat that storm," Del said. "I got this feeling I can do it."

"Beat it where?" Ginny said. "We don't know where we are or what's ahead."

"That's true," Del said. "All the more reason then to get there soon as we can."

Ginny stepped out and viewed the world with disregard. "I got sand in my teeth and in my toes," she complained. "I'll bet that Moro Gain knows right where storms'll likely be. I'll bet that's what happened, all right."

"Seemed like a decent sort to me," Del said.

"That's what I mean," Ginny said. "You can't trust a man like that at all."

The storm had seemed to last a couple of days. Ginny figured maybe an hour. The sky looked bad as cabbage soup. The land looked just the way it had. She couldn't see the difference between sand recently gone or newly arrived. Del got the van going again. Ginny thought about yesterday's bath. East Bad News had its points.

Before they topped the first rise, Possum Dark began to stomp on the roof. "Vehicles to port," he called out. "Sedans and pickup trucks. Flatbeds and semis. Buses of all kinds."

"What are they doing?" Del said.

"Coming right at us, hauling timber."

"Doing *what*?" Ginny made a face. "Damn it all, Del, will you stop the car? I swear you're a driving fool."

Del stopped. Ginny climbed up with Possum to watch. The caravan kept a straight line. Cars and trucks weren't exactly hauling timber . . . but they were. Each carried a section of a wall. Split logs bound together, sharpened at the top. The lead car turned and the others followed. The lead car turned again. In a moment, there was a wooden stockade assembled on the flats, square as if you'd drawn it with a rule. As stockade and a gate. Over the gate a wooden sign:

FORT PRU
Games of Chance & Amusement
Term · Whole Life · Half Life · Death

"I don't like it," said Possum Dark.

"You don't like anything's still alive," Ginny said.

"They've got small arms and they're a nervous-looking bunch."

"They're just horny, Possum. That's the same as nervous, or close enough." Possum pretended to understand. "Looks like they're pulled up for the night," she called to Del. "Let's do some business, friend. The overhead don't ever stop."

Five of them came out to the van. They all looked alike. Stringy, darkened by the sun. Bare to the waist except for collars and striped ties. Each carried an attaché case thin as two slices of bread without butter. Two had pistols stuck in their belts. The leader carried a fine-looking sawed-off Remington Twelve. It hung by a camou guitar strap to his waist. Del didn't like him at all. He had perfect white teeth and a bald head. Eyes the color of jellyfish melting on the beach. He studied the sign on the van and looked at Del.

"You got a whore inside or not?"

Del looked him straight on. "I'm a little displeased at that. It's not the way to talk."

"Hey." The man gave Del a wink. "You don't have to give us the pitch. We're show business folk ourselves."

"Is that right?"

"Wheels of chance and honest cards. Odds I *know* you'll like. I'm head actuary of this bunch. Name's Fred. That animal up there has a piss-poor attitude, friend. No reason to poke that weapon down my throat. We're friendly people here."

"No reason I can see why Possum'd spray this place with lead and diarhetics," Del said. "Less you can think of something I can't."

Fred smiled at that. The sun made a big gold ball on his head. "I guess we'll try your girl," he told Del. "Course we got to see her first. What do you take in trade?"

"Goods as fine as what you're getting in return."

"I've got just the thing." The head actuary winked again. The gesture was starting to irritate Del. Fred nodded, and a friend drew clean white paper from his case. "This here is heavy bond," he told Del, shuffling the edges with his thumb. "Fifty percent linen weave, and we got it by the ream. Won't find anything like it. You can mark on it good or trade it off. 7th Mercenary Writers came through a week ago. Whole brigade of mounted horse. Near cleaned us out, but we can spare a few reams. We got pencils too. Mirado 2s and 3s, unsharpened, with erasers on the end. When's the last time you saw *that*? Why, this stuff's good as gold. We got staples and legal pads. Claim forms, maim forms, forms of every sort. Deals on wheels is what we got. And *you* got gas under wraps in the wagon behind your van. I can smell it plain from here. Friend, we can sure talk some business with you there. I got seventeen rusty-ass guzzlers runnin' dry."

A gnat-whisker wire sparked hot in Del's head. He could see it in the underwriter's eyes. Gasoline greed was what it was, and he knew these men were bent on more than fleshly pleasure. He knew with androidial dread that when they could, they'd make their play.

"Well now, the gas is not for trade," he said as calmly as he could. "Sex and tacos and dangerous drugs is what we sell."

"No problem," the actuary said. "Why, no problem at all. Just an idea, is all it was. You get that little gal out here and

I'll bring in my crew. How's half a ream a man sound to you?''

"Just as fair as it can be," Del said, thinking that half of that would've been fine, knowing dead certain now that Fred intended to take back whatever he gave.

"That Moro fellow was right," Del said. "These insurance boys are bad news. Best thing we can do is take off and let it go."

"Pooh," said Ginny, "that's just the way men are. They come in mad as foamin' dogs and go away like cats licking cream. That's the nature of the fornicatin' trade. You wait and see. Besides, they won't get funny with Possum Dark."

"You wouldn't pray for rain if you were afire," Del muttered. "Well, I'm not unhitching the gas. I'll set you up a stage over the tarp. You can do your number there."

"Suit yourself," Ginny said, kissing a plastic cheek and scooting him out the door. "Now get on out of here and let me start getting cute."

It seemed to be going well. Cheerleader Barbara Jean awoke forgotten wet dreams, left their mouths as dry as snakes. Set them up for Sally the Teach and Nora Nurse, secret violations of the soul. Maybe Ginny was right, Del decided. Faced with girlie delights, a man's normally shitty outlook disappeared. When he was done, he didn't want to wreck a thing for an hour or maybe two. Didn't care about killing for half a day. Del could only guess at this magic and how it worked. Data was one thing, sweet encounters something else.

He caught Possum's eye and felt secure. Forty-eight men waited their turns. Possum knew the calibre of their arms, the length of every blade. His black twin-fifties blessed them all.

Fred the actuary sidled up and grinned at Del. "We sure ought to talk about gas. That's what we ought to do."

"Look," Del said, "gas isn't for trade, I told you that. Go talk to those boys at the refinery, same as us."

"Tried to. They got no use for office supplies."

"That's not my problem," Del said.

"Maybe it is."

Del didn't miss the razor tones. "You got something to say, just say it."

"Half of your gas. We pay our way with the girl and don't give you any trouble."

"You forget about *him*?"

Fred studied Possum Dark. "I can afford losses better than you. Listen, I know what you are, friend. I know you're not a man. Had a CPA droid just like you 'fore the War."

"Maybe we can talk," Del said, trying to figure what to do.

"Say now, that's what I like to hear."

Ginny's first customer staggered out, wild-eyed and white around the gills. "Godamn, try the Nurse," he bawled to the others. "Never had nothin' like it in my life!"

"Next," Del said, and started stacking bond paper. "Lust is the name of the game, gents, what did I tell you, now?"

"The girl plastic too?" Fred asked.

"Real as you," Del said. "We make some kind of deal, how do I know you'll keep your word?"

"Jesus," Fred said, "what do you think I am? You got my Life Under-writer's Oath!"

The second customer exploded through the curtain, tripped and fell on his face. Picked himself up and shook his head. He looked damaged, bleeding around the eyes.

"She's a tiger," Del announced, wondering what the hell was going on. " 'Scuse me a minute," he told Fred, and slipped inside the van. "Just what are you doing in here?" he asked Ginny. "Those boys look like they been through a thrasher."

"Beats me," Ginny said, halfway between Nora and Barbara Jean. "Last old boy jerked around like a snake having a fit. Started pulling out his hair. Somethin' isn't right here, Del. It's gotta be the tapes. I figure the Moro fellow's a cheat."

"We got trouble inside and out," Del told her. "The head of this bunch wants our gas."

"Well, he sure can't have it, by God."

"Ginny, the man's got bug-spit eyes. Says he'll take his chances with Possum. We better clear out while we can."

"Huh-unh." Ginny shook her head. "That'll rile 'em for sure. Give me a minute or two. We've done one Nora and a Sally. I'll switch them all to Barbara Jean and see."

Del slipped back outside. It seemed a dubious answer at best.

"That's some woman," said Fred.

"She's something else today. Your insurance boys have got her fired."

Fred grinned at that. "Guess I better give her a try."

"I wouldn't," Del said.

"Why not?"

"Let her calm down some. Might be more than you want to handle."

He knew at once this wasn't the thing to say. Fred turned the color of ketchup pie. "Why, you plastic piece of shit! I can handle any woman born . . . *or* put together out of a kit."

"Suit yourself," Del said, feeling the day going down the drain. "No charge at all."

"Damn right there's not." Fred jerked the next man out of line. "Get ready in there, little lady. I am going to handle *all* your policy needs!"

The men cheered. Possum Dark, who understood at least three-fifths of the trouble down below, shot Del a questioning look.

"Got any of those tacos?" someone asked.

"Not likely," Del said.

Del considered turning himself off. Android suicide seemed the answer. But in less than three minutes, unnatural howls began to come from the van. The howls turned to shrieks. Life underwriters went rigid. Then Fred emerged, shattered. He looked like a man who'd kicked a bear with boils. His joints appeared to bend the wrong way. He looked whomper-eyed at Del, dazed and out-of-synch. Everything happened then in seconds thin as wire. Del saw Fred find him, saw the oil-spill eyes catch him clean. Saw the sawed-off barrels match the eyes so fast even electric feet couldn't snatch him out of the way in time. Del's arm exploded. He let it go and ran for the van. Possum couldn't help. The actuary was below and too close. The twin-fifties opened up. Underwriters fled. Possum stitched the sand and sent them flying ragged and dead.

Del reached the driver's seat as lead peppered the van. He felt slightly silly. Sitting there with one arm, one hand on the wheel.

"Move over," Ginny said, "that isn't going to work."

"I guess not."

Ginny sent them lurching through the scrub. "Never saw anything like it in my life," she said aloud. "Turned that poor fella on, he started twisting out of his socks, bones snapping like sticks. Damndest orgasm I *ever* saw."

"Something's not working just right."

"Well, I can see that, Del. Jesus, what's that!"

Ginny twisted the wheel as a large part of the desert rose straight up in the air. Smoking sand rained down on the van.

"Rockets," Del said grimly. "That's the reason they figured that crazy-fingered Possum was a snap. Watch where you're going, girl!"

Two fiery pillars exploded ahead. Del leaned out the window and looked back. Half of Fort Pru's wall was in pursuit. Possum sprayed everything in sight, but he couldn't spot where the rockets were coming from. Underwriter assault cars split up, came at them from every side.

"Trying to flank us," Del said. A rocket burst to the right. "Ginny, I'm not real sure what to do."

"How's the stub?"

"Slight electric tingle. Like a doorbell half a mile away. Ginny, they get us in a circle, we're in very deep shit."

"They hit that gas, we won't have to worry about a thing. Oh Lord, now why did I think of that?"

Possum hit a semi clean on. It came to a stop and died, fell over like a bug. Del could see that being a truck and a wall all at once had its problems, balance being one.

"Head right at them," he told Ginny, "then veer off sharp. They can't turn quick going fast."

"Del!"

Bullets rattled the van. Something heavy made a noise. The van skewed to a halt.

Ginny took her hands off the wheel and looked grim. "It appears they got the tires. Del, we're flat dead is what we are. Let's get out of this thing."

And do *what*? Del wondered. Bearings seemed to roll about in his head. He sensed a malfunction on the way.

The Fort Pru vehicles shrieked to a stop. Crazed life agents piled out and came at them over the flats, firing small arms and hurling stones. A rocket burst nearby.

Possum's guns suddenly stopped. Ginny grimaced in disgust. "Don't you tell me we're out of ammo, Possum Dark. That stuff's plenty hard to get."

Possum started to speak. Del waved his good arm to the north. "Hey now, would you look at that!"

Suddenly there was confusion in the underwriters' ranks. A vaguely familiar pickup had appeared on the rise. The driver weaved through traffic, hurling grenades. They exploded in clusters, bright pink bouquets. He spotted the man with the rocket, lying flat atop a bus. Grenades stopped him cold. Underwriters abandoned the field and ran. Ginny saw a fairly peculiar sight. Six black Harleys had joined the truck. Chow Dogs with Uzis snaked in and out of the ranks, motors snarling and spewing horsetails of sand high in the air. They showed no mercy at all, picking off stragglers as they ran. A few underwriters made it to cover. In a moment, it was over. Fort Pru fled in sectional disarray.

"Well, if that wasn't just in the nick of time," Del said.

"I hate Chow Dogs," Possum said. "They got black tongues, and that's a fact."

"I hope you folks are all right," Moro said. "Well now, friend, looks as if you've thrown an arm."

"Nothing real serious," Del said.

"I'm grateful," Ginny said. "Guess I got to tell you that."

Moro was taken by her penetrating charm, her thankless manner. The fetching smudge of grease on her knee. He thought she was cute as a pup.

"I felt it was something I had to do. Circumstances being what they are."

"And just what circumstances are that?" Ginny asked.

"That pesky Shepherd Dog's sorta responsible for any trouble you might've had. Got a little pissed when that Possum cleaned him out. Five-card stud, I think it was. 'Course there might have been marking and crimping of cards, I couldn't say."

Ginny blew hair out of her eyes. "Mister, far as *I* can see, you're not making a lot of sense."

"I'm real embarrassed about this. That Dog got mad and kinda screwed up your gear."

"You let a *Dog* repair my stuff?" Ginny said.

"Perfectly good technician. Taught him mostly myself. Okay if you don't get his dander up. Those Shepherds are inbred, so I hear. What he *did* was set your tapes in a loop and speed 'em up. Customer'd get, say, twenty-six times his money's worth. Works out to a Mach 7 fuck. Could cause bodily harm."

"Lord, I ought to shoot you in the foot," Ginny said.

"Look," Moro said, "I stand behind my work and I got here quick as I could. Brought friends along to help, and I'm eating the cost of that."

"Damn right," Ginny said. The Chow Dogs sat their Harleys a ways off and glared at Possum. Possum Dark glared back. He secretly admired their leather gear, the Purina crests sewn on the backs.

"I'll be adding up costs," Ginny said. "I'm expecting full repairs."

"You'll get it. Of course you'll have to spend some time in Bad News. Might take a little while."

She caught his look and had to laugh. "You're a stubborn son of a bitch, I'll give you that. What'd you do with that Dog?"

"You want taco meat, I'll make you a deal."

"Yuck. I guess I'll pass."

Del began to weave about in roughly trapezoidal squares. Smoke started to curl out of his stub.

"For Christ's sake, Possum, sit on him or something," Ginny said.

"I can fix that," Moro told her.

"You've about fixed enough, seems to me."

"We're going to get along fine. You wait and see."

"You think so?" Ginny looked alarmed. "I better not get used to having you around."

"It could happen."

"It could just as easy *not*."

"I'll see about changing that tire," Moro said. "We ought to get Del out of the sun. You think about finding something nice to wear to dinner. East Bad News is kinda picky."

ABOUT THE EDITORS

In addition to his role as editor at *Isaac Asimov's Science Fiction Magazine* (for which he has won three Hugo Awards for Best Professional Editor), Gardner Dozois is an award-winning author: he received Nebula Awards two years in a row, for "The Peacemaker" (1983) and "The Morning Child" (1984).

Mr. Dozois is also a celebrated anthologist, whose Best of the Year collections are generally considered the standard against which all others are judged. And, with Jack Dann, he has edited a series of anthologies available from Ace Books. He lives in Philadelphia with his wife, Susan Casper, who is also a writer, and their two cats, Hobbes and Stuff.

Sheila Williams joined *Isaac Asimov's Science Fiction Magazine* in 1982 and has been the managing editor since 1986. She received her bachelor's degree from Elmira College in Elmira, New York, and her master's degree from Washington University in St. Louis, Missouri. During her junior year she studied at the London School of Economics.

Ms. Williams has coedited two anthologies for young adults and is the editor of a third, *The Loch Moose Monster: More Stories from IAsfm*, which is forthcoming from Delacorte in early 1992. She also coedited *Writing Science Fiction and Fantasy* (St. Martin's Press) with the editors of *IAsfm* and *Analog*. She lives in New York City with her husband, David Bruce.